The Fisherman's Daughter
The Roaring Twenties

by

I.J.WORKMAN

This is the Second of the Series that tells Emily's story through her life and the times of the twentieth century

Cover photograph by curtesy of *Tyne and Wear Archives*

Publisher: Independent Publishing Network.

Author: I.J.Workman
                 i.workman10@btinternet.com
                 Nether Shannochill, Aberfoyle, FK83UZ

Facebook: I.J.Workman

I would like to send my grateful thanks to Clare for all the encouragement, the editing and her persuasive talents to keep me going in the many moments of procrastination. To Charlotte for her artwork talents in cover design and drawing. And, last but not least, to the members of my local Creative Writing class for their friendship and support over the years.

Glossary

Alreet readers, because ah wes born in Northumberland ah speak in the book with a modified Geordie accent like. Some words look different on the page but if read phonetically the meanin' of what ahm sayin' will become obvious. But te avoid confusion ah've listed below some translations. Ah hope ye enjoy the second part of me on-gannin story: *The Fisherman's Daughter – The Roaring Twenties.*

Emily

Ah	I	*fer*	for
ah've	I have, I've	*gan*	go
ahm	I am, I'm	*gannin*	going
alreet	alright	*heor*	here
an'	and	*hyem*	home
anywa'	anyway	*Ma*	Mum
aye	yes	*me*	my
bairn	child	*oot*	out
bettor	better	*pet*	friend
brotha	brother	*te*	to *(not all)*
howay	come on	*thankye*	thankyou
bonny	good, handsome	wes	was
canna	can't	*whey aye*	hello,
canny	great, good, nice		yes, that's right
Da	Dad	*ye*	you *(not all)*
dee	do *(not all)*	*yeor*	year
divvent	don't	*yer*	your, you're
doon	down	*yerself*	yourself

Prologue

My life, my adventure to describe and unfurl:
Born to a fisherman's family, the eldest girl.
I looked after the bairns and helped with the cleaning.
I gathered coal from the beaches for cooking and the heating.
Then one night Da and two older brothers, died, drowned in a storm.
My uncle moved in. A drunkard, a lecherous beast. He left poor Ma
ragged and torn.
I killed him.
But Ma took the blame and for three years in Durham Jail she spent.
No option, me and Con to the Orphanage were sent.
For three full years we suffered and stayed,
the manager, on little boys, he constantly preyed.
The matron, a hero of mine. For me, a nursing post she did find.
Together we schemed to get rid of the man, the most deviant of all
mankind.
The treatment of women, the needs of the poor, all drew me to fight.
Determined to make a difference, to better their plight.
So, the Suffragettes I joined. The windows I broke.
The banners I waved. A house I left in smoke.
My Mhairi was snatched while I was away.
My heart is now broken. I cry for her, every single day.
The 'War-to-end-all-Wars'. To the battle lines of Flanders I went.
We collected the injured, the burnt, the gassed. Comforted, treated
and finally patched.
Caught by the enemy then held my young brother, killed in a blast.
I waited for my lover, the noise of the battles fading at last.
I jumped into his arms and I hugged him so tight.
To celebrate the Peace. The end of the fight.

5

The Fisherman's Daughter
The Roaring Twenties

Chapter 1 - 1922

With hands clutched behind my head I lie back onto the grassy bank and gaze dreamily into the azure blue sky. Behind and around me bees are buzzing, the spring flowers are waving spreading their scents and refreshing the skin of my face, bliss. I divert my eyes down to my body to check, yet again, my swelling bump. I smile, yes, my third pregnancy. I close my eyes. I couldn't be happier.

I think back four years to Flanders, the end of the war but the start of my new life. My Freddie standing there in front of me, smilingly at me with love in his eyes, and very much alive. I grin, not caring if anyone notices and wonder at why he chose this name. Gunther was not a name to shout out loud within a victorious but crippled country but why Freddie?

But I don't care. It got him through the boredom of the POW camp and, with the help of his tutor at Oxford, into the RAF. With his perfect English accent few people know of his ancestry. He saves his favourite German words just for me 'to show my depth of feelings' or so he explains!

I remember his joy when I could confirm my pregnancy and the great care he shows especially when we make love. "I have to look after you and our two babies". I am certainly thankful when Florence stays fast asleep in her small cot bed in the corner of my tiny apartment bedroom. An inquisitive three-year-old is not much of an aphrodisiac!

As always, my heart skips when I think of my children, my joy of our Flo and the stab of pain of my Mhairi. She will be eleven years old, wherever she is. No matter how much I love Freddie and our children my heartache for her never wanes. It's always there and, I suppose, always will be. For some reason I have never told my 'husband' and my friends never mention her in his company. Am I ashamed, embarrassed? Is there a fear of his rejection? He'd probably be cross that I haven't told him but I will explain, at some time.

I hear a distant low throb and my eyes flick open, my ears picking up the increasing volume. I sit up, head tipped skywards. Others swing open the hut door and stand on the veranda heads tip to match. I can see a black speck and a trail of smoke. I stand and concentrate. The black spot enlarges gradually transforming into a head-on view of the biplane, Freddie's biplane. My fingers clench, my eyes widen. It's the worst time - for me. He's so close and yet I know it could all end here in front of my eyes. But it doesn't. He lands with a slight bounce and cheers from the watchers who then retreat back in to the hut. They know we are rarely together and they kindly allow us some privacy.

He unties his helmet, swings effortlessly down to the grass, smiles and waves at me then runs over. I can only make it down here to his base at Catterick on the odd occasion so we take full advantage of every possible minute.

"Fancy a trip around the place"

"Ye took me round an' introduced me te everyone last time ah wes heor."

"No, I mean up there." He points to the sky.

My eyes widen in horror. "What! But, but, um..ah divvent know if ah like heights. Anywa' there's only one seat."

He has a glint in his eyes. I can see he wants to show off. He plays his trump card. "Not this one we've got an Avro trainer in the hanger."

7

I can't speak. Part of me wants to try but most of me is saying you've got to be joking.

"Come on I'll kit you out, fuel up and we'll be away in no time."

"What about ye lookin' after me an' yer children like?"

"You'll be as safe as houses in old Gertie, come on."

I follow him into the hut and he cajoles his friends to get me 'kitted out' while he fetches Gertie.

"And you lot be careful; she can tie up her own buttons and belt! Don't worry about boots she'll be fine with what she has on."

"But ah haven't agreed yet an' ah have te catch the train back te Newcastle an'..an'...."

But Freddie has gone, leaving the door ajar. I can see him striding purposefully over to the hanger. I feel terrified, I'm thinking why does he do this? I want to be with him but on the ground. I close my eyes and shake my head but then smile. I know I want to do it.

"Here you are Emily, try this on for size."

I've got to know all the pilots and most of the fitters, they all love Freddie. They say he's a 'natural' and should have been with them in the air battles over France. Little do they know. Reg hands me a long, black leather, fleece lined coat.

"I've left your hat, gloves and goggles on the table over there."

I'm kitted out in no time and feeling warm and fully protected but visibly quivering. I haven't managed to say a word. He sees I'm nervous.

"You don't have to worry. Gertie is a safe old bird and Freddie, well you know how good he is, unorthodox but brilliant."

I can only mumble 'umm'. Unorthodox is not a comforting word. I can hear another plane approaching us, it must be this Gertie. I walk out on to the veranda to look at her. She looks older than the others and lumbers along like an old horse and cart. She has two seats, one behind the other. Freddie jumps out of the rear seat on to the grass and waves me over. I take a deep breath and walk towards my fate.

"Have fun Emily." Another pilot shouts after me. I manage a weak smile and a feeble thumbs up. There's no turning back but I now feel a surge of excitement welling up inside. I just know I'm going to enjoy the flight.

With Freddie's help I scramble between the struts and in to the front seat. He ties me in and speaks in sign language telling me not to touch the pedals or the joystick and shows me the speaking tube so he can keep in contact. I nod, he blows a kiss and disappears.

For the next fifteen minutes I'm treated to an experience of a lifetime. Taking off is exhilarating, the noise deafening, the views breath-taking and his messages through the tube were tingling! I was in awe of the plane holding together with such a buffeting from the wind. The wings seem to wave independently as we turn and swoop, apparently gently, as he lets me know after we landed. And the landing, well, that is the scariest bit by far! But we make it and as we taxi towards the hut, I pat my bump. I've already decided that if you're another girl then your name's going to be Harriet - the first woman to fly the English Channel.

Chapter 2

We have a short time before I have to leave for the train and five of us are left sitting around a log fire relaxing, chatting and drinking tea. I'm never too sure of the pilots' duties in peacetime. Sometimes training cadets, other times testing aircraft after repairs completed and, rarely, patrolling the Yorkshire coast for smugglers. It all seems very laid back. I wonder what would happen if no-one turned in for the day. Would anyone notice?

"Ok, suppose you have a boy what shall we call him, one of the Wright brothers?"

This sets the others laughing out loud. "What, Orville or what was his brother's name?"

"Wilbur."

I pull a face. "Isn't there a famous flyer with a British name like?"

"How about Freddie!"

"Ah think one Freddie's enough." This sets the other pilots laughing again but I can see my own Freddie missed the joke. I change the subject quickly. "We'd best get gannin if ahm te get hyem tonight."

He's very quiet driving me to the local Catterick station. He parks close by and very gently explains his reaction. "My father is called Frederich."

"But ye always call him Wilhelm

"Yes, that's right Wilhelm Frederich."

"Oh pet, ah didn't mean te insult him. Are ye very upset?"

He says nothing more, just looks out through the windscreen.

"Ahm so sorry." I hold his hand. "What can ah dee te put it right."

He says nothing more until he turns to face me looking very serious. "Catch the next train."

My eyes lift then I realised his ploy. "So, yer not really upset, ye want te have yer way with me".

His smile returns immediately. "You know me too well. I can drive you to Dalton you can catch the same main line train to Newcastle."

I give him my most annoyed stare but I can't maintain it before I grab his hand and whisper. "But we must be quick."

It has to have been the fastest U-turn and journey back to his digs. Our clothes litter the floor and we make love for the second time in the day. After, we cuddle naked in his bed I whisper in his ear. "Yer father's name isn't Frederich is it?" He just shakes his head and buries it in to my bosom embarrassed.

I've said so many times before but men are just a different breed altogether.

I catch the connecting train, just, and find a seat by the window. He stands by the gate to the platform. I think he looks so smart in his uniform, so handsome and best of all, he's mine. I know we won't see each other for a while and I feel sad but at least I know we can make contact with the new telephone system now spreading like tree roots.

With a doleful hoot the train slowly pulls out the station leaving us waving at our shrinking figures. Once he's out of site I slump back into the seat and close my eyes to re-live my wonderful day.

****

I have some very special friends at the hospital. We've known each other from our student nursing days over 12 years ago. Millie of course I've known ever since my days in the Workhouse. I don't know what I would do without any of them. Rose left the hospital when she married and now has two boys, plus one girl today because I've left my Florence with them to see Freddie. Leaving my daughter is

11

always difficult, that will never change, but I have complete trust in all my friends.

Returning home from Flanders in January 1919 was lovely and heart breaking at the same time. Lovely because I could see my friends and sad because Freddie had to remain under guard, armistice or not, in an officers' POW camp in Ripon until well into 1919. I also had the little problem of being heavily pregnant.

On top of all this my mother received an unfortunate letter from Sister Brogan at the CCS at Brandhoek. It said that I was missing and she feared probably killed by a squad of German infantry attacking the Station. Assuming the worst my nurses flat had been released and my staff nurse position filled so there I was: no job, no home, no husband to support me and pregnant.

The letter also had the effect of my family at home, Mum with my twin sisters Gertie and Flo, emigrating to America with her new partner Davey. I knew about the idea before I returned to Flanders just after Christmas 1917. It seems, from what Millie tells me, that after the death of my young brother Con on the battlefield and my reported death, their last reason to stay was gone.

My arrival at the hospital complete with kitbag and bump caused pandemonium. Millie, bless her heart, had to leave the room and come in again to check if she was dreaming! What followed was a wonderful reunion in the Sister's office with all my nursing friends. I garbled my missing nine-months-story and received repeated hugs from everyone, I think to make sure I was real and not a ghost. For the time being the patients were completely forgotten.

My return coincided with the first wave of the Spanish Flu pandemic. The thoughts at the time were that returning soldiers brought it back from their unhealthy and cramped conditions in the trenches. I could only agree, for the good of myself, my baby and the hospital patients, I would have to be isolated at least until the baby was born and I was showing no ill effects. So, for the next two months I was stuck in a tiny but comfortable one bedroom flat in Gateshead. Thank goodness all my friends helped me through this time, visiting, shopping and most of all making sure Florence arrived safely, if not painlessly.

****

Less than an hour later the train steams in to Newcastle station but the light is now fading and I really want to pick up Florence and have a chance to walk home through the park. I board a steam tram and within 10 minutes I'm standing outside Rose's terraced cottage waiting for an answer to my knocking. But there is no answer and I let myself in, I know she never locks the door. I search around but the silence tells me there's no-one home. Automatically I tense, where could she be? Has there been an accident? Has she run away and they're all looking for her? I stop, stand erect and breathe deeply. I tell myself not to be so stupid she'll be back, yes she will, any minute, breath Em, breath.

"Emily yer back already. Look Flo, yer Ma's back."

I slump with so much relief. "Hi Rose, hi boys." I bend down to give Florence a hug, too tightly. I'm fighting in vain to stop my tears.

"Divvent cry Ma, ah've had a canny time."

I feel ridiculous. I quickly wipe my face and put on my excited smile. "Ah that's great, have ye been playin' in the park?"

"Aye an' ah can run nearly as fast as Bobby."

The children start chattering and run up the stairs oblivious of my emotional stress. Rose grabs my arm, gives me a hug and says, "Ah think ye need a cuppa pet."

"Sorry, ah feel so stupid." I slump down on a chair but I've recovered.

"How's that bonny flyer of yers?" The tension has gone, I'm back to normal. It's in the past and we're talking as friends talk but I know I must try to control this fear and I will.

"Ye did what!"

"That's right, up in the clouds. Well, actually it wes a clear day an' dee ye know the wings flap up an' doon."

"What, yer mad. I divvent think me husband would allow me to dee it anywa'."

"But if ye wanted to would ye let him stop ye?"

"Probably. Ye see ahm not ye, ye Suffragette."

"Ah know, sometimes ah wish ah wasn't. But ah do know ah wouldn't know what I'd dee without ye."

We finish our tea as the noise from upstairs increases a notch. "Right ah think it's time ah took me little monkey home an' get her to bed."

We do walk through the park despite the deepening gloom. We race together and she is a fast mover, at least until she trips on a stick and bangs her elbow on the ground. The rest of the journey she spends howling on my shoulders. I smile, it's a frustrated cry there's nothing broken. I know, I'm a nurse!

Chapter 3

With my Florence fed, a Beatrix Potter story read and now tucked up in bed asleep I can put my feet up and look forward to being Mum to my daughter for another 2 days, all to myself. I love my work at the hospital but I've taken three days off to allow Flo's nanny, my best friend Millie, to visit her boyfriend's parents in Scarborough.

Poor Millie, she married Frank, a lovely man from our Workhouse, in 1913, but he died in the war despite being a permitted conscientious objector. He had to be conscripted but in a non-combative role - a stretcher bearer. But it didn't save him. They had tried to start a family for years without success. It was all very sad for such a lovely, bubbly person. Now, just last year, she met and moved in with a shipyard welder and in no time was pregnant. She took no chances, left work immediately and did as little as possible outside of looking after her new boyfriend. It worked and they have a son. No sign of getting married but that's Millie. Left as a baby on the Workhouse steps, probably born out of wedlock and like me, not tied to convention.

I was a kept woman for over a year after Florence was born. Financed at first by the little bit I saved as a QAIMNS nurse then by Freddie. It was probably my happiest year of my life. Walking and singing along to my baby girl in the park, meeting and chatting to other Mums, looking forward to Freddie's visits. It was heaven, such a change from the years of tensions and challenges before. Inevitably though I felt the seeds of change growing deep inside. It wasn't the Suffragette movement, the vote for women had been won, at least partially and further progress was being made by the Pankhursts. No, there was a desire to put my years of nursing experience to good use again. I discussed this with Millie who agreed immediately and it was she who suggested that she could look after Florence along with her young Frank. They knew each other anyway, Flo acting the Mum. Freddie agreed readily. He knew not to try to change my mind!

So now I'm nursing again, a staff nurse, in the same hospital and working under the very same Sister and with some of the nurses from my old student nursing days. These long friendships have benefits: I don't work night shifts and I can always rely on help when I'm needed to look after a sick Florence or when Freddie is in town.

I can't help but compare the present health problems and treatments with those I experienced and endured in the CCS back in 1917/18. It's not just the difference in the age range of the patients or the conditions and facilities available. Then I had to make immediate decisions, decisions that often meant a young man surviving to fight another day, or not surviving at all. Here there are processes, systems, rules and regulations and crucially there is more time. Today's regime is of course much the better of the two for the patients, for everyone really. But I do miss the immediacy, the responsibility and, despite the long hours, the excitement, the adrenalin rush.

I say to myself: 'don't be so daft'. I remind myself of the heartache and pain of the soldiers, the all-consuming fear of the fighting just a few miles away but I can't stop myself. I have this inner drive for adventure and to make a real difference for groups of downtrodden people – women, miners, the poor – people who have been unfairly treated by the powerful. I do love my life. It's comfortable, loving, productive, but, pregnant or not I have to make changes or at least make plans. Life is so exciting.

But I don't know how or where.

Either way today is going to be an adventure. We're off to see a friend from my Suffragette days. Celia is now happily married with two children and living in Sunderland. This is her second marriage. Her first was a huge mistake. The brute of a man beat her constantly to get what he wanted. The sight of her scarred body covered in bruises and lacerations will never leave me. She put up with this treatment far too long. It was only after my insistent persuasion that she left him and went into hiding for six months. Conveniently, her husband was locked up for ten years for badly maiming some other poor creature. Only then could she venture out and lead a normal life. She soon married a good man, a coal miner from Monkwearmouth Colliery, and had her first son Jake, my god-son, now six years old and at school. A second arrived three years later, Thomas Junior, and we'll be seeing them all today.

The journey is by bus and tram and will take over an hour but we don't care, it's all part of the excitement. We're at the tram stop waiting. Flo is full of it. She's jumping around freeing her curly dark brown locks from my carefully clipped hairstyle. She points at this and that then talks to surprised passer-byes. Generally, they smile sometimes they stop and have a conversation. I think she'll be a people's person.

Looking about the busy street I spot the headlines emblazoned on a paper seller's billboard: *Miners Walk Out.* I'm not surprised. The last time we visited Celia she talked about the pit problems. The owners want to reduce the men's wages and increase their hours saying they have no choice with all the competition from Europe. I immediately recalled my last conversation with Ma's new partner Davey when I was home on leave from Flanders. He knew then changes were going to be made, changes for the worse. The war years demanded coal and for a short while after to help rebuild the country, but now?

The tram arrives and of course it's a race to the top deck front seats. Fortunately, they're vacant. Flo beats me hands down. I'm puffing slowly behind carefully lifting my bulk up the curling steps. I have to admit it is my favourite seat. The sights of the city fascinate me with the variety of buildings and vehicles on show intermixed with a moving swarm of pedestrians like ants busy in the back yard. Horses are still well in evidence despite the growth of motor cars

17

wheezing fumes and adding to the general cacophony. It's a real treat for both of us viewing the moving scene from above so different from my childhood days. But then I realise of course Florence knows nothing else. I immediately feel guilty. I should take her to my fishing village show her the beaches, the little harbour and my friends, my bat cave..... My eyes fill with tears for my family now all gone, dead or far away.

I feel ridiculous. I know I must enjoy each day and give Flo a squeeze. But I will take her back to my home, maybe when Freddie returns. The three of us will go, my own family.

Oh Mhairi, where are ye?

The tram seems to glide along, twitching a bit over crossings and bends but generally a smooth ride. Soon we arrive at the edge of the city and the end of the tracks and have to change onto a bus for the last leg of the journey. A much noisier affair and we have to make do with seats away from the prized top front positions. I manage Flo's disappointment by pointing to the passing estates, factories and pits through the side windows. These are mixed in with fields and woods and we talk about farms and animals. We rarely have a chance to talk like this and although my knowledge of the countryside is very limited, I'm able to conjure up stories about the lives of Peter Rabbit and Squirrel Nutkin.

The bus stops at a large warehouse by the River Wear where the bus half empties and we take our chance and rush to take over the front seats. We are now on roads lined each side with houses. Some of them are new Council houses replacing the old terraced two-up two down flats. They look lovely, some with gardens at the back and the front. I know Celia would love one of these but her family live in an ancient pit house near the colliery. The one good thing is that it's rent free!

The bus passes the entrance to the colliery and I point out the typical mining buildings and winding gantries behind and the spoil heaps alongside. Everything is covered in black dust very different from the green countryside we've just passed through.

"This is where yer Uncle Thomas works."

She looks over but doesn't seem interested and wants another animal story. I see a small gathering of men outside the gates some holding placards and talking to the miners coming and going. This mine is obviously still in operation, the Walk Out headline maybe just a threat. I hope so. There is a miners' benevolence fund from Union contributions but a long strike would quickly reduce their living standards to the breadline. I have to admit their present wages are better than most, certainly better than in nursing, but from what I hear and read the mine owners will not hesitate to make cuts if their profits are affected.

The bus grinds on past the pit and I can spot our bus stop. I point it out.

"Ah can see Auntie Celia an'......"

"Thomas." Florence jumps off the seat ready to fly down the steps. I stop her in time and we wait until the bus stops.

I lift her off and shout our thanks to the conductor. He bends down to Flo.

"Ye have a bonny day young lady an' look after yer Ma." He gives her a wink then looks at me, smiles and tips his cap.

I smile back thinking that you're very nice but not a patch on my Freddie.

Flo has no such thoughts and runs over to the waiting Celia and Thomas.

Celia is now thirty, slightly taller than me and always tries to dress in the latest fashions. Her statuesque figure is squashed in to a tubular dress making her look ready for a Charleston. Me, I feel under-dressed in my every day dress with a waistline on my waist! Pre-war fashion I know but there again the bus conductor didn't complain pregnant or not.

Thomas and Flo recognise each other but seem to lose their voices until Flo brings out her toy wooden horse and thrusts it under his nose. His eyes widen recognising the model and all tension disappears and they start chattering happily.

"Yer lookin' amazin' Celia pet. Ye look as though yer ready to dance."

Celia smiles and gives me a hug. "Guess what ah made this dress from off-cuts ah bought at the market. Copied a picture from a newspaper. What d'ye think like?"

"It looks very modern what does yer husband think about it?"

She frowns. "If he wasn't so canny ah think he would say he prefers the dress ah wore when he first met me."

"Ah assume he means all bust an' bum then."

"Mmm, but what dee ye think?"

"Ah think ye should wear what ye want no matter what anyone thinks. After all, ye haven't changed underneath. Remember: Never Surrender!"

She laughs out loud at our old Suffragette slogan. We turn and start walking back to her house behind our three-year olds still engrossed.

"Let's have a cuppa then we could have a walk in the park. These two can let off steam."

We've been friends since we first met in 1913 going down to London on the train to set fire to the MP's house. Abused by her husband she may have been but she has guts and determination. Like me she was arrested and imprisoned where she joined the hunger strikers until released to 'regain her health'.

After she changes out of her 'flapper dress' we walk through their local park arm in arm.

"Now tell me about these Walk Out rumours."

"Tom thinks it's all sabre rattling an' nothin' will happen. There is an agreement with the owners from yeors ago guaranteeing their wages an' hours. Ahm not so sure. There were rumours last yeor even when the amount of coal sent over to Europe wes at an all-time high. He's very trustin'."

I know that owners and shareholders are only interested in profits. Agreements can be ripped up so easily. I don't share Tom's optimism. Our conversations are never serious for long and we laugh and joke recalling and reminiscing our past adventures. Like my nursing friends she could hardly believe that Freddie took me on a flight in his plane but unlike most of my nursing friends Celia was envious.

"But Celia ye have a bonny family to look after, ye canna go gallivantin' like."

"Aah really. An' what about Florence, Harriet on-the-way an' ah know ye rarely mention her but Mhairi is somewhere."

She's right of course. "Tell ye what I'll ask Freddie if he has a trainer fer two buddin' pilots."

There's a sudden glint in her eyes. "An' they wear such sexy uniforms." We both crease up laughing. Other walkers must think we're quite mad.

We slowly make our way back to her house and are surprised to see a glum faced Tom in the kitchen.

"What's wrong Tom."

"Hi pet, alreet Emily. Well it's happened, they've cut our wages by 10% an' they want us to work eight hours underground a day. So, we've walked oot. We're on strike.

Chapter 4

Freddie's driving up to Newcastle today in his new car or rather a borrowed car. One of his fellow pilots has gone away and left it at the aerodrome for anyone to use. So Freddie stepped in immediately claiming he has to see his pregnant wife. A good enough excuse as far as I can see although of course we're not married!

We're going to visit the village where I was born and bred at least until I was fourteen. I can't wait. I'm standing at the window alongside Florence sitting on the back of our settee both looking down on to the street waiting eagerly. Our bags are packed, a picnic made and ready we just need transport and of course my loving pilot. He said ten o'clock. I look at the clock. My shoulders slump, it's still only ten to ten. I look away to make sure everything in the room is tidy.

"Ma, look, a car."

I twist back around and look down. "Aye, that's yer Da let's gan an' meet him."

We're soon outside and on to the pavement. Freddie has already leapt out over the door and is beaming. He grabs us both in a double embrace "Well what do you think of her?"

I look at the car in wonderment. "It looks real canny, so new lookin' an' there's no roof. Is it safe?"

"Of course, I'm a pilot!"

"Mmmm. Well come an' help with our bags an' we can get gannin."

We're soon driving through the city heading north. Bags stuffed into the boot and Flo on my lap in the passenger seat

I shout above the noise of the traffic and the wind. "Ah hope it doesn't rain."

"Don't worry there's a hood tucked behind the seats. But it's not going to rain I've ordered sunshine all the way on both days."

22

In no time we've crossed the bridge shot through the outskirts and now we're out in to the countryside. We're moving fast, much faster than anyone else. Pedestrians and other drivers stare and point and some honk at us. I have travelled in automobiles before but only over short distances and certainly not at this speed. It's exhilarating. I've given up trying to keep my hair in place and both mine and Flo's long curly locks are flailing behind us. I can't help but compare this journey to previous trips in omnibuses and even the horse and cart rides before and during the war years. Then it took hours and hours and the roads were rough. Now, although not exactly smooth, I think we'll arrive before midday, amazing.

There is very little conversation possible but I do point out the sea to Flo as soon as we hit the coast road. She has been to North Shields and Whitley Bay but I'm so keen to show her my beach. But when we approach familiar landmarks for some reason I'm overcome and lose the power to speak.

The tide's well out and there it is: my cave. I tug at Freddie's arm and manage to shout to stop. I step out still holding Flo in a vice-like grip and just stare. Without a word I hand her over to Freddie before making my way down the bank to the beach itself. He seems to understand that I want time to myself and they quietly follow on behind.

I sit on the rock outside the cave and the memories flood back. The stories I made up for my young brother Con and twin sisters Gertie and Flo. The way we relived our dreams when we gathered sea coal for the fires. Bennie our old horse plodding along the track head bobbing. My older brothers and Da and their heart wrenching deaths at sea, and of course my Ma now so far away.

I feel sad but I refuse to cry. They've now all gone from here but the memories are still with me and they are mostly happy ones. I make myself smile, wider and wider. I can laugh now and I turn throw my hands out wide in time to meet my Freddie and Flo and give them a huge hug. I'm so pleased to be here, it's been so long.

I take Flo in to the cave and I just know what will happen and she screams and holds me tight when the bats fly out.

"These are me friends an' this is their cave. Let's wave at them."

That's what we do and Freddie joins us and joins in.

"Howay ye two, let's see if ah recognise anyone in the village." I realise of course that anyone who knew me would think I'd been killed in the war. I explain this to Freddie.

"It'll be a nice surprise then."

"An' if they die of shock it'll be yer fault. After all it wes ye who saved me."

He becomes serious. "No, my lovely Emily it was you who saved me." Forgetting Flo for a minute we kiss passionately and hold each other tightly before I feel a tug at my jacket. Seeing what was happening Freddie lifts her on to his shoulders and shouts.

"Come on we're going to beat Mummy back up the beach to the car."

"No ye won't." I've got a head start but can't stop laughing to race a man shouting rude German words and a flailing three-year-old gripping on to his neck just behind.

As far as I can see the village is completely unchanged. We pass through and park at the harbour. It is quiet with just a few fleeting glimpses in the distance. The fishing fleet is away leaving only the odd rowing boat tied to the quayside. The gutting sheds are furnished with tables, baskets and bins but empty of life. The only sounds are the flapping of flags, the soft lap of waves against the walls and the sharp call of the gulls. But the scents of the sea are all around enveloping me in waves of nostalgia.

Freddie is standing stiffly by the quayside looking down in to the water but with one hand gripping a bollard.

"Ye feelin' ok pet?"

"Of course."

"Shall we all gan fer a paddle on the beach then?"

He springs away from the quayside and walks towards the gutting sheds. "Not for me thanks. Is this where your Mum worked?"

Freddie seems uneasy. "Aye, before ah wes born an' after she wes released from prison. She loved the sea an' the company. Ever wanted to be on the boats?"

"No." Let's walk back along the main street perhaps you'll see someone you remember."

"Ok pet." I grab his hand and with the other holding Florence we start to wander back along the road. He holds my hand tightly, he feels warm, hot even, contrasting Flo's cool palm. I wonder if he's worried or not feeling well but after a while his grip relaxes and we chatter normally. I was about to question him when a door to the shop opens and a woman steps out ready to shake a mat. I recognise an unchanged Mrs Maxwell. She sees us, smiles and batters the mat against the wall. Then she suddenly stops, drops the mat and swings round to face us again. One hand goes to her mouth the other points at me.

"Na, it canna be, but yer ...Emily Mulligan?"

"Aye Mrs Maxwell it's me Emily. How are ye?"

She doesn't answer. Both hands now cover her mouth. The poor thing is completely overcome. I walk up to her and bring her hands down. "Aye, it's me. Ahm alive an' this is me husband Freddie an' me daughter Florence."

I can see tears welling up in her eyes. "But we all thought you'd been killed an'...an' yer Ma's gone an' yer sisters. "She wipes her eyes. "Sorry ahm actin' daft. It's so canny to see ye." Her eyes light up and she grabs my hands. "Come on we must gan an' see Ettie, she's in, come on. She won't believe it." She pulls me along the road as if I don't know where she lives. Freddie holding Flo follows along behind smiling.

25

I'm wrong. Ettie has moved in to my old house next door. Somehow, I'm actually very pleased, perhaps because it's now still in the 'family'. Typically, we don't knock on the front door but go down the snicket, through the back gate and in to the yard. Again, there's no knocking but we let ourselves in and give Ettie the surprise of her life. She repeats the same emotions of shock and wonder at my sudden surprise appearance and it is with great relief that eventually we're all able to sit down and talk around her table boasting cups and a large pot of steaming tea. I don't want to go into any great detail about how I survived or that Freddie is German and we're not actually married. I really want to know about Ma, Davey and my twin sisters Gertie and Flo.

Ettie has changed. She looks frail and now needs sticks to get around. But I can never forget her and how kind she's been to my family. I have to explain to Freddie how she looked after us all when Ma was imprisoned. She had no option but to place me and Con in the Workhouse when her own husband died but still looked after the twins single handed.

"Yer Ma didn't want to gan even after ye' an' Con died, no, oh ye know what ah mean. But Davey wes very unhappy doon the pit an' he convinced her that America will be a new an' exciting place te live. They left just after the war finished. We were all sad te see them gan." She pauses not knowing what else to say, then. "Ah hope ye' divvent mind me movin' in here but ye Ma an' Davey offered it an'.... it has a built-in bath." She smiles wickedly and we laugh. She continues "The folk who moved in to me old place are very canny."

I'm feeling tense asking my next question. "Ettie, have ye their address in America?"

Ettie eyes widen. "Whey aye an'..." She stands up, gathers her sticks and walks over to the sideboard. She takes some letters out of one of the drawers and lays them down in front of me. "an' they sent some photographs. These arrived only about a month ago."

I eagerly but very carefully take out the letters from the envelopes and with one of them I find the photos, three of them. I feast my eyes. They are very formal: one of the twins, another showing a seated Ma with Davey standing behind and the third showing them altogether.

I can't speak. They are so smartly dressed and the girls so grown up their blond curls tied back, proper ladies. I show them to Freddie. He studies them and holds my hand.

"You have a lovely family Emily."

Chapter 5

We were due to find a hotel further North in Bamburgh or even Berwick but Ettie offered my old bedroom for the night. In fact, she insisted. I'm not sure Freddie altogether approves. I think he was looking forward to a romantic evening by ourselves. But he could see we have no choice and keeps smiling through. I'm going to make sure all three of us have an enjoyable and relaxing night in the very room I slept in for fourteen years mostly shared with my brother Con.

The afternoon is filled with smiles, laughter and gasps bringing each other up to date. I explain how I volunteered to help at a Casualty Clearing Station in Flanders and this is where I met and nursed Freddie injured in battle. They think it was all very romantic, if only they knew. They spoil Florence and give me more cuddles when they realise I'm pregnant and not just a bit overweight! It seems there have been few changes in the village and to my surprise Bennie our horse is still alive and enjoying himself in the field behind.

"Ye must all three of ye gan an' see him." Ettie looks at Mrs M. nods then adds, "We'll get some dinner together fer when ye get back."

I think we all need some exercise so we set off for the field. On the way I point out particular houses and landmarks and even look in to the 'The Fishers' pub. It's empty, quiet, not a soul about. I know how different it will be when the fleet returns.

Bennie, the dear old boy, trots over when we arrive at the field gate. I wonder if he remembers me but his head, now much greyer, bobs in what I feel is certain recognition, I think! He was always a steady, docile Cob and I have no worries that Flo is safe on his back. I would love to have a bare-back ride myself but I have to consider his great age and my own increasing weight. At the top of the field I gaze again at the panoramic sea view now visible over the village rooftops.

"What a view."

Freddie looks but says nothing. I study his face. He's staring out to the horizon but not with pleasure or desire.

"Ye divvent like the sea dee ye pet?"

He looks over to me, then smiles. "I'd rather be up in the air. Come on we'll get a couple of bottles of beer from the pub. What would the ladies like?"

"Gin perhaps."

We stroll back, bottles clinking in our pockets, taking our time giving ourselves the chance to chat. "So, what's this Davey like?"

"He's a canny man, so different from most men. He's kind an' considerate an' Ma just loves him so much. An', a very different breed: he doesn't drink an', as far as ah know, has never hit Ma!" I smile and drop my tone, "Ah knew about the new bath the last time ah visited. Guess what, they used to get in together. Now me Da would never ever dee that."

"But he worked down the mine, he would be black with dust."

I grin widely. "Whey aye. They would have to wash each other doon after like. Isn't that romantic?"

He smiles. "You British are full of surprises. Shall we re-enact tonight."

"Certainly not, can ye imagine Ettie's face? But we can dream about it, perhaps."

"Why was he unhappy? I thought the mines are busy."

"Yes, during the war yeors an' for a yeor or so after when we were rebuildin' but now there's lots of competition from Europe. This started even before 1914. Ah also think the mine owners are bein' greedy. They're causin' a lot of unrest. They want to increase the hours worked an' reduce their wages."

I relate what I had heard from Celia's husband Tom and their recent 'Walk Out'. It only lasted two days but everyone knows there will be more trouble on the way.

"I smell a Cause in your voice?"

I haven't really thought about it that way before but maybe he's right.

Freddie stops and gently pulls me back. As I turn, I can see he's looking serious and whispers to avoid Florence hearing. "I can see what you're thinking. No more of your hunger striking young lady."

I smile and shake my head. That was a bad, grim time for me. I will always remember those long weeks in Holloway jail. The continuous head throbbing, the weariness, the confinement in a stone walled box, the forced feeding but...I know I don't regret it, any of it. Except the inescapable fact that if I hadn't gone down to London, I would still have my Mhairi. I shake away the daily heartache of my lost daughter.

"Ye can talk. Fightin' in the trenches fer yeors wasn't exactly a picnic!"

"But I had no choice."

I drop my head. I understand the difference. I volunteered to go and I volunteered to help in Flanders. I ask for trouble and I get it. I know this but I have this inner drive. I can't ignore it. I wouldn't be happy just 'putting up with' as Ma used to say. I have to Make a Difference for women and for all the downtrodden.

He lifts my chin with his hand. I see him smile and we kiss tenderly and then cuddle with Florence squashed between us. My lovely family of four, well nearly.

Eventually with the encouragement of a wriggling daughter and with my head tipped back allowing the sea breeze to fill my senses, we continue down to the village, hand in hand.

Dinner was, surprise, surprise, Ettie's favourite, fish pie. I remember it well. I was never ever sure what was in it. I suspected it was the leftovers after most of the catch was boxed. I soon realised that if I didn't examine the contents too closely it tasted delicious. My brother Con never agreed. He particularly hated squid and had to examine every morsel before eating.

After dinner Mrs Maxwell has to get back to re-open the shop for the afternoon. Ettie after some persuasion settles down in to her armchair and with the help from her tot of gin, soon nods off for a well-earned afternoon nap.

Florence has no such desire and demands a paddle in the sea. Freddie initially volunteers to stay with Ettie.

"Yer comin' with us, no excuses. Ahm gannin to introduce ye to the sea, my sea. Ah lived with it every day fer fourteen yeors. If ye divvent dee anythin' daft, she'll look after ye an' you'll love it."

"Come on Daddy. Ah can paddle up to me bottom."

I take his hand and whisper. "Ettie will be fine an' so will ye. Just stay with me."

The sea is at its most tranquil. The tide is turning but the strip of sand is still visible and with the sun at our backs, shoes and socks off we let the surging water cool our feet. Flo is dipping her hands into the water, splashing with her feet and squealing. She's having the greatest fun. I hold on to Freddie's hand. As we walk, I feel him relax, his grip loosens and the tension in his face eases.

"Dee ye want to tell me about it?"

He looks past me and out to the sea horizon. "It's a family thing, my brother really, but not now I'll explain later." He pauses and continues walking. "Thank you, my love for bringing me here. I think talking about it will do me good but not now."

"That's ok, in yer own time."

Flo runs over, she looks cold. It is cold. Summer or not this is the North Sea and I've never known it warm.

"Right, ye know what we dee to stop us shiverin' divvent ye?"

She looks up at me questioning. "No Ma."

I grab her hand and Freddie's and shout, "Run."

She squeals and we run and splash and shriek and laugh until we're wet up to our knees. Then we turn and run back on dry land to shake the water off our clothes. Freddie grabs a handful of small stones and starts throwing them in to the waves to make a splash. Then gives some to Flo who does the same. Father and daughter enjoying each other's company.

I watch them but then notice a coble fishing boat behind them. I so wanted to see it and there it is. I know it and I know who's in it. Three men are waving and I'm so happy to see them: my Da and two older brothers, Brendon and Pat. I know they're dead, drowned in a stormy sea when I was fourteen but somehow the sight of them makes me so contented. It's as if they're looking after me. I wave back and continue waving until they disappear into the mist. Freddie and Flo don't notice anything. The vision is not really for them. My younger brother Con and my twin sisters Gertie and Flo used to see them and perhaps Ma. It's a family thing but it doesn't make me sad, it's just the opposite.

With shoes and socks in our hands we walk carefully up the beach to the rock at the entrance to my cave. It's sheltered and warm giving our clothes a chance to dry. I explain to Freddie why we had to visit the beach almost daily to pick coal.

"Most of the bairns had to dee it. It kept our families warm an' cooked our food like. We were known as the 'Coal Gatherers'. Ah didn't know it at the time but ah've learnt that the coal seams pass under the sea an' sometimes bits break off an' get washed ashore. They'll be some heor now like."

"You're full of surprises. You've led a very full, varied life so different from most."

"Ah suppose ah have." I give him a knowing look. "An' it's not gannin to change now. Divvent ye forget ah want some flyin' lessons!"

He smiles but there's a twinkle in his eyes. He grabs me and thrusts me up in to the air on to his shoulders and starts to run up the beach, "will this do for flying." I scream, shout and wriggle all to no avail until we reach the track where he lowers me down carefully looking sheepish. "Sorry I forgot about Harriet."

I can only smile, I can't be cross. I know our baby will have to put up with a lot worse.

We walk back to Ettie's hand in hand with Flo running on in front. "Darling, why were you waving at the sea back there?"

I try to explain my happy vision that gives me a warm, contented glow.

"That's something very special. You're lucky." He pauses while we walk on. "Sometimes I get visions but they're not so nice."

I feel the sharp pain of realization of his suffering. I understand and try to explain that so many of the war wounded I nursed in Flanders and even now four years later ex-soldiers still have terrible mental problems. We call it 'shell shock'. I hope and believe they will improve over time.

"I hope you're right."

I squeeze his hand and pray that I am right.

We continue quietly down the hill and through the village. Florence remembering the way dives down the ginnel to the back of the house. I hope Ettie doesn't get a rude awakening.

Chapter 6

Ettie has in fact been busy clearing up after our dinner and preparing my old bedroom ready for the three of us. While Freddie is playing with Flo outside in the yard Ettie sidles up to me and smiles conspiratorially. "Remember ah told ye about yer Ma havin' a bath fitted divvent ye? Piped hot water from the big copper an' everythin'." I nod, "Well, yer Gertie, bless her, let it slip that yer Ma an' Da sometimes shared it, together, ye know, at the same time." Her eyes light up as if I wouldn't believe it.

I go along with it, it's her revelation. "No, really?"

She nods vigorously. "Aye, an' um....if ye like, ye an' Freddie can dee the same." Her face flushes pink then. "Ah can look after Florence."

I can't help but smile broadly. "That would be nice. I'll see if Freddie is up fer it. Maybe Flo can join us, make it a threesome?"

Her hand covers her mouth in shock but recovers. "Whey aye, she's only wee. If only yer Ma was heor."

"There wouldn't be any room fer her as well!"

"No, ah divvent mean ...."

I put my arm around her shoulders. "Ah know, Ahm only jokin' Ettie. A bath does sound relaxin'. Yer very kind."

After a round of tea and orange juice the excitement of the day caught up with Flo. Her eyes were closing despite her best efforts so a quick wash and teeth clean followed by an impromptu story from her Dad and she was fast asleep in the middle of the bed.

As we leave the bedroom Freddie whispered "I can see this is going to be a romantic night!"

"It will be cosy an' warm. Anyway, ah've got a surprise fer ye." I open a door off the kitchen revealing Ma's bath she and Davey had fitted. "Ettie wants us te take a bath, together."

"Ahh, now you're talking. You can have the tap end."

34

"No way an' you'd bettor mind where ye put yer feet."

"When, now?"

"Certainly not. When Ettie's in bed." I smile at his eagerness.

He smiles back and rubs his hands. "I can wait."

The evening passes pleasantly accompanied by tots of gin and glasses of beer. Our conversation turned to the prospects of the families in the village. The catches of the fishing fleet appear unchanged. Some good days, some not so good. Unsurprisingly the local coal mines are suffering the effects of cheap imports like those around Newcastle.

Inevitably I get on my soapbox and poor Ettie and Freddie are battered by a tirade of my social and political views and demands.

It seems the boom time of the post war years is over. Industry particularly the heavy industries of mining, shipbuilding and the steelworks are feeling the pinch. Not the owners and management of course. They'll make sure their personal well-being is maintained. Likewise, the pontificating politicians. They were voted in, now they should ensure fair play and provide opportunities. But, as always, it's the many thousands of working men and women and their families that suffer.

Ettie is listening and sipping her gin but I don't think much is going in. Freddie drinks his beer but stares at the floor. He understands what upsets me but is very aware of the deprivation in Germany and the effect it's having on his parents living there. It's time for me to change the conversation.

I smile at them both. "Enough from me. Ah think it's bath time!"

Ettie's eyes spring open. "Aye, there's plenty of hot water like, an' towels. Ah hope ye both enjoy it." She blushes pink again. "Ah think, if ye divvent mind, I'll gan to bed. Ah've really enjoyed today but ahm a bit tired."

Freddie finishes his beer in one gulp and politely stands up. "Of course, we don't mind Ettie. You've been so kind to us."

"It's been a real pleasure." Then looks at me. "Ah knew of course that those nasty Germans wouldn't get ye." She laughs and totters unsteadily towards her bedroom. "Help yerself in the mornin' if ahm not up, goodnight."

I smile as I watch her close the door behind her. I turn to Freddie and pat my lump. "Little does she know that one nasty German did get me!"

"And I'm going to get you again. Come on and let me strip off those clothes."

I hold my hand up. "At least wait until she's asleep."

He walks over to my chair and tugs my hand. "Oh no. I've waited all day. Us nasty Germans have no patience."

I have to give in. He hushes me and quietly leads me into the bathroom. With steaming water filling the tub he begins to undress me, very gently, especially over Harriet. The bath is lovely, not sure it was made for two but we manage somehow. We wash each other. He is so gentle, never rough or rushed. I just relax knowing I'm in safe hands. Drying each other takes forever. He likes to concentrate on certain areas just to make sure they're perfectly pristine. He says you can't be too sure! Hmmm. I don't complain.

We slip into bed squashing but not waking Florence. There's no love making. That'll have to wait for a less squeaky bed and just the two of us.

I awake with a kick in the tummy from an awake Flo. The morning light is streaming around the curtain edges and I can hear movement from the kitchen. The two of us creep out of the bedroom to join Ettie, leaving Freddie still snoozing.

She's at the stove stirring a large saucepan of porridge. I smile when I recognise her old striped pinney still in good use.

"Morning pets. Sit yourself doon ah've got some porridge on the go. Did ye have a comfy night?

I don't get a chance to answer before Flo pipes up. "Ah got a bit squashed by Ma and Pa. They kept cuddlin' each other an' ah wes in the middle."

Ettie turns holding the saucepan ready to dish out. "Ah 'spect it was only to keep ye warm an' cosy pet. Now get some of this doon ye it'll keep ye gannin all day. There's milk an' honey on the table. Ah 'spect yer Ma will help ye."

With Flo concentrating on mixing in the honey Ettie turns to me and whispers. "How wes the bath?" She gives me a wicked smile within the same embarrassed pink bloom in her cheeks.

"It wes canny, so relaxing. So much bettor than the old tin bath."

"Ah still have it. It's in the stable. It's bonnie fer Bennie's hay in Winter."

"He looks in canny condition Ettie. Dee ye mind lookin' after him?"

"He's bonny. Yer Ma told me what to dee but ah had a good idea. Ah think ah've known him longer than ah've known ye! Ah can get up to the gate in the field an' he trots doon fer his treats. In snowy winter days old Jock brings him doon heor an' helps me. We get on just fine."

We have to get back to Newcastle in time for Freddie to drive back to Catterick. It has been a heartening weekend for me. I've been able to show Freddie and Flo where I grew up, to be with my childhood friends and, a surprise, to discover the address of Ma and my sisters. I kick myself because why haven't I visited before? Why have I unknowingly tried to blot out my past? I resolved to write to Ma as soon as I get back but how to explain, what will she think of me?

It's another glorious Summer day so we can travel with the car open to the wind. After hugs and kisses and promises of a re-visit we start our return journey waving furiously to our small group of well-wishers gathered in the street. We also wave as we pass my beach with my bat cave only just visible in the retreating tide. I haven't seen any coal gatherers during our visit. I suppose the arrival of gas for heating and lighting has reduced the need. The children now all go to school during the day which I know must be better for them but...

The noise of the open topped car restricts conversation but I want to be quiet. My brain is full of emotion and I need time to think and to reminisce.

We stop about half way home at a field gate. We stretch our legs and look over to a peaceful, tranquil view of a flock of sheep quietly grazing. Ettie has made us some sandwiches for our journey and we settle down to our picnic on a blanket.

Flo is busy adding extra flavour into her sandwich by including a bunch of wild flowers thriving by the stone wall. Freddie and myself are leaning back against the gate when out of the blue he asks.

"Do you think you're a communist?"

I have to admit I haven't even thought of it. "Ah suppose ah might be but...ah've read about the millions that have died in Russia in the last five yeors with Lenin takin' over from the Tsars. This bloodshed is unbelievable, ah mean there must be another way fer everyone to get their own fair share?"

"We're in such a dire economic position in Germany that people want change and some see communism as a way forward. It may even happen here. The government are scared stiff. Some foresee a repeat of the bloodshed, and, more to the point, they're worried about their own livelihoods."

I smile at his cynicism but the thought of millions more dying appals me.

"Ahm hopin' the new Labour party can do somethin' fer us like. At least they seem to support the needs of the workin' man. It's a pity ahm still too young to vote." I turn to Freddie and give him a wicked smile. "But ahm not too young to make a fuss."

He gives me a knowing look. "Come on you I've got to get this car back to Catterick tonight. This is no time for making devious plans."

He jumps up and helps me to my feet. We wave good bye to the sheep and the pastoral scene and we're soon packed up and away at top speed flying along the winding country lanes. My mind, still full of plans for action, is blissfully unaware that Freddie is concentrating hard.

"What's that noise?"

I jump at his sudden shout. I look over surprised. "That noise. Can you hear it?"

The air is full of rumbles and crunches as we run over lumps and bumps of the road but I can't hear anything new. I shake my head.

"Look we'll stop at the next town there may be someone who can help."

We slow down and with the reduced wind noise I can hear a clanking, whirring sound. It suddenly dawns on me that we could be stranded if the car breaks down.

Slowly we drive in to the outskirts of Ashington. The new noise is now very obvious. People we pass look over wondering what's wrong. Freddie spots a complex of factory buildings with two lorries parked outside. "I'll try over there. They may have a mechanic who can help."

He soon appears with a man in grubby clothes wiping his hands on a cloth. I can see that he likes the car but shakes his head at the strange noise. They spend the next half an hour gazing under the bonnet racing the engine and making some adjustments with a spanner but still, worryingly, looking glum. Finally, Freddie closes the bonnet and comes over looking serious.

"I'm sorry Em love, he says he can probably repair her but not until tomorrow. I'm going to have to stay here the night. I can wire the base to let them know what's happening." I must have looked alarmed. "Look, I know you're working tomorrow but a friend of this man has to drive one of these lorries in to Newcastle tonight and he offered to take you and Florence home. Would that be alright?"

My heart sank. All I could muster was an Ok. He bent down and kissed me on the cheek. "I'm sorry to have our weekend spoilt like this but if he can repair it, I'll drop by the hospital on my way back. I'll just go and find out when he's going."

As he walked away, I reflected that something horse-drawn would have got us all back tonight albeit late. Marvellous these inventions until they break down.

Chapter 7

I'm in the lorry's cab with David. The three of us squashed in to a small space separated by old cushions and covered by blankets with our case squashed in behind. I've lifted Florence on to my lap so that she can look out the windows. Poor Freddie. I can still see his frustration at having to stay behind while his family disappears down the Great North Road which, I'm now told, is the A1. It's frustrating for me but Florence is fascinated by the new experience. Raised above her normal sight lines she maintains her continuous stream of questions pointing at distant hills, buildings and anything really. David is quiet concentrating on his driving. A young man dressed in clean blue overalls has a mass of curly brown hair surrounding a cherubic face. He has been very polite, making sure we have all we need for the journey. He seems very different, thoughtful. We soon leave the terraced houses, factories and pits behind us and we're in to the countryside. The steady rumbling of the engine has a relaxing effect on Florence and now she's slumped into my comfortable shoulder and chest pillow. I start a conversation.

"Dee ye live in Ashington David?"

He looks over, notices my sleeping daughter and smiles. "Aye, all me life. We stay in one of them Woodhorn pit houses."

"Dee ye like driving lorries."

"Aye. ah've only just started like. Ah really want to gan on to drive buses. Take families on holiday te Whitley Bay, a park or to the shops in Newcastle." I quickly realise he is very sociable and likes to talk but what he says next completely surprises me.

"Ah worked doon the pit for the last ten yeors but never liked it. In fact, ah hated just about every minute. Ah like to be outside ye see."

"But why did ye stay in minin' so long? And, if ye divvent mind me sayin', ye divvent look old enough."

He scratches his curly haired head. "Had no choice. My Da died in Woodhorn Pit an' me Ma had no other income. Ah started when ah wes twelve."

I knew kids worked down the mines, but twelve? "What happened?"

"Ma says it wes a gas explosion. We all felt the tremor, even in the house. She just knew it wes from the pit. The story goes that the safety checks were never done. The Colliery Manager was taken to court."

"Wes he convicted?"

He looks over to me, grimaces and shakes his head.

I look away in disgust but unsurprised at his whole story. I can never forget the under-age soldiers fighting in the war. One in particular: fourteen-year-old Michael we nursed in Newcastle. What a lovely, brave and determined boy he was. I often wonder how he is now. But I feel certain whatever he's doing, on his parent's farm or anywhere else, he'll be making the best of it despite his missing leg.

In one aspect Michael was a big lad for his age. David on the other hand doesn't look twenty-two so I can guess he never looked twelve ten years ago. But the Manager employed him. He may of course have understood that his family needed the income and he wanted to help. I feel confused, what is right?

"Me younger brotha now works doon the Pit so Ma's ok, an' it gave me a chance te dee something ah really wanted. Anyway, the coal owners are threatenin' to reduce the hourly rate an' increase the hours worked underground. That wes the last straw for me like."

"So, what's the Miners' Federation doin' about it?"

"They're threatenin' this an' that an' the other. Each pit seems to be different. It all depends on the owners. There's no co-ordination."

"But that's what the Federation is fer."

David just shrugs and continues staring ahead concentrating on the road. Our conversation dries up. My head fills with my usual frustrations with the worker/owner/politician relationships. It's all so wrong and it has to change.

We're into the Newcastle suburbs and soon cross the Tyne into Gateshead and we draw up outside my flat.

"Thanks David we dee appreciate ye gannin to all this trouble. Dee ye fancy a cup of tea?"

"Better not ah've got to get this stuff delivered. Ah hope yer husband is back soon." Before I leave the cab, he smiles and adds. "Divvent worry about the miners they're always moanin' about somethin' or other."

"Ah suppose so. Good luck with gettin' yer dream job drivin' the coaches."

I slip down to the pavement clutching a waking Florence, give David a last wave and slam the door shut. I watch him carefully making his way down the street avoiding errant children and footballs. I can see neighbours chatting at their front doors probably wondering what has happened. But I just wave for now. I'll speak to them later after we've eaten our tea.

Chapter 8

My 'Poor' ward has been quiet today. We call it such because the patients haven't had to pay anything because of their circumstances. The 'Posh' ward is upstairs reserved for those who can pay the allotted amount. It has been decided they should be kept apart. I disagree completely. It's divisive, they should be integrated. The level of service is the same, well, nearly. I admit there are more patients for every nurse down here but they're as comfortable as they can be. The proper name for my ward is 'The Edith Cavell' ward, the British nurse who treated soldiers from both sides without discrimination. When I think of this, I remember Freddie's words: They should call it 'The Emily Mulligan' ward. I smile, I feel proud with what I did in the war but there is a difference: I had to look after the German injured, I had been captured, I had to do it, I had no choice. There's also another difference: I'm still alive.

I'm sitting opposite Sister Parker. The same sister who caught me truanting at my very first Suffragette meeting in 1911, who looked after me when I gave birth to my illegitimate daughter Mhairi and supported me throughout my nursing life. My life would have been very different without her - for the worse.

"So, Emily, what do you think of that?"

I'm flabbergasted. Sister has called me in during my break and given me the most amazing news: she has put my name forward to replace Sister Richardson in the 'Posh' ward. She is retiring next year.

"But Sister ahm too young an' ahm pr..."

"Emily, we've known each other for over twelve years now. Call me Evelyn, and you're not too young and I know and can see that you're pregnant. We've agreed that you should have your baby in here and after a period you can return to work in the hospital. All as you did before with Mhairi and Florence but this time you can come back as a Sister."

My words have dried up but my brain is tumbling over with questions. I know I would love the position. Normally Sisters are well into their forties. What would the other Staff Nurses think? Who would look after my children? But what a challenge it would be. I want to get up and give her a big grateful squeeze but I just give her a smile.

"Thank ye Evelyn, ah dee appreciate it. Yer very kind."

"It's nothing to do with being kind. You're perfect for the job. I've seen how you cope in emergencies and, I might add," she gives me a big knowing smile, "so has Matron. I know it's still a while to go yet but it'll give you time to take it all in and prepare."

****

My shift has finished and I'm walking back to collect Florence from Millie. It's been a glorious Summer day and it's still warm. A gentle cooling breeze is blowing along the Tyne. I'm taking the long route back giving myself time to think. I know I would enjoy the challenge. Evelyn makes it all look simple. There's rarely any staff dissent. She has a happy knack of combining authority and friendliness but there have been problems in the Mary Seacole ward, the 'Posh' ward. Complaints of intimidation, arguments and threats are behind the high turnover of staff. I can see this is something I will have to change. There is also the inevitable heartache of leaving both my children every day adding to the pain of losing my Mhairi but I can feel my whole body stiffen with steely determination. This time it will be different. I will not be away for weeks and, crucially I know I can trust Millie. Not that she knows anything about it yet!

I've decided to speak to Freddie before anyone else. It has to be a joint decision. I grimace and almost laugh out loud. Who am I

45

kidding? I know what I want. It'll be a challenge and that's what I need. I will accept the offer no matter what. If it actually comes of course.

****

Millie is happily chatting about her day with her Frank and my Florence while we sit in her tiny but sunny back yard and the children play around our feet. I concentrate and laugh and speak at the right times. I don't want to mention my news yet. It'll wait while I think it through.

"Well Em, tell me all about it. Somethin's on yer mind isn't there?"

My eyes widen in surprise. "What makes ye think that. Ahm probably just a bit tired like that's all."

She laughs and grabs my hands with hers. "How long have we known each other. Ah know ye bettor than ye know yerself." She sits back and grabs her cup. "Come on, tell me all about it."

I stare in to her face. I try to keep to my story….but I can't. I can't keep any secrets from my very best friend, I never could. I smile and start slowly but accelerate to express speed telling the whole tale almost without taking a breath. I finish and look at her. She has her hand to her mouth. I can see she's so pleased.

"Well, what dee ye think?"

"What dee ah think? Emily it's marvellous, ye should be celebratin', tellin' the world. You'll be the youngest Sister in the hospital an' you'll be brilliant, an'," she grabs my hands again. "I'll love te look after Harriet, or maybe Harry."

Tears seep through my eyes and down my cheeks. I realise I was worrying that Millie may not have wanted the extra burden. But the invisible weight has lifted, I get up and pull her up at the same time

and grip her tight, my head on her shoulder. I know Freddie will
agree! I then realise what she said and hold her at arm's length.

"It'll be Harriet, ah just know it."

Chapter 9

I look into Harry's face, his eyes closed concentrating on feeding. His blonde curly locks swirling over his head. The early morning sun is beaming through the window behind me warming the chilled air of my sitting room. Florence is playing quietly at my feet. It's so peaceful. I know it'll change any minute but I'm enjoying the silence while it lasts.

Harry arrived nearly two weeks ago now and this is my first week at home. He arrived quickly and almost painlessly, by far the easiest birth of the three. The staff at the hospital spoilt us rotten. I can still see their I-told-you-so smiles. I had been convinced and even made a pink bonnet and, probably out of stubbornness, he wears it at every opportunity. There's nothing wrong with pink! But I have to smile myself, a nurse, an expert in such matters getting it completely wrong. However much it was embarrassing, I'm so pleased.

Freddie arrived too late for the birth. He burst into my private room followed by Sister and then proceeded to spend the next five minutes gawping and playing with his son ignoring me completely. It was only after Sister left that he turned to me with a devilish smile. He stripped off his coat and shoes and to my horror slipped into bed besides me. I had no time to complain.

"So, my fraulein, where is Harriet."

I had no time to answer before he locked me into an enveloping embrace. I was still feeling very fragile but he was gentle and we kissed lovingly before I had to shoo him out lest Sister returned.

He stayed in Newcastle for a full week, staying in my house, visiting me daily and looking after Florence during the day. I feel proud of him, a man taking on the role of a mother, well, until bedtime when Millie came to pick her up! Each afternoon they boarded the tram for the hospital loaded with presents they had either baked or made out of bits of wood and cloth.

The morning of the day I was due to leave he pushed Florence's pram all the way to the hospital. I guess I expected some other form of transport would be on offer, but no, not my Freddie. Always the one to surprise. Fortunately, it was another warm autumn day. Our return journey was taken in easy stages and connected a warm farewell from the staff to an excited welcome at home from Millie and the children.

On his last full day, we had a family day out at Whitley Bay. It was my suggestion and only after some persuasion did Freddie agree. Our day began with the usual tram ride and then at North Shields, a coastal tram for the scenic route to complete our journey. It was yet another sunny day which, inevitably, attracted the crowds. I held Harry in a comfy, home-made, shoulder sling while Freddie carried the bag of food, clothes and our bucket and spade all in one hand and Florence eager but nervous clinging tightly to the other. I have to say he did look a little stressed but he had no choice I've just given birth so I was going to relax in the warmth.

The promenade was crammed with noisy but happy holiday-makers competing with bicycles and the odd car squeezing its way through. I had my eyes open for a vacant beach hut. I needed some privacy not just to change our clothes but also to feed the fidgeting Harry. We dropped down on to the sand. It looked as though we were out of luck when a lady beckoned me over.

"Ah can see you've got a young-un, we're just off to the Spanish City. Come in before someone else grabs it."

Her words were a god-send and I thanked her gratefully. She gasped when she looked at Harry.

"My she's a bonny wee thing."

I wasn't going to correct her. I didn't have to. Florence piped up immediately and at full volume. "It's a boy he's name's Harry."

I could only nod, hopefully not turning pink like his bonnet but she just laughed and turned to Flo. "Sorry ah meant to say: he's a bonny wee thing."

I suspect Freddie will now never let me forget how I dressed our son in girls' clothes.

We changed into our beach costumes and ate our sandwiches while I discreetly fed Harry. Flo then decided it was time to paddle and tugged on Freddie's arm. He could see there was no alternative and I watched them as one ran and the other followed walking at a pace to keep up. They returned as Harry had finished and was now sound asleep drunk with milk. I laid him down, comfortably wedged between our bags. While Flo was making good use of the bucket and spade, I beckoned Freddie to sit with me.

"Well, how wes it?"

"Cold."

"Are ye gannin to tell me about it?"

"Yes." He studied the sand in front of him, obviously thinking, then. "I killed my brother."

I couldn't speak. I was stunned. I waited.

He couldn't look at me but just stared out to the horizon. I waited hoping he would explain. "I was supposed to be looking after him but…. I was reading, while I should have been looking after him. When I looked up, he'd disappeared. I thought he must have gone back up the beach to our parents." He shook his head remembering. I took his hand in mine, immediately he swung round clasping mine in his, eyes glistening.

"He must have run into the sea, he couldn't swim. I knew he couldn't but I just carried on reading."

"Oh pet."

"My parents never really forgave me."

"But it was their responsibility, not yours. How old were ye?"

"Nearly six, Bertie was four."

50

I shook my head. "That's far too young. Ye canna place such a weight on a five-year-old's shoulders."

"My parents were strict. You did as you were told. I knew that and I didn't. They returned to Bavaria soon after, but not me. I was sent to Newbury school and that was that."

"Did ye see them at all after that?"

"Oh yes, my mother came over each year and she used to write."

"But not yer Da?"

He shook his head. "The next time I saw him was in 1914 when they took me back to join the army."

I shuffled my seat closer and put my arms around his shoulders. They were shaking. He was crying silently. I held him until I felt him relax. "Ah want te gan an' see them. Show them our family. Tell them what a hero ye were in the war. Ah want them te be proud of ye."

He sat back into his chair and gripped my hand. "I've always said that you saved my life and not just in Flanders. You've shown me what life can and should be like and I'm not sure I deserve you. It's a kind thought of yours to meet my parents but it'll be difficult to arrange and I'm not sure what our reception will be like."

I don't care about the reception. They need to see each other, to forgive, lay past ghosts and start again. Either way I felt determination seeping through me. It's possible, even with two children. We will manage somehow.

"Well, we'll see won't we!"

My mind switches back to the present. Harry is still sleeping. Florence is tugging at my dress.

"Mummy, can we gan for a walk in the park now please?"

51

Chapter 10

I watch the countryside slipping by, clouds of steam float across my view and absentmindedly I hear the clickety-clack of wheels on rails. Since Harry appeared this is my first trip down to Catterick to meet Freddie. Evelyn has confirmed my promotion to Sister and has allowed me to choose a date to fit in with Harry's progress. I'm being spoilt, lucky me!

I want to discuss my ideas to visit Freddie's parents. I do hope he's still ok with it. We've spoken on the telephone but the line was crackly. I think I heard the right words but not the enthusiasm. I suspect he would back out if I didn't keep the pressure on. Either way I know it has to be done, to give them a chance of a proper reunion.

Our two-month-old Harry is sleeping in his baby basket. I've managed to feed him without too much embarrassment to the other passengers although one older lady tut-tutted loudly and turned the other way. In my view it's a natural process and, providing I don't flaunt any bare flesh, I'm in my rights to feed my child. I've left Florence with Millie. She loves having her. Flo's company for her young Frank and I can see this reduces the full time needs of a single toddler.

We soon arrive at Catterick station and I immediately spot Freddie on the platform in his RAF uniform. I feel so proud that he's mine and no-one else's. I get up when the train stops and I'm noticed by a kind old railwayman who opens the door and takes my bag down from the luggage rack. He even helps me step on to the platform while I clutch Harry's basket. Freddie runs up and offers him a tip.

"No thank you Sir, it's my pleasure. Have a good day you two"

He almost gives us a salute. I shout thank you before he walks away to wave his flag.

"What a kind man."

"He is and so am I. Give me a kiss you. How's my Harry?"

We now have the platform to ourselves and take our time before we leave to drive to the aerodrome, or so I thought. He gives a little cough and confesses that he needs to fetch something from his digs first. I smile. I know him too well. But it has been a long time since we've been able to make love and I've really missed him. I just hope Harry stays asleep.

I lie back on to the pillow completely relaxed and loved. My body has just about returned to its pre-pregnancy shape and condition apart from of course my milk-laden breasts still over-large. But there are no complaints there. I do believe he prefers them this way. It's a shame they have to return to their normal size but at least my clothes will fit again.

I listen to him clearing away our dinner plates. He is very tidy and organised, some man. He comes in with a tray laden with everything for afternoon tea including cake bought locally.

"When dee ye have te gan te work?"

"Tomorrow, I managed to fiddle a day off today. But I've got a special treat for you providing Harry behaves himself."

"What is it?"

He smiles roguishly. "You'll find out, tomorrow."

"Whey aye, sounds interesting."

I get out of bed, slip on one of Freddie's dressing gowns and pick up a gurgling Harry from his basket. Through our tea, try as I may, Freddie doesn't reveal any more clues. The tea was just how I like it, warming and satisfying. I've taught him well. We then turn our attention to our son, playing with him on the bed. I know I've been lucky. Rarely have my babies been a problem. Little persistent crying except when wanting a feed. But there's always the nappy change and this is that time!

"I can handle him, I've got a bucket for steeping, some towels and nappies. Remember I was with you when you came out of the hospital."

53

I watched, a little nervously, but there was no need to be. He managed with great care and gentleness and returned him clean and even smelling of talc. Timing it beautifully for his feed. I can never imagine my Da having anything to do with it. He used to turn his nose up at the smell of dirty nappies and disinfectant despite himself honking of fish most of the time.

With Harry fed, changed and back to sleep in his basket Freddie managed to slip his hand under my dressing gown wanting more passion.

I grabbed and withdrew his hand. "No Freddie, ah want te speak te ye about our trip to see yer parents."

"We can do that tomorrow."

"No, now. This is me idea or rather Evelyn's: We catch the train doon to London then Dover. There's a ferry over to Calais an' we catch another train to Munich changin' in Paris. Easy. Ye did say yer parents lived in Munich didn't ye?"

Freddie sighs, holds his head in his hands then eventually looks up at me. I wait patiently for his answer. I can see he's not keen, but I'm determined.

"Well?"

"They live about fifteen miles out of Munich in a village called Starnberg. It will take us days and we'll need bags and bags of luggage and who's Evelyn anyway?"

"Ye know her, Sister Evelyn Parker. She knows someone who travelled to Strasbourg. It's on the same route."

"I'd rather fly there!"

I ignore this and continue. "We can stay in Dover an' in Paris. It will be fun."

"With a three-year-old and a baby? And what about the cost? We'll need to rob a bank."

I also ignore this. "If ye wanted te see yer parents ye would agree immediately. Besides ahm gannin te be a Sister. They get well paid."

He shakes his head, I think, I hope, he knows he can't change my mind.

"Ok, ok, I'll talk to the RAF, see what they say. I'll get you another cup of tea." He smiles for the first time but there's a devilish look in his eyes. On condition...."

I know instantly what he wants. I pull off my dressing gown and slink under the bed covers as sensually as possible.

He undresses and pulls back the covers revealing my naked body and starts to kiss his favourite spots. I think, how easy it is to get around a man. But I have to admit it's all worth it.

****

It's the middle of the morning on the following day and I'm staring out of the airmens' hut at the aerodrome. Harry is asleep in his basket in the quietest corner. But it's all quiet and I'm wondering what's happening. All the men including Freddie are in the hanger next door getting their aeroplanes ready. Only Alec the clerk is quietly working away in his office, head down. He arranges the rotas, reports and, well, everything really, leaving the pilots just to get on with the flying.

He's been out to see me, just to say hello. His answer to my question to try to discover what's happening was 'oh they're only sorting flight details'. He immediately ran back to his office shutting the door securely behind him. Mysterious.

The sky is cloudy and there is a chill in the air, a typical October day. All I can see is the tree lined grass runway and a limp wind-sock. I can't hear anything but then, making me jump, an engine starts and then a minute later another one. After a few minutes I look to the right, a biplane appears out of the hanger, then another. They trundle over to the runway and stop. Another engine starts and again after a few minutes Old Gertie appears still lumbering like an old horse and

55

cart and I can guess who's sitting in it. My heart leaps, yes, he's going to take me up again. I have to admit I was hoping Freddie's surprise was going to include another flight.

The old girl hisses and wheezes towards the hut. The quiet, relaxed morning has disappeared replaced by a vibrant, mechanical cacophony. I run over to check on Harry who thankfully is still blissfully asleep after his last feed. Alec appears smiling holding in one hand the same long, black fleece lined coat I wore before and in the other a fleece lined hood, goggles, warm gloves and best of all, fleece lined boots.

He speaks quietly. "Better put all these on Emily it's not exactly warm up there." The door opens, he sees Freddie and walks back in to his office. He seems to be a shy man and doesn't want to interfere.

Freddie gives him a thumbs-up. "Thanks Alec. Now get all this gear on and we'll be off. How's Harry."

I shush him and whisper. "He's canny." I give him a cuddle. "Thankyou." The clothes fit me perfectly and I really feel the part, I feel snug, warm and eager to fly.

Walking over to Gertie I gesture over to the other two planes and shout over the noise. "Are they comin' with us?"

"Of course. you're a V.I.P. you need an escort. I'll help you up."

There's no time for any other questions. I climb in to my seat between the struts, he follows me up and makes sure the straps are tight.

He shouts into my ears. "Remember you can turn with your stick control and the rudder. So, if you're going right, stick to the right and lightly press the right rudder pedal. If you want to climb stick towards you, and away from you for going down. Have a practice."

I look at him quizzically.

"Go on try, see how it feels."

I do remember from the last and the only other time he's taken me up, but I never actually touched anything. So now I'm getting a feel of the controls. They are certainly doing something, the movement is precise, nothing loose or wobbly. It feels exciting, daring. I know I would really like to fly for real. He gives me a thumbs up and leaves to climb in to his own seat behind.

I hear his voice through the speaking tube. "Ready?"

I answer the same and we're off down the runway, the engine is roaring, the wheels are bumping and as we accelerate the wind increases. We lift off the ground and the noise reduces down to the roar of the engines. The sky is directly in front, the ground disappearing quickly each side and it feels totally exhilarating.

Looking at the altimeter we level off at about 800 feet, I think it is. I can now see the hills in front of us. I look over the side for a view of the Yorkshire Moors passing below interlaced with stone walls and the occasional lane and tracks. The engine noise is increasing. I look to my right between the wings and to my horror another biplane is now flying alongside. My eyes are wide open in shock. He is so close, what is he doing? The pilot waves and points to my left. I look over and there's another aeroplane equally close with the pilot holding a banner in one hand reading in big red letters the word HAPPY. He then waves to me and points to my right to the first pilot who now has his own banner reading BIRTHDAY. I can't believe it and of course I hear Freddie trying to sing to me through the tube. I wait for him to finish and wave at the pilots each side. I can only smile but still nervous of them being so close. I grab the tube and shout. "But it's not me birthday until next month!"

"I know, but I may not get the chance then. So, today's the day."

I give the pilots another wave each and they veer off and suddenly we're by ourselves in the wide-open sky. What a treat. I can guarantee no-one has had such a present before.

I shout down the tube. "Thank ye, ah love ye."

"I've not finished with you yet. I want you to climb to 1000 feet. Off you go."

"Yer jokin' right?"

"Pull the stick slowly towards you."

I silently swear but I think, yes, I'm going to and I take a hold of the stick. Slowly, steadily, I pull, immediately the nose starts to rise. For some reason the noise from the engine increases.

"Leave the throttle to me. A little more on the stick. Ok, now slowly push it away until we're level."

For the next ten minutes we dive, climb again, turn right and left using the stick and the rudder pedals. I'm flying a plane. I want to fling my arms in the air in celebration but I don't want to release the controls.

"Ok love, I'll take over. You're a natural, well done. I'll bring her into land. Make sure your straps are tight."

I release my hold and slump back into the seat overwhelmed which soon changes into a relaxed exhaustion. But Freddie isn't finished. He can't resist some acrobatics: tight turns, sudden lifts and drops. As a finale we do a low pass over the aerodrome and waggles his wings at his mates before we turn and land in front of them.

I manage to extricate myself from the cockpit and jump down to the grass but I'm still in another world. I just know I want more but for now I just fly at my smiling Freddie, arms outstretched. He catches me in mid-air and swings me round, my legs clasping his waist. "Thank ye, thank ye." I kiss him full on the mouth something that starts a series of whistles from our audience.

We walk hand in hand to the hut. I thank the two other pilots for their antics. I couldn't have asked for a more enjoyable day. Inside I spot Alec holding a bundle of blankets looking very pleased with himself.

"Well Harry was happy at first, gurgling and kicking his legs but then I think he realised he was hungry and started whimpering. So, I hope you don't mind but I picked him up and we've had lots of conversations and he loves my badges."

I can see Harry is happy....until he sees me and screws up his face and starts bellowing.

"Yer a born father Alec, thank ye fer lookin' after him. I'd bettor find somewhere te feed him."

"Mmmm, please use my office. I'm off for a walk anyway."

He looks a little embarrassed but I take up his offer and settle down with my baby. While everyone else continues with their day I need time to sit back and relax and relive what has happened. I just can't stop smiling.

Chapter 11

Millie doesn't believe me. She's shaking her head, hand to her mouth. "Yer tellin' me that ye actually flew an aeroplane?" I nod for the umpteenth time "Ye lucky thing." She paused. "An' ye didn't crash into the ground?"

I laugh. "Of course ah did, lots of times! No, he didn't let me land." I smile, "Maybe next time."

"Ah bet no-one in the whole of Newcastle has been up in an aeroplane let alone fly one!" She pauses thinking. "Does the RAF know about yer escapade?"

"You're joking. Officially ahm from the local newspaper wantin' a flying story. If anyone in authority finds out who ah really am poor Freddie won't heor the last of it. He'll probably have te leave. It's a bit risky." I smile widely. "But ahm gannin te have another try. It's so canny."

"The Flying Sister. That'll be a great story. You'll be famous. Again!"

We're sitting in the park wrapped up keeping warm in the clear Autumn day. Frank and Florence are playing with some sticks while Harry sleeps in my sling. I arrived home at midday having caught the early train, after the most wonderful day ever. I know it could land Freddie into trouble but he trusts the team at the base. And, there is no doubt, the 'reporter' will be calling again! I'm going to make the best of my time at home with my children, meeting my friends, making plans for my new Sister role and of course arranging our trip to Germany. Not sure how we can afford it but something will turn up. Life is all good.

****

Our mid-Winter journey to Dover has been completed smoothly and efficiently. Freddie travelled up to Newcastle to help me get everything together and to board the train. He's been in a good mood chatting about his early days in Germany. I think he's looking forward to meeting his parents. He's accepted that I won't change my mind and I believe, now that we're on our way, the heavy burden of guilt held all these years is being released. He made all the travel arrangements himself and booked the hotels both here, in Dover, and in Paris. His friends at the base have helped. This was obvious when I revisited the airfield last month for another flying lesson. Although I feel certain they believe it is just a holiday trip and have no idea we're going to meet his German parents.

He is like a magician. Somehow, he managed to get us both first class train tickets all the way to France and in reserved compartments. It was so much easier. No problems with Florence playing noisily or Harry bawling. No embarrassment breast feeding or from amorous approaches from my 'husband' or, occasionally, the other way around! Equally, the hotel looks one of the best and we have a wonderful room overlooking the harbour. Freddie boasted that no less a person than my heroine: Harriet Quimby, stayed here just before her cross-Channel flight in 1912. I feel very honoured.

"Sorry love but when we get to Calais the RAF's generosity runs out and we'll have to rough it for the rest of our journey with everyone else!"

I smile at this revelation. "Ah divvent want te know about the fiddlin' that's been gannin on. Ahm just gannin to enjoy it while ah can." I stop and look around the room in wonder. "To think Harriet stayed here." I sigh. "Ah hope ah can follow in her footsteps."

"Oh no you don't. She crashed and died in the same year and I'm not letting you to do that. She was only in her thirties."

I'm shocked. "Oh, poor hinney." I look over to Freddie. "But ahm determined to keep flying when ah can an' maybe get me pilot's license."

"I know and you will. Also, today's aircraft are much safer so you've got a better survival chance."

Now lying awake in bed I'm thinking back to my last flying lesson. There were no Happy Birthday stunts like before but plenty of circuits and exhilarating climbs and stalls and tight turns. I feel super confident – but as yet I haven't tried taking off or landing. Maybe next time. It's difficult to sleep and when I do, I suspect I'll be dreaming of flying over the English Channel, Harriet style.

This morning we're huddled together trying to keep warm on the deck of our ferry: *The Maid of Orleans.* I know it's warm down below but I want to be reminded of my journeys over to France during the war. The smell of the salty air, the excitement, the dread, the nervous fear of the unknown - especially the first time. This time there are far fewer ships about, no navy frigates or corvettes, no lurking submarines and no-one in military uniform. This is a different ferry but memories flood back.

We leave the harbour and as Britain slips away, we wave at the White Cliffs and shout goodbye and see you again soon. Florence is bemused and excited. Harry is asleep and at nearly six months old she's getting heavy. Freddie is brave enough to volunteer to take over the burden but not the indignity of the sling. Instead he takes him in his arms and walks proudly forward. I just hope he doesn't trip!

There are few families on board. Instead most of the passengers seem to be businessmen in smarts coats and hats, or couples dressed in the latest fashion walking along the decking as if on parade. I feel dowdy in my practical but warm and comfortable clothing. It shows my bust and waist where they are and not flattened and dropped almost to my knees. The men's clothing is loose and looks comfortable, very much like Freddie's attire. It suddenly dawns that perhaps he would like me to wear the latest trends.

"Don't even think about it. You wear what you feel comfortable in." He looks at the fashions exhibited around him and smiles. "Either way you'll never get into those things."

"Are ye saying ahm f.."

"No, you're just the right shape and just to prove it." He hands over Harry and sits him on my hip. "There we are, a perfect fit."

I give him a look and then realise that a certain baby needs a nappy change, again. I sigh, grab my bag and handover Flo. "Look after our daughter while ah deal with this." I give him a tight-lipped look but he slips his arm around my waist. "No, I'll come with you. I've seen enough of the sea for now."

We spend the rest of the short journey in the warmth of the covered lounge playing with the children and chatting to other passengers. I know he likes me as I am, which is as well, because I'm not going to change!

Our onward journey to Paris isn't exactly like my squashed-in, khaki journeys of 1917/18 but not that much different. At Calais railway station the announcements, posters, signs and the uniformed staff direct passengers to the first class only 'Orient Express' luxury train. But not for us. Ours is on the adjacent platform looking like a poor, lost cousin, distinctly third class. We settle in our seats amongst an all French speaking clientele. I gaze wistfully at the departing super train complete with whistles blowing, flags flying and smiling, waving passengers. Ours follows along ten minutes later without any such fanfare.

I hope we could manage our normal routine of feeding, changing and controlling the children in such a limited space. Freddie, of course, can speak French and I can still remember words and phrases from 5 years ago. It becomes immediately obvious our fellow passengers love children. Full of smiles they play with Florence and admire Harry in his sling. Some unpack snacks and tit-bits and offer them around. It's like one big happy family. The train stops at wayside stations allowing an interchange of passengers. A young lady with a baby settles in opposite and immediately starts breast feeding. There is no embarrassment and she can even speak some English. I take advantage, start feeding Harry and happily converse with my new friend, Helene. She's travelling home after spending time with her mother. Our children are the obvious first topic but our conversation inevitably moves on to what we did in the war. I explain my role as a nurse at the Casualty Clearing Station in Flanders. Shockingly she tells me how she lost both her brothers and her father fighting. Our conversation ceases. She looks down. I can see she's thinking about them. I reach for her hand and try to console her in my mixture of languages.

"Pardon Madam. Ah know how ye must feel. Ah lost family as well." I tell her about Con and then my own father and older brothers.

"Ye know, ah see them sometimes in their fishin' boat. They wave. It makes me believe they're still with me, lookin' after me like."

She looks up, eyes wide, she nods. "Oui et moi aussi. Mais..not at sea, along the lane by our ferme, in uniform, and they wave." She grabs my hand and smiles broadly, "It is nice."

I can only nod and agree, "Oui, it is nice."

"Ma Mere she not see them. She hates the Germans."

"Do ye?"

She shakes her head vigorously. "No….only the generals."

"Bon."

She gets off at Amiens and we wave as our train jolts back into action and accelerates out of the station. I sit back and wonder at the co-incidences of our pasts and our visions of our departed relations. I fabricated the story of us holidaying in Paris. I'm very defensive about Freddie and his German nationality. I shouldn't be, Helene doesn't hold a grudge and that's how it should be.

By the time we reach the Gare-du-Nord in Paris it's getting dark and we're all needing a quiet time. Florence particularly is flagging, having been the centre of attention throughout the journey she is now grumpy and whiney. Harry has an easy life: feeding, being changed, sleeping and reacting to admiring passengers. For the parents, our need is to find our hotel and slump somewhere. Thoughts of dinner can wait.

No chance.

The city is heaving with humanity. It is London times two. We stand and stare, then twist round trying to take in everything, the nose-to-tail traffic, the cacophony of different sounds and wondering how on earth we can find our way.

"Vous etes perdu?....Lost?"

An automobile has stopped besides us, it's a taxicab. The driver is looking at us hopefully. Freddie shows him a piece of paper showing our hotel details.

"Ahhh, the Roma Sacre Coeur in Montmartre. It is only cinque minutes." He demonstrates by showing one hand.

"Ok Em? We could walk if you want."

"With all our cases an' Flo an' Harry, no thanks. We'd probably get lost anywa'."

He smiles. "Where's your adventure?"

"Mmm. Let's settle in, then adventure!"

It takes fifteen minutes but the journey is fascinating and the destination stunning. I gaze up at the grand hotel with its ornate balconies and carvings. We can hear music from a café opposite, delicious spiced aromas surround and envelope us. It's another world. I leave Freddie to pay the taxi and sort our booking at the reception. The clanking lift delivers us to the very top floor and once in our room we run to the window to gaze over the city. And there's the Basilica of the Sacre Couer gleaming white before our eyes, its dome thrusting high into the blue cloudless sky. I've heard about it, read about it and now I can see it.

Built in the last century as an atonement for the savagery of the war with Prussia and amazingly funded by public donations. The war to end all future wars. Little did they know. Little have we learnt.

Our bedroom of brightly coloured walls includes a little cot for Harry and a double bed which will do for the three of us. Our weariness has vanished in the rush of adrenaline. We all bounce on the bed, cuddle and shout. 'We're here, Paris, the capital of France'. Little Harry's eyes are glued open in shock, poor Florence thinks we're mad. Perhaps we are, but I want to have fun.

I look at Flo. "Let's gan over to the café opposite an' see what they have to eat, shall we?"

She nods, "Will they have lemonade?"

"Oooh, let's find out."

We find a change of clothes each, pocket some French francs and make for the lift. Flo gets there first and presses the button magically starting the rumbling and clanking far below us. We can see the lift arrive behind the grill and soon we're inside and dropping back down to ground level. Flo grips my hand tight. It's all so new, so exciting. The café is warm and inviting. A smiling elderly man wearing a black beret is playing his accordion in the corner and even manages to wave at us in welcome. Food is chosen and arrives within a few minutes.

"What's this Ma?"

"It's called Croque-Monsieur. Actually, it's French cheese an' ham. It's lovely an' there's yer lemonade." Freddie and myself feast on spicy baguettes helped down with a glass of wine, or two. I can sit back and take in the atmosphere while Freddie manages to eat and hold Harry at the same time. The comparison with nearly twenty years ago strikes me. I could never imagine Pa ever doing that. How times have changed, for me at least. I suspect most men would still resist such a temptation! I wonder if Ma's new companion, Davey, is like Freddie. I think he is. Perhaps they're doing the same as us in America. I hope so, she so deserves it. I do miss them all.

It's late when we finish. Flo and Harry should both be tucked up in bed. But this is special day. We join the happy throng of Parisians and walk along the streets listening to their accents and taking in their different dress styles, all so very exotic and exciting.

The warmth soaked up in the café is now being cooled by the Winter breeze and I can see Flo shivering. Freddie picks her up and we make our way back to our hotel. By the time we get back they're both fast asleep in our arms and only need tucking up into their beds. I know Harry will need feeding soon but for now the drama of the day has caught up with both of us and we slump down on to the sofa.

"It's been a canny, how are ye feelin'?"

"Tired, ready for bed."

I look over, he's eyes are closed. I smile to myself but just a little disappointed. But then one eye springs open. He smiles devilishly.

"But not too tired."

"Good, but we mustn't wake Flo."

He pats the sofa. "So, what's wrong with this?"

Whether it's the cushions or our advancing ages we just can't get comfortable. So, with great care, Freddie transfers Flo from our bed to the sofa, making sure she's still asleep, then we both strip off and slip between the bed covers. It feels delicious. We kiss, cuddle and make love several times until we fall asleep in each other's arms totally satisfied with our day.

Chapter 12

The morning of the next day was not so good. I'm feeding Harry, Freddie and Flo are still fast asleep and my head feels very heavy. I guess this is the effect of the wine. It was lovely at the time but I'm not used to it and if this is the effect it has then I'll go without in future – or at least try something different!

It's still dark outside. It must be early but I'm not sure how early. Haven't been able to focus on the clock. I want to slump back onto the pillow, back to sleep. I'm sure I would feel better if I could but Harry continues feeding and I haven't changed sides yet. I sigh and wonder what today will bring. A change of country, certainly, then a meeting with Freddie's parents. I look over to his prone body just visible. He will be nervous. I hope it'll go well. It'll make all the difference to him. I want his deep-rooted shame to be removed. He needs resolution, an understanding by both parties.

Our next and last part of our journey is the longest. It will take all day with a change of trains at Strasbourg near the German border. While Freddie is buying the tickets, I've been stationed around a bench seat on the concourse of Gare d'Lest railway station surrounded by our children, suitcases and new bags of food for the journey. The high ceiling with its imperious arches makes the space inside feel calm and organized certainly more relaxed than the Gare du Nord. I feel excited, I do like train journeys, but a little anxious about the duration.

I need not have worried. The children are either entertained, eating or asleep. Freddie however is getting more tense and impatient the closer we journey to Munich. He is nervous. He has no idea of the reception we will have. Someone is going to meet us to take us the last step to Starnberg. Father, mother, friend, driver? I don't know. He hasn't spoken to his father for many years, his mother, no more than once each year. Will they be polite but formal or will they show some degree of forgiveness or even love?

Bavaria seems to be a really beautiful place: huge forests, magnificent mountains to the South and pretty villages and towns. Rolling into Munich itself is a delight, dominated as it is by huge elaborate towered churches, rows and rows of colorful crimson tiled roofs and wide thoroughfares. Peering through the windows I notice the fashions for women are similar to those I've seen in Paris or London but already I've noticed the men and boys often wear lederhosen or plus-fours. This reminds me instantly of my days in Flanders working in the German hospital and being shown family photos. I rather like the difference.

Freddie is first out of the train, completely distracted.

"Pet, can ye help me please?"

He's looking along the platform. Hearing me he turns around. "Oh, sorry love, give me those." He points to the cases, then grabs them. "Come on, they'll be waiting for us."

I grab his arm and pull him back. "Ah think we're a few minutes early, there's no rush." I smile trying to make him relax.

"Oh, I know, I know, sorry....mm....Let me help with Florence."

We make for the ticket barrier looking around for someone to recognize us. I see plenty of taxicabs and automobiles and some omnibuses but no obvious contact waves or shouts. Then Freddie recognizes something.

"Ah, there he is." He points to a horse drawn carriage pulling up alongside the kerbing further away. As we walk towards it, I have to wonder what I'm going to find at his parents' house. This man is obviously not his father. He's young, formally dressed in breeches and cap. The carriage is gleaming and the horse beautifully turned out. The driver sees us and opens the door.

"Sir, Frau." He actually bows.

"Danke. Das sind Emily und meine Kinder Florence und Harry."

He bows again. He helps me in and closes the door behind us then packs our cases into the back. I feel like a queen. I look around a little embarrassed at all the attention. We have certainly been noticed. Some of the older people are smiling but I do notice the younger ones, particularly the men, are ignoring us, some even sneering. I'm shocked and very pleased to get on our way.

Our final part of our epic journey is so different from anything else. The carriage sways comfortably along the smooth surfaced road all the way to Starnberg. Out of Munich and into the countryside the only sound is the trotting of the horse and the occasional domestic animal call. We have blankets to keep us warm although Freddie and Flo ignore them completely: Freddie trying to keep calm pointing out landmarks, Flo just too excited running from side to side enjoying the ride.

Starnberg is a small picturesque town set on the slopes of a hill at the head of a large lake.

"We used to sail our model boats in a small cove down there." He points to a quiet area surrounded by leafless trees away from any houses. "The water is shallow we could just wade in easily." He smiles briefly before quickly turning away.

"Were ye happy then?"

He looks at me quizzically. "Yes, I suppose I was but..I'm much happier now. I live in the real world. Then, I was guarded all the time, rarely by myself. My Kindermädchen or our chauffer were always with us.

"Kindermädchen?"

"Nanny."

"Freddie, how many servants did ye have?"

He laughs. "Many, but I don't know how many. My Kindermädchen was nice, very kind." He is obviously relaxing, reminiscing. "I'll always remember her but particular her bottom, it was huge, well huge to me, I suppose I was much smaller then. I

70

think my father also liked her." He shakes his head, "I saw him several times smacking it and smiling. She always gave him a small smile back." His eyebrows lift, "Oh, do you think they were….."

"Ah divvent think so. Ah only know a little about him but he seems very strict." I smile at him. "But it seems ye take after him with yer love of certain bulges."

His eyes widen in mock horror. "As if." He immediately slides over to my side and kisses me on the lips while sliding a hand under my coat to feel my own bulges.

I let him have his fill. I want him to relax as much as possible. But it's nice anyway.

We're climbing now, above the town and back into the countryside. The wide panorama of a distant mountain range appears, it looks just beautiful. Soon we slow and pass below an arch and through a pair of open ornate steel gates. We have arrived, apparently, but I can't see any sign of housing. Instead the road has changed into a neat stone track cutting through a neat field grazed by some cows and sheep and dotted with mature trees.

"Are we in a park?" Flo's eyes are wide open with the prospect of having lots of fun.

Freddie answers. "Well not really, it belongs to your Grandma and Grandpa. It's part of their garden."

Like me this information has stunned Flo into silence. The track follows a slow bend to the right slowly revealing what looks like a small castle. It's something I've only ever seen in storybooks. The three-storey building is complete with towers at each corner topped with conical roofs, castellations between and with a wide set of steps leading up to the front entrance.

"Oh Freddie it's beautiful. Why didn't ye tell me?"

"I thought it might put you off."

At first, I don't take in what he says. I'm so mesmerised by such a grand house in such a wonderful setting. There are other separate smaller structures in the grounds. One looks like a stable block then:

"What dee ye mean it might put me off? It's beautiful. It's like a castle in a magical fairy-tale book."

"Mmm, it might look it but it's not magical. It's a liability. There's always something falling down or leaking."

"Pet, when you've lived in a tiny cottage or a poky flat or a squashed-in terraced house all yer life then this is paradise no matter if the rain comes in – wear a raincoat! Is yer father a Duke or somethin'?"

"No, of course not. His title is: Count Feldafing. My mother is the Countess of course."

My eyes widen even further but it's too late to ask more questions, we're slowing then pulling up by the steps. I see the doors opening and someone moving smartly out to meet us. The chauffer opens the carriage door, Freddie jumps down, lifts Florence to the ground, takes Harry and helps me out. I can get used to this.

As we go through the big entrance doors, strangely, I'm taken back to my first day at the Workhouse. The main building was an old stately home but when I was interned at fourteen years old it was so run-down. Filthy dirty, broken furniture and it stank like a dungeon, the opposite of this spotless palace.

We're shown into the Reception Room. The doorman makes sure we're comfortable.

"Ich werde deine Mutter wissen lassen, dass du hier bist"

"Dankeschön"

He leaves closing the door quietly behind him. "What was that, something about yer Ma?"

"Yes, he's going to let her know we're here."

So, we wait. I look around the room. It's very grand with its huge windows and high ornate ceiling, bookcases on two walls, portraits filling the other two. There's a large drinks cabinet, settees and an open fire slowly burning timber logs. I'm feeling nervous myself, I wonder if I have to curtsey to the Countess, shake hands, bow. Freddie says. "No, just say hello."

Must be at least twenty minutes later and we're still waiting. Florence is getting fidgety, Harry is hungry.

I have to decide which is best: a struggling, noisy, hungry baby or giving the first view of her son's 'wife', bare breasted. "Sorry Freddie ahm gannin te have te feed him." By now, I'm an expert at discretion and can feed my child without showing much bare flesh. I settle down to the task. Almost immediately the door opens and in sweeps the Countess, a tall, slim majestic woman. I jump, Harry is surprised, stops feeding, leans back and starts yelling revealing my chest in its full glory!

"Oh."

Chapter 13

"How are you Mother?"

Freddie's mother re-composes herself quickly while I re-adjust myself. "Oh, how lovely to see you Gunther." She takes in Florence and myself. "And your wife and children."

"This is Emily, our daughter Florence and son Harry."

She speaks to me. "I'm so sorry to burst in on you I didn't realise...and your children, they are so lovely."

I've decided to stay seated and extend my hand. "Lovely te meet ye Countess. Sorry ah canna stand at the moment. Ah want to keep Harry quiet."

She sits down next to me on the settee. "You must make yourself at home and please call me Brigitte." She plays with Harry's blonde curls. "So like my son's." She gets up quickly, I think embarrassed by her remark. "I'll get Karl to show you to your room. Dinner will be ready in one hour."

"Thank you Mother, but I'm afraid we only have casual clothing. I hope that's acceptable?"

"Of course dear. We rarely dress for dinner these days." She leaves the room closing the door quietly behind her.

"Oh dear, ah think she's embarrassed. Ah assume Bertie wes blonde?"

"Mmm. Come on, I know the room we've been given. Our bags will be there, let's go."

****

The house is simply sumptuous, stunning, so very different from my quarters in Newcastle. The staircase rises grandly, watched over by portraits of family members. Our bedroom is enormous. The two huge windows provide panoramic views over more gardens and the

74

mountain range in the far distance. A gardener is packing up for the day, pushing a wheelbarrow full of swept leaves and garden implements. In normal circumstances the tranquil setting would relax me, but not today.

Florence however is in her element. She has her own bed and is now bouncing as high as she can. "Can ah have a bed like this at hyem please, it's so springy."

I know she wants her own bed. Sharing with her Ma is not the best but it'll have to do until I can afford something larger. "One day Flo, ah promise."

There's even a cot-bed complete with lacy side curtains. I can guess who used this last. I lay a fully fed Harry inside hoping he'll stay asleep at least until we finish. I know he'll want some action before we can get to bed for the night.

But the best is for Freddie and me, a four-poster bed big enough for all of us combined. I sit, sink into it and ponder: why is there such a huge difference in standards between most people and the few in the Upper Class? Is it good for the working class to accept and look up to the wealthy? Or bad to know that some live like this when most survive in comparative squalor?

"Come on dreamer. Best get changed. And don't think I don't know what you're thinking. This country, like Britain has suffered or enjoyed the class system for generations and it's not going to change overnight. If it does at all. So put your communist ideas aside for now."

"Ah know. Anyway, stop reading my mind. Ahm not gannin te worry about that. For now, ah have te remember how te eat in the proper manner!" I look over to Flo still bouncing. "An' hope our daughter behaves herself."

Dinner has passed without too many embarrassments and we have adjourned into a sitting room. Wilhelm, Freddie's father, is absent on business in Berlin and won't be back for a couple of days. I'm thinking that this might be a good thing. Brigitte seems nice. She's obviously very pleased to see her Gunther (I have to remember to call him by his German name). She also likes children and helps to entertain Florence so she may try to influence the Count when he returns. However, our conversation inevitably turns to politics. I learn more about the conditions in Germany.

"The Weimer government is weak. They've lost control of inflation. People in Bavaria are starving and they're turning to militant organisations in desperation, especially the communists." God knows what will become of us if they come to power."

Freddie asks. "What about the Nationalists?"

"I'm not sure they're any better. They want to emulate that Mussolini man in Italy. You know, he took over the government and he's now their dictator. I suppose we may do better with them, but there's another problem: they blame the Jews for the present mess and they promise to remove them from the country and stop all immigration." She hesitated. "What they actually said was that they would destroy all Jews!".

Freddie shook his head in disbelief. "If this government can't sort out this inflation then your alternatives are bloodshed or bloodshed."

I took my leave with Flo to check on Harry leaving Freddie and his Ma to continue their talk. Sitting on the floor playing with my children I can't help thinking. Communism v Dictatorship. Communism, surely, is better for the majority but then I think of the millions killed in the Russian Revolution. In reality I know a Democracy is best, after all what have I been fighting for over the last ten years. The rise of the British Labour Party has given me hope for the future. A party elected by the majority who will stand up for all Classes. This must be the best option. For Germany's sake I have to believe the current government will sort out the economy before the country starts to look at alternatives.

Sometime later Freddie joins us.

"How's yer Ma? She wasn't too embarrassed by me?

"Certainly not, in fact, just the opposite. I gave her a brief resume on your life. She wishes she could have been more like you. To stand up for herself."

"Thanks love an' how's yer father?"

"By the sound of it he hasn't changed."

"Well, we'll have te see, won't we? Anyway, let's just hope the German leaders sort themselves out like an' not give these extreme parties a chance. Ah mean who can vote fer someone threatenin' to 'destroy' entire races of people?"

"Mother's really worried."

"But why?"

"She's Jewish."

Chapter 14

Over breakfast we agreed to accompany Brigitte to Munich. Despite the Winter weather and the failing economy, the weekends bring the Bavarians out to enjoy themselves in the cafes and bars or just for a walk with their families. Our transport is yesterday's elegant horse and carriage with our chauffeur, Hans.

We stop alongside the River Isar. Hans helps us dismount, then, before we set off, I notice him speaking to Brigitte. He looks anxious and whatever he's saying he's causing her some concern. Freddie joins in the conversation but whatever it is I have no idea of the problem. I assume they will let me know some time meanwhile I snuggle Harry into my sling, take Florence by the hand and we peer through the railings at the flowing river. It is a clear but cold day but we're warmly wrapped and ready to enjoy the city.

We're soon through a gate in to a park strangely called the 'Englischer Garten'. Freddie explains that the design was built to resemble an English country garden and was actually managed by the military – to give them a grounding in farming and gardening operations. He adds, cynically, that it didn't stop them blowing the countryside apart in wartime.

We stop at a café outside a Chinese style building and they manage to produce a pot of tea for me while Freddie and Brigitte have coffee. A lemon drink arrives for Flo and there is a plate of German baking delights. The park is enormous and very popular. More and more walkers arrive, not just families on a day out but large groups of men and women have gathered. I'm beginning to wonder if there is some special fair being set up when I hear music in the background. Disjointed at first, the musicians quickly get into rhythm. It is a brass band and although they are out of my sight, the music is delightful and we can relax in the warming Winter sunshine.

Having completed our mid-morning meal, we leave to visit a children's play area. The band has stopped for a well-earned break. Their music has been replaced by someone speaking through a loud hailer.

All in German of course but I'm still interested to watch but Freddie and Brigitte are steering us away from the speaker. I stop and try to get a sight of the speaker through the crowd forming. "Can we have a look at him?"

Freddie shakes his head vigorously. "No, we must leave now, the play area is this way."

I look back at him. He is obviously worried. His Ma has lifted up Florence and is now striding away in the opposite direction.

"But, it's only one..." Before I could finish a group of determined, brown uniformed men run past us, push into the crowd and stride towards the speaker. Seconds later I hear new shouting and then, unbelievably, shots are fired. The crowd immediately backs towards us, people turn and start running. Freddie grabs my hand and pulls me away. I try to run. I squeeze Harry to my chest. I don't know what's happening. I can't hear any more shots, just shrieks and cries from the retreating, panicking mass of people. I'm running, still pulled by Freddie. I must not trip and crush my baby. What am I doing running away? Someone may be hurt they may need help.

We stop at last and look back.

The area has changed. The bustling happy gathering has gone, replaced by deserted buildings. The grassed area is littered with debris left by the crowd fleeing for their lives. Then I see them, bodies in amongst the litter, some moving, others are still. I must help them. I'm a nurse. I can help. I hand Harry over to Freddie and retrace my steps. The first injuries I find are elderly women and men trampled by the human stampede and abandoned. They are in shock. There are no obvious injuries but I comfort them as best I can and try to tell them not to move and wait for medical help. Nearer the platform is a young man in a suit with an armband. He is not moving. His eyes are closed but he is breathing. Blood is seeping through his clothing from a chest wound. I look for a cloth to stem the flow but I hear a noise close behind me. I look up and see one of the brown-shirted men looking down. He's holding a gun loosely in his hand. He's staring at the injured man. He's very young, in his teens. He looks frightened.

I try to communicate. "Have you a cloth?" I show him the wound.

"Use this." I hear Freddie behind me. I turn and grab his handkerchief and immediately apply it to the wound.

"Ah need a bandage. He needs te get to a hospital now. Can we get yer carriage heor?"

"My mother has already gone to fetch him." He turns, "Here they are now."

I do the best I can using one of my stockings for a bandage. Freddie and Hans load him carefully in to the carriage.

"Look after the bairns love. I'll stay heor with these others."

Freddie looks at the frightened man. "What about him?"

"Divvent worry, he's in shock. Ah can manage, he's harmless now."

Freddie approaches him and carefully removes the gun from his hand. "The hospital is only a few minutes away. We'll be back as soon as possible. Stay here won't you."

I nod. He jumps in to the carriage and they're away.

The young man is now slumped on to the grass his arms clutched around his knees. I can hear him sobbing. I go up to him and put my hand on his shoulder, I try to remember some German words. "*Warum*, why did ye do this?"

He looks at me. I think he half understands what I'm saying. He shakes his head and speaks in stuttering German. "*I never meant to shoot him, I'm sorry.*"

I don't know what to say. I know what I would like to say but he wouldn't understand so I just hold his clutched hands and we wait.

Some relations of the injured have returned. I go and meet them and to re-check the injuries. There is nothing serious but I try to indicate that they should see a doctor just in case.

The police arrive. I look around, but the young man has gone.

Chapter 15

We're discussing this morning's tragic happening in Brigitte's sitting room. The last we heard the injured young man was still alive but the doctor was not optimistic. The bullet is still lodged in his chest, his lungs are damaged and there is internal bleeding. Others affected have reported to the hospital, some have been kept in as a precaution but, thank goodness, there's only the one fighting for his life.

"This is not the first time. The injured young man is a communist. His attackers are the Nationalists, 'The Brown Shirts'. They can see the government is falling out of favour and they're fighting each other in the race to take over. I despair. Wilhelm favours the Nationalists. He thinks we'll be better off. He doesn't believe they'll carry out their threat on the Jewish people."

Freddie agrees. "It sounds as if they're using the politicians 'Blame Game'. Trying to convince the voters who's to blame for the mess Germany's in. There's no way the Jews are responsible and made to just disappear."

"But I've heard their leader at a local rally. He is very convincing. They have a huge following here in Bavaria."

"What's his name?"

"Adolph Hitler."

****

In bed that night we go through it all again but in a whisper with Flo fast asleep besides us. Then before we drift off to sleep.

"I'm very proud of you. You remind me of Edith Cavell."

"Ah've looked after hundreds of you Germans." Memories of the months I spent in the German hospital in 1918 flood back. "Pet, ye divvent know where Sister Schwimmer is now dee ye? Ah remember

82

she comes from Munich an' has a son. Ah forget the name but he must be nearly twenty now."

We lost touch in 1919 but I guess she may still be here. "Ye know she had a 'thing' for ye, divvent ye?"

"The only 'thing' I had was for some other lady. Now what was her name?"

Not wanting to wake Flo I just had to give him a withering stare. "Just ye wait 'till mornin'."

He reached over and gave me a sexy kiss on the lips. "I can't wait."

"Mmm, night, night."

****

I've fed Harry and we're dressed for a walk around the grounds. It's a clear, cool morning just the tonic for both of us. I leave Freddie and Flo, both still fast asleep. I meet Brigitte downstairs.

"Morning Brigitte, do ye mind if we have a walk around yer gardens before breakfast. It looks so invitin' out of our window."

"Of course not, Emily. Go and see our Summer House." She pauses. "Oh, Michael, our gardener usually lights a heater inside but he's off today. Their son isn't well. So better take a coat." She sighs and continues, "I'm afraid that communist died last night, poor man. The police are looking for the murderer. I expect they'll want to speak to you sometime today."

I was so much hoping he would live. Now there will be recriminations and so it goes on. I shake my head, disappointed.

Brigitte held my hand. "You did all you could. I do admire my daughter-in-law."

"Thankyou. Ah just hope it ends there. But, from what you've told me, ah doubt it."

The anticipation of my walk in the garden has been overshadowed by the news. I find the Summer House, which is just about the size of my home, and I sit and gaze at the view of the mountain range and chatter to Harry in his sling. But my mind is elsewhere. The futility of it all. Where will it end? More murders, rebellions, wars?

I often talk to myself and get curious looks not least from my children but I find it helps. I need to be positive get the joy out of everything. Some people seem to be just evil but they must have a reason to do what they do. I need to look at the problem from their perspective and maybe I can moderate my own views. This way I'm not looking and feeling angry, upset and bitter. I want to cheer up people not transfer my misery onto them. So, this morning, I've thought it through. The current Weimer government will find a way to improve conditions in the country to raise everyone's spirits and give people hope. Even those in the extreme parties. So, with a smile on my face, I continue my garden walk, talking to Harry and breathing in the bracing atmosphere.

"Come on ye lot. It's time ye were up. Me an' Harry have been around the garden already. Breakfast in half an hour. Come on" I rip back the bed clothes revealing the sleeping couple.

"Oh Mum."

"Oh darling. Come in and give me a cuddle." Freddie tries to grab my arm, misses but feels my cold hands on his face.

"Ahhh, right you." He swings out of bed and makes another grab but misses again and I make for our bathroom. He follows me in. "I know, let's all have a bath together?"

"Ok, at least we'll all be awake."

Fortunately, it's a large bath and there's plenty of room with the children playing between our legs. The water's hot and the soap bubbles clean us thoroughly. The early sad news started my day off badly. It is still sad but I'm not going to let it spoil my day. The bath is a tonic and we all arrive downstairs full of life.

84

Just before we enter the dining room Freddie whispers in my ear. "Best not mention our joint bath to Mother. She'll have a fit."

I smile. I think I know Brigitte better than he does. We enter the room and she's already in position drinking her coffee.

Before she even sits down Florence, eyes wide, pipes up. "We had a bath this mornin', all together." She looks to Brigitte for a reaction. I see Freddie's eyes rise to the ceiling

Brigitte smiles broadly. "Oh, that's wonderful. Do you know that we used to do that, Grandpa, your father, Bertie and me? It was so much fun, wasn't it Gunther?"

I had to smile. Freddie even looked embarrassed. "Yes mother."

****

While Freddie and Florence go off by themselves to enjoy time together in one of the play areas in Munich. Harry and I stay with Brigitte. Outwardly she appears elegant, somewhat aloof but this is just a veneer. We have long chats mostly in her homely study or on walks around her beautiful gardens and she tells about her life.

Her family moved to Germany from Poland forty years ago to get away from growing persecution. She was just seven years old, an only child. "We opened a shop in Munich. I used to love helping out, filling the shelves and talking to the customers." She adds proudly, "I could speak two languages and a bit of Russian at that age and still can, plus English of course. I used to love showing off to my parents. Their German wasn't good so they used me as an interpreter!" She smiles, "I was a quick learner, well, in languages anyway. I'm not so good with figures much to my father's embarrassment." She shakes her head, "You see Jewish people are supposed to have mathematical brains but not me. I met Wilhelm when I was just fourteen. He was my first and only boyfriend. He was six years older and studying at the University. I was tall for my age and I lied! I told him I was sixteen. I didn't know he lived here and his father was a Count. I really didn't know what a Count was anyway. I certainly didn't care. He was very handsome and charming and we were very naughty!" She smiles colouring up slightly. "Inevitably I got pregnant with Gunther. His parents never knew."

Although I try not to look surprised, my face must have shown it. She takes my hand.

"I can see you're shocked, I'm sorry, I hope you don't think we're awful people but we were very happy. I looked after the baby with the help of my parents for nearly a year. It was all a big secret. As soon as he left university we moved to England. He worked for the German Ambassador as an interpreter. We lived in Epsom, that's in Surrey. Do you know it? It has a famous racecourse there. It's where the Derby takes place."

I nod but I know very little about horse racing and have never been to a meet even in Newcastle. "Ah've heard of the Derby an' have been to London a few times, but ah divvent know Epsom."

"It's a lovely place, rolling hills, the people seemed friendly and relaxed." She added smiling, and they have a sense of humour, unlike most people here! Wilhelm took the train every day and I just looked after my boys." She went quiet and thoughtful.

I'm determined to talk about it. I want to remove the shadow over our visit. "Brigitte, Gunther has told me all about Bertie an' how he died. It's very sad. Sad fer everyone."

She stops walking and looks at me. There are tears in her eyes. She obviously wants to talk, she does, but it only comes in stutters.

"Bertie was a lovely little boy."

"I blame myself."

"I shouldn't have left him with Gunther."

"He didn't understand his problem."

I must look surprised. She continues in an avalanche of words.

86

"You see he was mentally sub-normal. He had no fears, no sense of danger. He would throw himself down stairs, walk in to walls, do the unexpected. We had to be with him, hold his hand, watch his every movement. Poor Gunther, he could see what we had to do but he didn't understand and, on the beach….."

I hold her hand tightly. She dries her eyes and continues. "Wilhelm blames him completely. I mean how can you blame a five-year-old? He's disowned him. He said I must never talk about him and never see him again. We even left him all alone in a boarding school in England. I had to beg to see him every year." I felt her hand grip and saw her body tense. She suddenly spoke in German, her eyes glaring: *Until the bloody war started then of course he brought him back to learn to fight. To learn some discipline!*" She relaxed her grip and sighed. "Sorry Emily. I must learn to control myself."

"It's good te talk Brigitte. Ye have te get it off yer chest. Maybe even shout it te the heavens."

She smiles at me. "Thank you Emily. I know you're right." She stops and we walk on. "You know he'll be home soon. He doesn't know you're here."

"Oh."

She looks uncomfortable. "I thought a surprise might be better. He probably won't even recognise him from the odd photographs I've shown him."

"Ah've known him since 1917. He wes brought in to our Casualty Clearing Station in Flanders badly wounded. Everyone thought he wes gannin to die." Brigitte gasps, hand to her mouth. I briefly give her my story of nursing on the frontline, our capture, and my period in the German hospital. "Ah can tell ye that he wes a war hero. In the last months when it became obvious the end wes close. He made sure as many of his men survived as possible. He retreated when necessary. There were no futile fight-te-the-last actions. He wanted

his men te get back to their families. He wes brave, courageous an'
kind. You an' Wilhelm can feel very proud of yer son."

She hugs me tightly. I can feel her sobbing, her body shaking. I
hold her until I can feel her body relax.

When we release, she looks at me through her tear stained eyes.
"Thankyou Emily, that does make me feel proud. I didn't hear from
him for months, then we received a telegram saying he was lost-in-
action possibly captured. I assumed the worst. It wasn't until early
1919 that we heard he was in a prisoner-of-war camp in England. I
could hardly believe it. I still had a son."

"An' now a daughter-in-law an' two grand-children."

She laughs and we walk back arm in arm still chatting together.
She's a lovely lady. We return to the house and approach the front
door. Hans, the chauffeur is busy unloading cases from the carriage.

"Der Graf ist zurückgekehrt."

She turns to me surprised. "Wilhelm is back."

Chapter 16

Brigitte has rushed inside. I followed after a while so as not to spoil their greeting. Harry needed some entertainment anyway. I guess that gazing at scenery and listening to his Mum and Grandmother have only a limited appeal to a six-month old baby. Kicking legs and gurgling turn to frustration for not being able to crawl very far and then to food demanding howls. So now I sit at the window in our bedroom, gaze at the views and let him satiate his hunger pangs. I can now relax and recall this morning's chat with Brigitte. It's been interesting and surprising. What a start to their liaison. Romantic really, sad for Wilhelm's parents but inspiring to learn of their determination to have their baby, my lover, and be together. I wonder if they are really married. They are the Count and Countess for all to see, but, I just wonder. I smile, it may run in the family. A noise outside breaks in to my reverie. The front door slams and a figure walks quickly to the carriage. He doesn't wait for the chauffeur to open the door but flings it open himself and jumps in. Before it moves away, I see a motionless man inside. His face is set, there is no joy, just pent-up, controlled anger.

My heart sinks. I suspect our arrival unannounced has not gone down well. I wait for Harry to have his fill and lay him down for a rest before I venture downstairs. Brigitte is sitting in her study facing away from me but her head is bowed and her shoulders are shaking. I don't know whether to approach her now or wait a while. I go for it. I walk up to the chair and hold her hand gripped to the armrest. She jumps up immediately and mops her eyes with her hankie.

She speaks without looking at me "Sorry Emily I just needed a quiet few minutes after our walk. Wilhelm had to rush off to Munich for a meeting."

"Ah saw him leave. Brigitte, he's upset, isn't he?"

"No, no, surprised. He'll be fine when he gets back." She turns, she smiles, she's controlled but her eyes are pink and moist. "Let's have some tea." Without waiting for an answer, she rings for Karl.

He soon arrives with a tray of cups, pots and biscuits. He lays it down on the small table between us.

I decide not to probe but, hopefully, allow her to confide in her own time. "How wes Wilhelm's business trip?"

"As well as can be expected under the present difficulties."

She sips her coffee and crunches on a biscuit automatically all the while staring unfocused at the wall of portraits. We sit together quietly. She is lost in thought then, "Sorry Emily dear. It's just that there have been demonstrations outside his offices - by the Communists. They're always demanding: more money, better conditions and so on. I think they actually want to take over. Wilhelm wants the government to sort out the mess. Either that or allow the Nationalists to take over." She shakes her head then holds it in her hands. I wait. "I just know that'll be the worst for Germany or at least for some of us. You listen to them, read the newspapers and you may think they stand for us all." She shakes her head again. "But they don't, they're divisive and so violent. People are dying every day. Like that poor man yesterday."

I know very little about German politics. I keep my communist tendencies hidden. They certainly would not help in this situation. Instead I verbalize my previous thoughts to Brigitte. "Perhaps the present government can sort the economy, improve the lot fer everyone. That way the extreme parties won't have the support."

She smiles at me. "You're always so positive. You're a delight. I should be more like you." Her expression changes, she looks nervous. "There is something else. Wilhelm was..." We're interrupted by a sudden wrap on the door and Karl enters. He's looking anxious, out-of-breath but manages to pass his message in German.

"Ich entschuldige mich bei der Gräfin, aber Michael ist hier. Sein Sohn ist sehr krank. Kannst du helfen"

Brigitte's eyes widen and translates for me. "Michael's son is very ill. They live in the cottage by the gate. I'll have to go and see him."

"I'll come with ye."

"Oh thank you Emily. There is no carriage but we have bicycles, can you ride?"

"Yes."

Karl has expertly adjusted the seat of mine and we both ride quickly through the grounds towards the cottage. The cattle hardly notice our passing. I'm hoping Harry stays asleep.

The front door is ajar and I follow Brigitte inside. Michael's wife, Hannah, is sitting by their son's bed, Michael himself standing behind. As we enter, she rises and gives Brigitte a small bow then speaks in rapid German.

"Thank you, Countess, for coming. Little Otto has had a very bad night, he's gasping for breath, coughing and look, his neck is swollen. We've given him linctus. I don't know what to do."

Brigitte introduces me as Gunther's wife and as a Krankenschwester. I remember well the German for nurse from my days in Flanders. I don't need to examine Otto. I recognise the symptoms. He is suffering from one of the most debilitating illnesses and one of the most contagious.

I speak to Brigitte. "He has Diphtheria an' we must get him to the hospital as soon as possible. There's a new antitoxin that may help but we have te act quickly. Also, the disease is contagious an' he must be isolated. Michael an' Hannah may already have it. Are there any other children?"

She shakes her head. "Otto is their only living child. Our carriage has not returned yet so we should cycle back and we can use our telephone."

I nod. "All three need te gan. Otto fer treatment, Michael an' Hannah fer observation."

Brigitte explains our actions to the parents and what they have to do. We leave them to get everything ready and we cycle back.

She manages to get through to the hospital and transport is due within two hours. She then delivers startling news: There is an epidemic. The hospital already has ten sufferers, mostly children and many more under observation. They have allocated two whole wards for Diphtheria treatment already.

I need to look after Harry but I warn Brigitte to just let the family know what's happening and not to expose herself to the disease any further.

I sit watching my son happily playing on the floor. I've already changed my clothes, washed and cleaned my teeth. I have to reduce the risk of infection as much as possible. I think of Michael and Hannah with their 'last living child'. I haven't asked but I can only assume at least two others have died. They must be terrified. I have always assumed my Mhairi is still alive, never considered anything else. I can't and I won't.

I recall similar epidemics in Newcastle. Anyone can catch the disease but children and older people are most vulnerable. Many were interned in the hospital but so many more suffered and died at home. Parents looking on as their child gasps for every breath until their last. Thinking about it makes my heart leap and my eyes fill with tears.

I mutter to myself, "Oh divvent be so stupid. You're a nurse. You've seen it all before in the wards. Be professional, efficient."

Damn it all, I know all that. But I'm also a Mother.

Chapter 17

It wasn't until early evening when transport for the family arrived. Brigitte explained the service was run on a voluntary basis and therefore relied on someone willing to come out this far from Munich. Not the best system for poor Otto. The frustration was that our carriage had already returned with Freddie and Florence, not realising the ambulance hadn't arrived. We all just have to hope and pray for his recovery.

****

Dinner is late tonight. Brigitte, Freddie and myself are waiting at the table in the dining room. Florence and Harry are tucked up in bed for the night.

"Is Father due home?"

"I hoped he might be but he must have been held up."

I look at Brigitte but she keeps her head down. Freddie knows that Wilhelm arrived but had to leave for a meeting in Munich, apparently.

"He's not coming is he Mother?"

Brigitte answers quickly, too quickly. "Of course he will. If he can."

There's a long awkward silence before Freddie reaches over and takes his mother's hand. "You didn't tell him we were coming did you?"

She looks at him desperately. "I just....I just thought he might see you and you could talk. You know, man to man. Put the past behind you. Start afresh. It was unfortunate that you weren't here when he arrived back."

"You know Mother it's been over twenty-five years since Bertie died. It was tragic, but twenty-five years! I've been without a father for all this time. All through my school years, not once did he visit, and you only came once a year. Every holiday, I had nowhere to go so I stayed in the school with a few other forgotten cast-offs. It was the same at Oxford." He pauses then looks straight into her eyes. "Mother, I was very, very lonely. It seemed to me that no-one cared whether I lived or died."

At this Brigitte burst in to tears, hands clutching at her face.

"Sorry Mother. I know you would have come to see me more often and I know why you couldn't."

Brigitte wiped her eyes on her handkerchief. "He changed when Bertie died. The loving, kind man I married turned in to a bitter and twisted individual. It was as if a tap holding all his fun and compassion inside, was turned on and all his goodness drained out. He rarely smiles, there is no joy in him."

She pauses and shakes her head. "It's not just about you and Bertie. I've never mentioned this to you before but...he felt let down by the German surrender in 1918 and humiliated by the terms of the Treaty."

Freddie is completely shocked by this confession. "Has he any idea of the state of our army? Does he not realise how demoralised the troops were? The Kaiser and his generals were panicking, the soldiers were surrendering in droves, the new recruits were kids with little or no training. There was no choice."

"He feels they should have fought to the last man."

"Well, he's mad." Freddie stands up, eyes flaring, pushing his chair back ready to leave. I hold his arm and shake my head. His eyes close, his body eventually relaxes and sits back down. "I'm sorry, but he is wrong. I was there. I could see it in their faces. There was no choice. We had already lost too many."

"Gunther, you don't have to convince me. His hatred of the Communists has driven him into the hands of the Nationalists. He listens to them at their rallies. He reads about them in the newspapers.

He's become indoctrinated. In Germany now, everyone is on one side or the other. You've probably noticed already how some look at us with hatred, particularly the younger men. My only hope is that the government can sort out the mess we're in. Only then will people lose interest and just get on with their own lives."

Our conversation is stopped by Karl and the maid coming in with our dinner. We eat silently thinking our own thoughts. My own revolves around Brigitte. How on earth has she stayed with this man and for twenty-five years? Someone so changed from the person she married. I can see the love is one-way only. She's now ruled by someone whose passion has been totally re-directed and she's right, he has been indoctrinated to nationalism. I know I wouldn't have stood for it. I need love and understanding from my partner not abandonment. I need happiness in my life.

But that's me. Brigitte is different: she's loyal and maybe, like Ma used to be, she puts up with what she has. I have to put my automatic Suffragette demands for woman's equality and respect to one side. I do like and sympathize with her but I've not even met Wilhelm. I have my own image of someone who doesn't forgive, who is proud of his position as the Count above anything else. I also have this doubt about his loyalty – smacking the nanny's bottom indeed. I really need to meet him and form my own opinion.

I realise, all this is about me. My Freddie is the one who needs to reconcile with his father. They have to talk, reach an understanding one way or another. After all that's the reason why we're here.

"It's such a shame. You come all this way to be met by a murder, a serious illness, a country in turmoil and a contrary Count. I want you to have some fun. It is still possible." She switches on her smile. "I thought tomorrow we could all have a trip on the *See*. It's only a small boat. Hans and his friend can stoke the boiler and steer. I can provide clothing for everyone but it does have a warm cabin and we can take a picnic."

95

I immediately look over to Freddie. To anyone else his expression hasn't changed but I know him well. It's probably the very last thing he wants to do. "That sounds lovely Brigitte and Florence would certainly enjoy the ride. I know Gunther gets seasick but he was fine on the ferry, weren't you pet?"

"Yes, of course Mother. Sounds interesting."

"I remember you used to paddle around in that tiny rowing boat with Bertie." Brigitte's face suddenly changes from jollity to concern and embarrassment. "Oh, sorry, perhaps we can go to the park. Yes, we can do that. Plenty to see and do there."

"No Mother. Let's have a boat trip. It'll be good for all of us."

****

With dinner finished we're now in our room discussing our conversation quietly. I'm feeding Harry while Florence is fast asleep in her bed.

"I can't see much chance of conciliation. He sounds set in his ways. All this nationalism rubbish. When I returned in 1914 to train in the army, he was all for the all-powerful German/Austrian alliance to take over Europe. It seems he hasn't changed."

From what I've heard and from my own intuition I can't disagree but I have to be optimistic. "Either way, after twenty-five years, it can only make it better te talk, about everythin' – Bertie, the war, the Treaty, yor Ma. Ye may not come te any agreement but ye can at least learn an' respect each other's opinions an' the reasoning behind them like."

He sits quietly while I settle Harry and get ready for bed myself. It has been a very long, interesting day but I'm very tired. I dump my clothes on a chair and reach for my nightgown already half asleep. I jump as I feel Freddie's hands slip around my waist and his kisses on my neck. He knows what I like but I'm just too tired.

"I love you, I'm so lucky to have you and I promise not to turn in to my father."

I smile to myself thinking this is his way to get around me. I tilt my head to enjoy the contact but confirm that if he does, I'll be off! He slides his hands up to caress my breasts, it's only then I realise he is also totally naked. I laugh and comment on his speed of undressing. He turns me round, gives me a tight squeeze and a long lingering kiss. Our intimate contact has completely driven off my weariness and he lifts me bodily into our four-poster bed for some luxurious and passionate love making. We finish both totally drained of energy and, still in each other's arms, we drift off to sleep - but not before I remember his last words and my answer: No, you had better not!

Chapter 18

Our trip on the *See* isn't quite how I expected. The 'small boat' is akin to the size of a collier taking coal from Newcastle to London and, I expect, far more comfortable! It is a long narrow lake with steep wooded sides only cleared for neat, tiny villages gripping to the slopes. Brigitte proudly indicates a group of houses that belong to her Estate. Only very slightly tongue-in-cheek does she pronounce: "That's Feldafing and I'm their Countess." Despite her problems she is obviously proud of her position and so she should be. I suspect she is a compassionate and fair-minded estate owner. I wonder if the responsibility all falls on her shoulders.

Freddie relives his childhood memories. So very different to mine but they both involved the excitement of playing and living close to water. Florence and Harry will miss out. We do live close to the Tyne but the poor old river surrounded by industry is badly polluted, not the best place to paddle or swim. Remembering the enjoyment of our recent trip to Whitely Bay I've made a personal vow to arrange some more family adventures to the coast. We're an 'Island Race' and we should keep reminding ourselves what an asset that is.

Hans handles the boat professionally and is likeable and friendly to all of us. His friend, a tall, muscular young man is sullen with a permanent sneer on his face. Fortunately, he spends most of his time feeding the boiler, out of our sight. We tie-up at a pier at the South end and eat our prepared lunch. The sun is shining but the wind chill drives us in to the warming cabin. Lunch is not sandwiches and tea but a properly laid out meal washed down with a local, white bubbly wine. This is a very different world and I can see the attraction. I'm not sure what effect this will have on Harry's milk but it makes me relax, even a bit tipsy!

Freddie and Brigitte are enjoying their renewed relationship. There is a good deal of smiling and laughter, a tonic for both of them.

The Count, however, is a completely different proposition but, even if that relationship doesn't work, our trip has been worthwhile.

On our return we play traditional German children's games on deck. They include the German equivalents of the popular: *Blindman's Buff* and *Grandmother's footsteps* but with slight rule differences. Either that or some are just cheating! Florence is in her element and from her expressions she doesn't understand the antics of the grown-ups. Possibly something to do with the alcohol bringing out the worst. I can't possibly comment.

Leaving the boat at the end of our trip I make a point of thanking Hans and his friend for their work doing my very best in my limited German. Hans is very appreciative and I even squeeze a smile out of his friend. There is hope.

We arrive home in good spirits. I'm ready for a relaxing walk in the garden but Brigitte helped by Florence convinces me I should take a tour of the stables first. There was no alternative. Harry, bless him, is now fast asleep in his sling. The day's fresh air has taken its toll. I hand him over to Freddie while I do my duty. In truth I love horses and the two of us make our way around the side of the house. Again, the differences compared to my childhood memories are obvious: the solid stone construction, tidy courtyard, separate tack-room, hayloft and I assume living quarters for a groom. My dear old Bennie had nothing like this but there again I don't suppose he minded.

Florence is the first to notice a horse looking over one of the stall doors. We walk over and I lift her up for a nose pat. The horse is what I would call a thoroughbred. A slender, proud, handsome creature very much like the one who hauled our carriage today. Between two stalls was a staircase leading I assume to the hayloft. Pulled by my inquisitive daughter we start to climb but I can hear movement above and some grunting. Near the top I peer over. It takes me a while to take in the view and what was happening. A couple, semi-naked, are making love on bales of straw. They are too intent to notice me. I pick up Florence before she notices and quietly, we leave them to their secret liaison. Unfortunately, I have recognised both of them. It was no longer a secret.

Sobered and numbed by the experience I walk around the garden with Flo. I have managed to divert her attention away from the hayloft and why we had to leave so quickly and now she runs ahead oblivious to what was going on. It is nothing to do with me and feel that I cannot mention it to anyone. It's their business but I am appalled.

We return to the house after an hour or so of trying to understand the situation. I wonder, should I perhaps mention this to Freddie. Certainly not to Brigitte. Inside we were met by an anxious Countess.

"I hope you don't mind Emily but I've ordered some tea for you." She looks down at Flo smiling. "And some lemonade for a certain young lady." She continues with news that Wilhelm is back home and is now talking to Gunther in the library. I thought we would leave them to it. Come into my study." She's excited. It seems they were, at least, polite and ready to talk.

Florence is eagerly describing our tour around the stables and the garden when the maid enters carrying a tray of drinks. I study her in a new light. Her long curly black hair is now tied back neatly into a bun revealing a full, pretty face. Her dress, hat, piny and shoes are immaculate. What she can't hide is her well rounded figure and a slight pink glow to her cheeks. She curtsies, turns and leaves, closing the door quietly behind her all very efficiently. I can surmise this is not a one-off situation.

I drink my tea and smile but I'm acting the part. My mind is elsewhere. Gunther's recollection of his father patting the large rump of his nanny obviously did not end there. As far as I can see this man is a habitual philanderer. He has a lovely and I'm sure loyal wife but takes a mistress when needed to fulfil his sexual desires. There is obviously no respect for Brigitte as a woman.

Flo has finished her description and her lemonade and is now on the floor studying some children's picture books.

"You have such a lovely daughter. She's so inquisitive, interested in everything. I'm so pleased for you and Gunther." She pauses, her expression changes, she sits with me on the settee then continues in a whisper. Her words completely stun me. "Emily dear, I do know about Wilhelm and our maid." She obviously is trying to find the right words. "Let me explain. You see, there were complications giving birth to Bertie and as a consequence making love is now extremely painful for me. That's why we've had no more children. We do still sleep together but an embrace is as far as it goes. I realise and have to accept that he needs to appease his sexual desires. All I insist is that he does it out-of-sight and not in our bed."

She looks at me and takes my hand. "I can see that you've seen them together but please understand it's by mutual agreement. I don't like it, not one little bit. I long to make love again but, it's impossible."

Tears fill my eyes. The strength of this woman amazes me. I don't think, no, I know I could never agree to that. Making love brings Freddie and me together. I need the intimate contact. I could never stand him having mistresses. But would I leave him because of that? Is our love not strong enough? I grip her hand.

"I'm so sorry fer ye, fer ye both. Ah divvent know what te say."

"Emily, just accept it. Please don't let it affect your judgement of him." She smiles grimly. "His political opinion is, however, an entirely different problem."

I look out the window to the garden. I see Wilhelm and Freddie walking together, chatting, smiling, working it out. I realise I must not mention this to Freddie. It's their business, not ours. I thought that I was a resolute and determined woman. Well I am, but I'm a step behind Brigitte.

Chapter 19

For some reason Harry has had a wakeful night. It seems like every few hours he woke up, whimpered then yelled demanding to be fed. I managed to tend to him without waking Florence or Freddie but as dawn enriched our bedroom, I felt exhausted. Thank goodness I've been left to sleep through most of the morning. When I finally surfaced into reality yet again, I find I'm alone, wondering where everyone else has gone. There's a knock on the door and without waiting for an answer in walks Freddie carrying a tray followed by Flo.

"Morning sleepy head. We thought you deserved a lie-in and...*tarrah*...breakfast in bed. Come on sit yourself up. Cook has served you eggs, tomatoes and a very special Bavarian treat – Weisswurst. That's white sausage. And a pot of tea of course."

"That's just canny, but where's Harry?"

"Don't worry about him, he's being spoilt by his grandmother. I think he must have had tummy problems last night but he's been bathed and changed and now smells like roses."

Florence pipes up holding her nose. "He smelt of pooh."

I laugh and hold up my face for a kiss.

"You deserve it."

I feel like a Duchess, let alone a Countess, waited upon so beautifully. "Thank ye, servants. Ye can go now!" I pour my first cup of tea and sip it regally. Freddie bends down and whispers in my ear something unsuitable – especially before my tea.

They leave me to my breakfast. Yes, I could just get used to this, but I do realise what a special family I have.

I appear much later having enjoyed the hearty breakfast and a warm bath. I have heard some commotion down the stairs and assume guests have arrived. Freddie and Flo are nowhere to be seen. I'm wondering where to go next when the study door opens and Brigitte appears, sees me and smiles broadly.

"Ah, Just the person I'm looking for. There's someone here to see you."

I assume it must be the police to talk to me about the murder of the communist speaker. I've been waiting nervously since that day trying to recall the details. I check my dress, breathe deeply and follow Brigitte back in to the study.

I look around the room and see a woman, not any woman. My nervousness vanishes.

"Sister Schwimmer, Brunhilda. Is it really you?"

"Emily, my dear, how are you?"

We hug each other. I'm so pleased to see her. I so wanted her to be alive and well but I don't know where to start. I turn to Brigitte. "This person took me in when ah wes captured in 1918, she saved me life." I nodded wanting to emphasise the point. "Yes, literally saved me from certain death."

"Yes, I know, Gunther has told me. I managed to find her working in the hospital here in Munich. I'll leave you to talk while I arrange some refreshments." She leaves the room leaving us alone together.

We repeat the hug and sit on the settee facing each other.

"I'm not sure I actually saved your life but you certainly helped me save many of our boys. It's so lovely to hear your accented voice. I'll never forget it but now tell me how are you doing. The last time I saw you was just after the ceasefire in the arms of a certain 'Oberleutnant 1st class'."

I garble a quick resume of the last nearly five years.

"I'm so pleased. I knew you two were in love from the moment we met."

"We're very happy but tell me about yerself an' yer son, Zach isn't it. He must be nearly twenty, isn't he?"

Her smiled disappears and I fear that something has happened. "He's nineteen, he's well and works with me in the hospital." She pauses before going in to detail. "But like all youngsters he wants to change the world. He's joined the Communist Party. He's been arrested twice in the last month for a breach of the peace. Not that there's much peace around here!"

"That must be very worryin' fer ye Brunhilda."

"It is." Her smile beams out again before continuing. "I'm getting married again and at my great old age! I met him as a patient. He's always smiling, he's kind and even gets on well with Zach."

"Ahm so pleased for ye."

We spend the next hour reminiscing and drinking tea and coffee. Being with her, my memories flood back clearly. Many very sad tragedies but also some happy events, even during the fighting. This is weird. Looking back, I realise this period was a good time in my life. I suppose I knew precisely what I had to do, there were no choices to be made, and I did it to the best of my ability. We looked after our boys, many were saved, many had a better future life because of our care and we were respected.

"Now tell me about that handsome husband of yours."

At that precise moment the door opens and my family troop in. As Freddie walks in holding Harry on his shoulders I couldn't help but watch Brunhilda. She absolutely swoons, blushing pink. I realise then that she had more than just 'a thing' for my ex-soldier.

A further hour is spent talking altogether and playing with Flo and Harry before she has to leave. We exchange addresses and keep hugging each other as if not wanting to part again. We wave until the carriage was out of site and I sigh. It was a lovely treat to meet her and talk. Tears fill my eyes but with happiness not sadness. I pull myself together and grab Florence's hand as we walk back up the steps in to the house and close the door behind us.

"So Oberleutnant 1st class, ye never had a thing with our Sister?"

"She was always very kind to me."

"Yes and…"

"Ok, we had a special relationship." He stepped in close and whispered, "but not a patch on a certain Staff Nurse."

Chapter 20

We've had five fascinating days in Bavaria but this morning we're getting ready for our return journey. The weather has turned from bright and cold to overcast, wet and still cold but I feel a warm glow inside. Freddie and Wilhelm have had two days together and I'm absolutely amazed how their attitudes have changed in such a short time. Their initial coldness and suspicion melted away like snow in May. The bitterness built up over many years has disappeared and has revealed a father/son relationship long hidden. It's hard to believe such a change was possible but I'm so pleased. I really hope they keep in touch with each other and maintain their friendship.

Another surprise has been Brigitte. What a woman. She is the backbone of their marriage. She maintains the standing of being a Countess but she has revealed a perceptive, compassionate and loving person underneath. She certainly has a lot to put up with: a husband with reactionary, political views and is unable to control his own sexual desires. All this despite her own frustrated needs.

She has also forged an unbreakable friendship with a certain four-year-old who seems sad to leave. I feel certain we'll be seeing each other again. Nothing has been arranged, don't know where or when, but I know it will happen.

With Harry comfortable in his sling we say our goodbyes on the doorsteps. I speak to Brigitte personally. "Thank ye fer lookin' after us so well. Ye can see someone here is unhappy to be leavin'. Oh, an' please let me know how Otto an' his parents get on won't ye?"

"I will, and Emily, it's been a real pleasure. You are a wonderful family. You've lifted my heart." She continued in whisper. "And you've both made such a difference to Wilhelm. He is so different. It's like a great weight has been lifted." She gives me a beautific smile between two pink cheeks. She doesn't have to explain.

While the men are shaking hands, I say Auf Wiedersehen to the staff I've got to know. They've all been so kind and supportive during our visit.

Wilhelm is courteous, shaking my hand and bowing. "I'm sorry we haven't spoken together very much but I've heard all about you from my son. You know women in Germany won the vote at the same time as you in Britain and I'm sure you and your Mrs Pankhurst helped."

All I can say was thank you. I sincerely hope my vision of him in the hayloft will fade, eventually.

We all waved from the carriage window as we made our way down the drive. I felt sad leaving and I could see Freddie and Florence felt the same. "Did ye enjoy yourself Flo?"

"Yes, she's nice."

****

Our long journey home is relaxing. We know what we are to do, where to go and what to expect. Our train journeys are still exciting: meeting different travellers, admiring views missed before and of course talking about our stay in Sternberg.

The shock that Freddie's parents are more or less Royalty and live in a palace with servants is the biggest surprise for me. I wonder why he hadn't warned me before. Modesty, embarrassment, shame? I don't know, but it has certainly opened my eyes to life in a world completely different to anything I have known, if only for a few days. To live without money worries is something unknown at home but I wonder if Brigitte has friends to help her or confide in, during times of crisis. I hope so. Wilhelm doesn't seem to fit that role, although, that may have changed since our visit. I just cannot imagine how trust can develop when one partner requires an occasional lover!

The best result, of course, has been the lifting of the emotional weights from the father's and son's shoulders. Their discussions have made a difference. I know from experience that talking always helps to understand each other better. Here, their long-held bitterness has been replaced with regret that it has taken so long. What a waste of family unity and fun.

An early train from Paris allowed us to forego the Dover overnight stop. Instead we stay in a small hotel in Greenwich.

"This area's ok and I can see there are some good views, but why here?"

Freddie has submitted to my request. I haven't explained but I do want to take a certain walk tomorrow morning. So, we've changed trains at London Bridge and we're settled into a small hotel in the gathering dusk. It's a guest house really. I suspect used by travellers and working men but comfortable enough for the four of us.

It's been ten years but when leaving the station building, memories flooded back: the terraced housing fronting towering warehouses and loading cranes and most of all, the all-pervading smell of the hidden River Thames meandering out to the sea, just behind.

Why I need to return, I'm not sure. My previous visit set off five weeks of my life I can never forget. The excitement of our battle plan, the shock of the girl's face at the window of her burning house and the long painful incarceration in Holloway. I know I was here. Perhaps it's a morbid desire to relive the occasion. Maybe to re-assess why we did what we did and, most of all, decide if it was all worthwhile. Did it really make a difference?

Previously, I've only described my time here generally with Freddie but now with Harry and Florence settled down for the night I go through my final Suffragette story in detail.

He listens quietly until I finish. He's quiet and just slides his arms around me and we cuddle silently.

"Thanks for telling me. I have read the news item. Your friend Millie showed me. You were all brave, but particularly you. Few people would have done what you did. Perhaps a walk tomorrow will answer some of your questions."

After breakfast, well wrapped, we leave the guest house. I have Harry in his sling and Florence is walking with Freddie holding hands. The station and the main road through are bustling with traffic and pedestrians but as soon as we head towards the river, down a side road, there's a calm. Only the occasional lorry passes us. We reach the riverbank and look over to the Millwall docks and I breath in the familiar salty sea breeze. The view hasn't really changed in ten years, the river still slides by looking somehow forbidding and mysterious under the leaden sky.

"Whey aye everybody, let's walk alongside the river maybe we'll see some big cargo boats."

Florence looks at me confused. She doesn't understand why we're here. I guess in the last few days with ferry crossings and so on, she's seen lots of big boats.

She looks over a low stone wall. "Ah divvent want te swim in there, Ma. It looks like the river at home."

"No, we're not gannin swimmin' today. We're gannin te see a house doon here. It's not too far."

"Who lives there?"

Freddie comes to the rescue. "Come on Flo let's beat your Ma and Harry." They break in to run. I follow as fast as I can.

It's actually not as far as I thought. It seemed further before and we were all in a horse drawn cart but I guess nervous anticipation stretched the remembered length of our journey.

There it is, the large stone-built house within a tidy back garden and the now visible main road passing the other side. The recess where we stacked the firewood is hidden behind a new conservatory. I also notice all the windows and surrounds look new. I can recall the

109

bangs of the exploding glass as the fire took hold. It is obvious the roof has been repaired with new slates but the walls still show stains from the raging inferno we started.

I stare at the building unfocused but remembering the terrifying vision of the young girl at the window trapped inside. My actions nearly killed her but, in the end, I saved her. No-one else saw her. It was just a fleeting glimpse in the smoke. How would I have felt if there was no glimpse and hearing the news the following day – Suffragettes' action kills a politician's daughter. I close my eyes but open them seconds later. But it didn't happen and hopefully she's alive and well. I can't beat myself up with something that didn't happen. I wonder who lives here now.

I break from my reverie when the back door of the conservatory opens and a woman holding a basket of washing walks out looking optimistically at the sky. She wears a piny and a small white hat, I suppose she must be a maid.

She notices us and asks. "What d'ya think of the weava, is it worth putting this lot out then?"

I smile. "Well ye must be positive like, the sun'll be oot an' there's a breeze so why not?"

Her eyebrows rise. "You're not from round 'ere are ya?"

"No, from Newcastle."

"Cor blimey you've really got lost ain't ya." She smiles at her own joke. But before I can reply there's a young lady at the door.

"Can I help you Vera?"

"No, it's ok Mary love. I'm just chattin'. They come from Newcastle, how about that!"

Mary smiles at us. "Nice to see you." Then turns and goes back inside.

"She's a lovely girl ya kna always tryin' to be helpful. Not like most these days."

110

I'm lost for words. I recognise Mary as the girl I saved. She must be fourteen now or thereabouts, a couple of years older than my Mhairi. She's still alive and she's a lovely girl – and so's my Mhairi.

"We must be gettin' back. Good luck with yor washin'." We say goodbye and start to move away. I look back to the house and see Mary at the window, she's smiling and waving. I wave back. I have to turn away, tears are filling my eyes.

Despite what happened to Mhairi when I was away, I now know my trip to London all those years ago, was worthwhile.

Chapter 21

We make our way back to Kings Cross and using our return first class tickets we enjoy our journey back to Newcastle in style. In the few quiet moments I plan for my new role as a Sister. I'm looking forward to the challenge but feel nervous. I know there have been personnel problems which I need to address. I'm also aware of the close relationship with the doctors. As a Staff Nurse I manage the nurses. Doctors' instructions arrive via the Sister. And then there is the Matron. A fearsome lady, stern-faced, large bosomed, frightening. I've had very little to do with her but that will change. Yes, it will be interesting. I know Sister Parker will help and advise. I only hope I can cope. I'm certain I will.

By the time we reach Newcastle the day's fading into the evening. On our way to catch the taxicab back to my flat we pass a news vendor he's shouting something unbelievable:

"The French have invaded Germany, read it here."

Freddie can't believe it. He buys a paper then stands and reads the front page. For some time, he can't speak, then. "I cannot believe this. It says that French and Belgium troops have taken over the German Ruhr. They say they're staying until they get the agreed reparations. If not, they'll take it in materials." He shakes his head in disbelief. "This is meat and drink to the Nationalists and the Communists. They'll be rubbing their hands."

My heart sinks. "What does our government say?"

He carries on reading. "It says here that Britain is against this invasion. It will cause bigger problems in Germany. Too right it will."

Home in my flat I feel tired and deflated. I feel for Wilhelm and Brigitte. We left them in a positive mood, their personal relationship stronger, but now?

The gloomy news seems to have affected everyone. Harry is unsettled wanting attention and feeds. Florence is quiet playing absentmindedly with her toys and Freddie is grumbling and looking miserable. I'm not putting up with this: politicians depressing everyone. I turn on my smile.

"Tell ye what let's have a game. We can play with yer new board game Auntie Millie gave ye - *Snakes and Ladders*."

Freddie joins me. "That's a great idea." He looked at Flo, "do you know your gran bought it for me when I was your age?"

The mention of Brigitte brightened her mood immediately and she runs off to fetch it. Even Harry's face lightens sensing something interesting's happening.

Several games later, mostly won by Flo, we've forgotten about the invasion. The children have settled in their beds and I'm cuddling Freddie on the sofa, head on his shoulder.

"Good idea you had about the game. I remember I used to love it. It was actually my grandparents. They brought it back from India, I think it was called something else and the board was covered in Indian figures – some good, the ladders and some bad, the snakes."

"Well ah think we're the ladders, an' the snakes, the politicians."

Freddie laughs. "They're not all snakes, just most of them. But you're definitely a ladder." He kissed me on the top of my head.

"Oh, very sexy, indeed!"

"Well how's this then." He turns me around, holds me face up on his lap and kisses me tenderly on the lips.

"Mmm bettor."

*****

Two recovery days later and we're now making our way to see Millie. We've waved off Freddie at the station after the most amazing holiday. Saying goodbye is difficult but I know we love each other.

We'll be meeting again soon and there's a trust between us. He loves his flying and I'm going to love my new job. But now I want to sit with my very best friend and have a comfortable chat over a cuppa.

I should have known better. Millie is full of the news. She loves international shenanigans. So, we have to talk about the invasion and what I've learnt about German politics.

I'm through my second cup of tea before I try to change the subject.

"So, tell me what's happened while ah've been away like."

"Nothin' new really. There's talk of more strikes at the pits an' now, even a hunger march te London."

My interest is kindled. "But how will they dee that? It'll takes weeks, how will they eat, where will they sleep?"

She smiles innocently. "Maybe they'll buy some first-class train tickets."

I screw up my eyes and frown "Mmmm." Luckily, I know she's joking. "Yer just jealous, divvent forget you'll be havin' the benefit of lookin' after two sweet bairns." An unfortunate statement just as a fight started between Florence and her Frank.

After a session of my no-shouting peace-making the pair are playing together again – as sweet as pie. We can continue our conversation.

"That was cannily done if ah may say. Ye should be out there sortin' the miners' problems oot."

"Well someone needs te. What about yor Sam? All peace an' quiet at the shipyard?"

Millie shakes her head and frowns. "Not so ye notice. The manager's been caught slowin' the clock doon so they all work longer. Would you believe that? Sam thinks they've been doing it fer weeks."

"So, what's the union doin' about that?"

"They're havin' discussions."

"Oh, that'll dee some good!"

Typically, I can feel my insides tensing from frustrations of not being able to make changes. I would like to try but it'll have to wait. I have an exciting job at the hospital to look forward to. That will fill my waking hours.

"So Em, ye lookin' forward te bein' the boss?"

"Why aye, ah am. Ahm a bit worried about the Matron but ah dee know she recommended me. So did Evelyn."

"Ye know ah worked on the Posh Ward. Well, the Sister wes ok ah suppose but she didn't have much compassion fer her staff. She certainly gave them a rocket when they made mistakes no matter what the reasons. There wes no arm around my shoulders when my Frank wes killed. She never got involved or wanted te know about our personal lives." She pauses thinking. "The patients were her only priority. Maybe that's the right way."

"Maybe not."

"Good luck anyway, not that ye need it, you'll be great."

We stand up an' hug each other. Everyone needs a friend an' ah've got the best.

Chapter 22

The past few months seem to have gone in a flash of an eye. Spring has most definitely sprung and I'm preparing for my first day as a Sister in the Mary Seacole Ward. I've made several visits already, meeting the ward staff, some talks with Matron and learning the routine from Sister Parker, my friend Evelyn. All seems calm and well organised but I've yet to find out how they all work together when something goes awry.

Talking with Matron has been a revelation. Before, our contacts have been limited to me holding the door open for her and the occasional nod of our heads when we pass each other. I expect each hospital is different but in Newcastle she runs the business. What she wants, goes and that includes management of the doctors! Ward control and discipline are the Sister's responsibility and Matron ensures that's done in the proper manner. The hierarchy is clear and strictly followed but the main priority for every member of staff from Matron to the tea ladies is, how it should be, the patients.

The surprise to me and I suspect to other nurses is how much she supports everyone in her own quiet way. She knows our names, our experience, even our personal details and problems. She's very aware of my three children all born in the hospital and all out-of-wedlock. She knows that I don't live in the nurses' quarters and the father is an ex-German soldier, now an RAF pilot. In most situations these would prevent me from working anywhere let alone here in the hospital but she has confidence in my abilities.

"Sister Mulligan, you have a natural way of getting the best out of everyone. You will need all that and more to handle the problems in your ward. It won't be easy but I have every confidence in you."

I won't forget these encouraging words. They give me confidence I can manage, albeit with some nervous anticipation.

*****

I'm cycling into work my mind a mixture of emotions. The children have been abandoned in Millie's kindergarten. Florence ran to her as if it's happened every day of her life. Harry waddled into her arms looking uncertain. I decided there's to be no long goodbyes and we just wave through the window as I walk away. This was all rehearsed yesterday but I still feel chilled to my core. As I wend my way along back streets and alongside the river, I'm concentrating on my first day back at work and completely slotting my children to the back of my mind – as if!

It's easier when I walk through in to the hospital and make my way up to my ward. Under my cloak I'm wearing my Sister's dark blue uniform. I know it's only a cotton dress but I feel honoured and privileged and it gives me a lift. I walk through the doors and into my office and straight into a heated argument.

Staff was berating a sullen looking nurse. I know them both and pretend not to notice their animosity.

"Good morning Staff, Wallace."

Staff gets up off my chair and ushers Wallace out through the door.

"Sorry Sister but she's driving me mad with frustration." She explains the problem. I know Wallace. She used to be a keen, lively individual.

"Perhaps she's just havin' a bad day."

"She's having too many bad days for my liking, she's lazy, forgetful, comes in late. You just have to do something with her it's not good enough. She's got to go. She's loading extra work on the others - and me."

I'm not getting into any argument with Jean MacNamara. Her final 'and me' is particularly significant.

"Ok Staff. Before anythin' else an' before ye gan off-shift ah want ye te take me round the ward fer an update on the patients."

She's still muttering as we leave the office to do the 'round'. I have met the patients already. The day-shift Staff took me yesterday. I wanted to familiarise myself before I started. I now need an update, either way I want this to be my future daily routine,

Talking to the patients is always a delight. Over the days the nurses get to know them individually. Not just their health problems but also their lives at home, good and bad. A relationship is formed some stronger than others. It is pleasing to see their health improving and sad in a way when they leave. Every ward receives Christmas cards from past patients still wanting to remember and in-a-way celebrate their time here. Often so different from their humdrum daily routine. There are, of course, patients that don't recover. No matter how often this happens it saddens the nursing staff. I felt this particularly in Flanders when young men died from their battle wounds. There I had to blanket my pain with the knowledge that we had done our very best for each of them. This same message I try to pass on here.

I manage to have a tea break with Evelyn. I want to learn about the new doctor due to take his round this afternoon. She warns me that Matron will almost certainly accompany him. She smiles, to make sure he behaves himself!

Before I left, she asks. "How was the night shift Staff?"

"Unhappy, but ah know her. Millie used te work with her."

"Oh yes, of course. Well good luck."

The new doctor was young, tentative and obviously terrified of Matron. I could only smile to myself. He's being trained to Matron's way. Before she left, she took me aside.

"How's your first day Sister?"

"Interestin'."

She smiled. "I thought it might be."

The rest of the day was uneventful. I took my turn at the ward centre table to allow Staff to take her break. I've managed to speak to all the nurses at some time. I found them mostly keen and able, some are nervous, they shouldn't be, they all know me. I intend to speak to them altogether tomorrow. I want to let them know my own ideas and views.

Arriving at Millie's after the shift was heart-warming. I was immediately surrounded by all three excited children with Millie standing behind looking just a little tired.

"How have they been?"

"They've been great fun an' noisy. My Frank is havin' the time of his life. He loves yer Harry, showin' him all his toys. Florence has been helpin' me de some bakin', haven't ye love?"

"Come over here Ma, we've made some cakes, look."

Millie whispers. "Ah just managed to stop her addin' soap flakes te the mix."

I laugh then, quietly, looking serious. "What de ye mean? We always de that at hyem. It washes our mouths oot, stops us sayin' rude words."

She smiles. "Ah haven't noticed."

"Cheek."

After a while Millie and myself are drinking tea at her table. I ask her about Nurse Wallace Wright. She's surprised.

"She wes always lively an' bright an' certainly never late fer her shift." She pauses. "Her family live in the Hebburn area, ah think. Her Da works in the shipyard but she stays in the nursing quarters like all the others."

She laughs when I tell her about the new doctor. "Terrified of getting' squashed by Matron ah 'spect!"

"Ye know she's not so bad. She certainly looks fearsome but there's a kind heart inside."

119

"Mmm, well ah wouldn't want te meet her on a dark night. It's not her heart that would flatten me. By the way Harry drank the milk no problem."

*****

The nervous tension and my adrenaline have vanished. Once I get my children home all I want to do is collapse and put my feet up but I know I must give them time before I put them to bed. I hope I can get used to this routine, otherwise... But I have enjoyed the day and I have plans for tomorrow.

I sit on the sofa giving Harry his last feed of the day He's not completely weaned. In truth I still like to breast feed him mornings and evenings, it's good for him and for me. I can sit, think and relax.

Staff Nurse Jean MacNamara and Nurse Wallace Wright are top of my list.

Chapter 23

I've managed to meet all my regular staff during the week and gave them all the same message: work is to be enjoyed and stressing the importance of smiling and having a positive attitude. I believe this will help ensure their duties are carried out in the proper manner and the patients get the best care possible. I just hope the message sinks in. I will keep reminding them until it does.

Some seem to be in awe of me maybe because of what I've done in the past or maybe just because I'm Sister. That's good either way, respect is crucial. Others sneer as if they know better. Maybe they do but I have some ideas involving changing responsibilities.

Then there is Wallace.

On many days she arrives late, rushing in pretending she's not. Smiles are rare. Her mornings consist of wide-eyed panicking movements replaced in the afternoons by drooping shoulders and frowns. I can see other nurses help her through the day which is good to see but she's suffering. Something in her personal life is bad and I want to help her if I can.

She's sitting alongside me in my office. Her whole-body shouts 'help me'. Emaciated, unwashed, unruly hair, scruffy uniform. So different from the lively, enthusiastic girl I've known before. I want to know the problem but there's little response to my questions. I offer a day off, different shift, all politely refused: "Thankye Sister but ahm fine." Before she leaves, I have to insist that she smartens herself up. "And yer must wash yerself an' yer uniform. All the digs have showers! Ye know cleanliness is crucial, divvent ye?"

"Yes Sister."

"Off ye gan then." Before she leaves, I try to encourage her. "You've always been a canny nurse. Divvent let yer standards drop."

"No Sister, thankye Sister."

She needs help. I feel certain it's a private matter, I don't want to pry. But there's nothing wrong in keeping my ears and eyes open. I may be able to help somehow. I'm cycling home, my mind full of possible problems. Shipyard workers are being laid-off, sickness in the family could be anything. I decide to talk to Millie when I collect Flo and Harry. She'll have some intuitive ideas.

"Sounds like she's helpin' out at hyem. She'll have some brothas an' sisters. If she's the eldest she may be getting' them up in the mornings an' off te school. Ah can't see any man doin' that. Her Da probably expects her te dee it."

I know this happens, when the mother falls ill or leaves home the eldest girl has to take over her duties whatever her situation. I'm so lucky I have Millie to help me. I have no relations to step in. I would have to look after them myself and certainly, there would be no wonderful work at the hospital. Immediately I feel bad. I love my children but...I suppose I just want both.

"My Freddie would help in that situation, ah think."

"Mm not sure if my Sam would." She pauses, "anywa' ah could ask a few questions. Ah know some folk from Hebburn."

"Thanks Millie I'll dee the same."

"Anyway, enough of all that. Look at this. Come on Flo let's show yer Ma what he can dee." She picks up my crawling Harry and stands him up onto his feet keeping hold of his hand and with Florence holding the other. Then both let go. Harry looks worried until he boldly steps forward towards me a huge smile creasing his face. Then crumples down into my open arms.

I pick him up jubilantly and shout. "Ye can walk." I hug him tightly.

"We were walkin' with him in the park today. Ah was behind holdin' both his hands up an' just let go an' he carried on all by himself."

"But then he fell on his face an' started cryin'."

"Hush Flo, yer not supposed te tell yer Ma that. It's only a little scratch like."

I smiled broadly. His very first steps. "That's really canny."

****

Pushing him slowly back home in his pram with Flo alongside I can't help myself. Tears are sliding down both cheeks. I'm thinking don't be daft Emily it's good news. Of course it is but, no matter what, I'm acutely aware I've missed his first steps in life, all by himself. I was there when both Mhairi and Florence had theirs but absent for Harry's. Is it really all worth it?

My route home takes the back streets to avoid the crush on the main road but eventually I have to join it and there I have to stop. There is a commotion. Crowds, controlled by the police, line the pavements. Some are shouting, cheering, others are just looking on, wondering. There are no vehicles on the road and then I spot the procession. Men walking arm in arm, some holding banners aloft. It's a protest against Hawthorn's shipyard redundancies. It's not unusual. There have been several recently, if not the shipbuilders then it's the miners or the steel workers. I think of all the families now destitute, dependant on local paltry Parish Payments. My tears have dried, replaced by concern and anger. I feel a hand on my shoulder. I turn and see a face I've not seen but thought about for many years.

"Hello Emily."

"Hello Stan."

Chapter 24

My old lover hasn't changed very much, still handsome especially in his police uniform. Maybe a few more grey hairs and now supporting a moustache. I look down and spot his sergeant stripes.

"Ye look canny an' promoted too."

"Thanks, an' so de ye. Are these yer bairns?"

I introduce Florence and Harry.

"How old is Florence?"

"She's four." His eyes widen. "No, she's not yers."

"Sorry ah didn't mean te...." His face reddens but recovers his composure, "an' Mhairi?"

I shake my head. I don't want to discuss my missing daughter. I think for some reason I partially blame him for her disappearance. Perhaps he should have been checking on her when I was down in London with the Suffragettes. I know this is unfair. She was my responsibility and mine only. I employed the Roberts to look after her. How was he to know they were scheming to abduct her.

We stand talking, bringing each other up to date as the demonstration is moving past us. He's married to the woman he was with when I returned from Flanders in 1917 and they've had their own daughter adding to her own two sons with her first husband killed in the war. I maintain the pretence of my marriage and I release my cloak to show off my Sister's uniform.

"Good fer ye, you've done so well."

I can see he still has feelings for me and realise I must change the subject. "How's the demo then?"

He relaxes and looks around to see the last men march past. "No trouble heor but big problems at the Yard a couple of months back." He related the fights and scuffles and then the arrests. "We held on te them for a week until everythin' settled doon. Now, of course, they divvent have jobs te gan back te. Hawthorn's all too eager te get rid."

He shakes his head. "This town is too reliant on the big heavy industries. Coal, Shipyards an' Steelworks. They're all strugglin'. We need smaller companies makin' products that are still needed. Ah divvent know what's gannin te happen but it won't be good."

We part company, no further meetings organised. How could there be. He raped me. It's over four years ago, I know he's sorry, but I can never forgive him. We were together for over six years and we had some great times but I know now I never loved him like I love Freddie.

*****

Two weeks have flown past and I'm pleased I'm getting used to the routine of delivering my children, working in the hospital then back to being Ma at our cosy little flat. Last weekend the three of us travelled down to see their Da and of course I had another flying lesson. Florence was transfixed most of the day gazing at the aeroplanes taking off and landing especially when her Ma appeared all geared up in her flying uniform.

"Ye look just like a pilot."

"Ah am a pilot pet. Yer Da has been teachin' me."

Her eyes widened in surprise. I have told her before but perhaps she didn't believe me. I feel confident I can handle the aeroplane. Taking off and landing are a piece of cake. I've even landed at other local aerodromes. Mind, I've only flown 'Old Gertie'. She's lovely. Ok she's slow and old but she has a personality all of her own.

But all this is totally illegal. Should the Wing Commander find out then we're both in trouble. But Freddie seems calm and confident and his fellow pilots and crew are always friendly and welcoming. So, I just have to hope our secret stays secret. I'm not going to stop flying no matter what happens.

It's a new week and I'm waiting outside the nurses' quarters to meet Nurse Wright. I want to talk to her before she gets to the Ward. It's a busy time and nurse after nurse pass by singly or in groups. They're surprised to see me. Some greet me and wonder what I'm doing. I recognise a friend of Wallace's and stop her.

"Mornin' Jane is Wallace comin'?"

She immediately stops, sees me, understands what I'm asking then looks away when she replies. "No Sister, ah've not seen her this mornin'."

"Wes she alright last night?"

"Yes Sister, ah think so."

"Alright Jane you'd best get te yer Ward." She goes to walk on but stops and looks round.

"Yes Jane?"

"Ah divvent know if ah should say." She pauses looking down.

"Say what?"

She fidgets shuffling her feet but then decides and looks at me. "Ye see Sister, she gets up two hours early every morning an' cycles hyem te look after her family. Then cycles back." She pauses. "She made me promise not te tell anyone but, ye see, she's sufferin' an' she's my friend an' ah hate te see her like this. There's nothing of her. She canna carry on like this. Sorry Sister." Her gaze diverts to the ground.

My eyes close. Millie was right. "Divvent be sorry. Dee ye know what's happened in her family?"

"Her Ma has te leave early to clean the offices. Wallace has te get her two sisters an' two brothers up an' get them ready fer school an' then get her Da's breakfast."

I nod. "Thanks fer lettin' me know. Divvent worry, ahm not cross with her. I'll wait here. Ye better get gannin'."

"Um, you'd better wait around by the cycle sheds she doesn't usually come back heor."

I walk around the back of the quarters and meet Wallace dismounting. She sees me and immediately colours up.

"Sorry Sister, I'll make up for it."

"Wallace, if ye divvent mind, ah want ye te tell me all about it. Ah know you've been home and ye gan home every mornin' before ye start work heor. Can you explain to me what's happened?"

She starts slowly then speeds up, her words tumbling over each other as if she's been wanting to explain many times before. "Da's lost his job, Ma's had te start cleanin' doon at the Yard an' ah have te get the kids up an' away an' things."

I suddenly realise. "Yer Da's been sacked by Hawthorns, hasn't he?"

She nods "But he's lookin' for a job all the time, but there isn't any about. He's tryin' everywhere."

I look at her. Her face is drawn and pale. Cheek bones jutting, hair a complete tangled mess. Her uniform is dirty, splattered with mud and torn in places.

"Wallace, you're not comin' on the ward lookin' like this. Ah want ye te take the morning off. Get te yer room, wash an' get another uniform from stores – tell them ah've sent ye. And, have breakfast yerself. Rest for a while an' return te the Ward after dinner."

"But I'll get into trouble."

"You'll be in trouble with me if ye don't. I'll clear it with Staff."

"Thank ye, Sister."

She turns and starts to walk away. "And Wallace, when ah see ye next, you'll have a smile on that face of yours, ok?"

She nods. "Sorry Sister."

The poor thing, if I was in her shoes, I'd be ashamed. She's bearing the brunt of her family demands but it's compromising the work I know she loves. I can see great determination. No complaining like many others would but gets on with everything as best she can. I know this is a very temporary cure but I'm not going to demand that she chooses home or her work, she deserves much better. But I don't have an answer, yet.

Back in the Ward I've explained to Staff Nurse McNamara that Nurse Wright has been re-assigned this morning but will be back for the afternoon. She frowns, tuts and mutters as she leaves my office. I ignore them completely. I've known her since I was a student nurse. She's lived in the same room in the nurses' quarters all this time, has few friends buts obviously proud to be a nurse. Demands high standards but is inflexible. She's someone you know will never change. Also, I suspect, is disappointed not to have been promoted to Sister here, on the Mary Seacole Ward.

I manage to grab a few minutes with Sister Evelyn Parker during the day to discuss Wallace.

"She may have to make a choice: home or hospital. That would be a shame, she's an excellent nurse. I'll give it some thought. By the way how's your Staff?"

"An interesting challenge."

She smiles. "I thought it might be."

Wallace returned to the Ward rejuvenated but over the next few days her workload is again taking its toll. Everyone who knows her agrees she has great potential. There has to be an answer that benefits both herself and the hospital.

Nearing the end of my final shift for the week, Evelyn leaves the usual a pile of notices on my desk. I notice she's written on one in particular. It's the Situations Vacant sheet.

Chapter 25

I have three days off. An internal private arrangement in the hospital allows an extra day and a half holiday but the pay-back is having to work eleven consecutive days. But I'm not thinking about that. We're making our way to Catterick again to live as a family if only for a short period. Planned trips include visits to York and Scarborough. Also, if the weather holds, more flying lessons in Old Gertie. I always feel nervous before any flight. This time he's promised me something different – a flight over the sea. We have to refuel at another aerodrome on the way. But I'm feeling positive. I have to. I gaze out the carriage windows but I don't see the scenery flashing past. I see me at the controls of an aeroplane springing up from the runway and soaring high in to the air. My heart lifts with it and my eyes close, I can't wait. I'm jerked out of daydream when my arm is repeatedly tugged back.

"Ma, ma, we're slowing doon. Are we nearly there?"

My eyes spring open, stare down at Florence, realise what's she's saying then turn to see the station coming into view.

"Why Aye, thankyou Flo. Get yer things together we divvent want te miss yer Da, do we?"

"My things are together an' ah've got all Harry's toys an' blankets in the bag already."

I look around and smile. What an organiser she is. "Well done Flo, come on Harry let's gan and find yer Da." I lift Harry up with one arm and grab the bag with the other leaving Flo to open the door once we've stopped. On the platform we look all around but there is no Freddie. The same lovely railwayman we always see, approaches. He's looking concerned.

"Morning Mrs Mulligan. I've just received a message from your husband. I'm afraid there's been an accident and he can't meet you but I've arranged transport to take you to the aerodrome. It's at the front of the station."

"Is he alright?"

"Yes, but an aeroplane has had an accident and he wants you there as soon as you can."

"Right, let's go children. Ah think yer Da needs some help." The porter takes my bag and we walk as quick as we can for the taxicab. But it's not a taxicab, just a horse and a trailer already loaded with boxes and bags.

"I'm sorry but this is all I could get for you."

"It'll be fine, we'll just squeeze into the back." I look at the children, "it'll be an adventure." As we head off, I shout a 'thank you' to the porter. He raises his hand but looks worried and so am I.

The driver hasn't said anything. There's no urgency, no galloping off to save the day at the aerodrome. He sits stooped holding the reins loosely allowing the horse to plod slowly away from the station.

"Can we gan a bit faster. Ah think there's been an accident."

"Righto."

"Ahm a nurse. They may need my help."

"Righto."

Our speed gathers some momentum but we can't seem to manage a trot even. I hold my breath trying to calm myself. Florence and Harry are holding hands for comfort rather than keeping balance. At this rate we'll be over an hour. I just hope any treatment can wait. I've just decided I'm going to take the reins myself when he pulls over, stops and opens a field gate. I look over and all I see is a small herd of sheep. I hold my head in my hands. This is ridiculous.

"Where are we gannin?"

"Aerodrome."

We're on a track through the field but it's still very bumpy and now all three of us are clutched together to keep balance. It's been fifteen minutes at least and I can see only fields and a wood in front of us. I'm resigned to accept that whatever route we're taking we will eventually get there. Trees now soar high above us hiding all views in every direction until our path bends slowly to the left revealing, unbelievably, the aerodrome.

We have made it quicker than if we had used the roads. I now recognise the woods as those that border the runway, a landmark I use when returning from a flying lesson. Our driver doesn't stop but continues on to the flat grassed surface heading towards a column of smoke drifting skywards. As we approach, I can make out the cause of the fire. A biplane is sat lurched at an angle. The wings on one side are crumpled into the ground the opposite wings pointing skywards. I can see the squadron's lorry and nearby, people, gathered together in a circle looking to a dark shape lying on the ground. This has to be the pilot.

But it's not the pilot. As I peer between the onlookers, I spot four legs in the air and a bovine head, eyes closed to the world. Yes, it's a cow!

One of the pilots has seen us approach and comes over.

"Hello Emily. A bit of a mishap I'm afraid. One of our chaps landed on this beast. Killed it stone dead, I think. Made a mess of the plane though."

"Thank goodness ah thought it was one of ye." I look around. "The pilot is ok?"

"I'm afraid not, Freddie's had to take him to the hospital, damaged leg and a few bruises and cuts. Flew out of the cockpit trying to evade the animal." Hopefully Freddie will be back soon. Sorry about this."

After making certain the children stayed in the trailer, I jump down to look at the prone animal. I could see immediately it was breathing. "Let's try an' roll him over."

This seemed to startle everyone but not into any action.

"Come on grab a leg an' pull."

With two on each leg on one side we only had to move it slightly when it sprang to life, scattering us backwards. The animal finished it's roll over and then, unsteadily, got to its feet. It shook itself and then casually walked away as if nothing had happened.

"It wasn't dead then."

I have to turn away before smiling. I wonder: do these people live in the real world? They might be great pilots but…

I turn back to the watching crowd. "Just a bit of concussion ah think. I'll take me bairns back te the hut if that's ok."

We plod back along the runway towards the base. With Freddie away looking after the injured pilot I have to wonder what we're going to do. It's a lovely Summer's day, perhaps a walk. Back at the huts I give my thanks to the driver who just nods before plodding off the same way he came. I can only assume he is what Freddie calls 'a typical Yorkshireman'. I hope he has been paid for his efforts.

I chat with Alec while he plays with Harry and Florence, he obviously loves children. He's called away as the telephone rings. He looks serious when he returns.

"Sorry Emily but HQ want Freddie to take over the recce over the coastline when he returns. Someone is bringing a replacement aircraft. It'll be here soon."

My heart sinks, looks like my flight's not possible. I still have some food left but I'm really disappointed. I hear some commotion outside. An RAF truck has drawn up and the door of the hut flies open. It's Freddie. Ignoring his children and Alec he picks me up and swings me round then gives me a long kiss right on my lips.

"When I get my breath back, I manage to get a few words in. "That's no way te treat a Ward Sister!"

"There's no other way." He reaches out again but I avoid his grasp and point to his children, Florence looking ashamed, Harry looking confused and Alec totally embarrassed.

"Ah there you all are. How's the cow?"

"Ma got her up an' she walked off."

"Ye see not only do ah treat sick patients, ah cure farm animals an' have te put up with amorous approaches from strange men."

"Who from, Alec, one of the pilots?" He smiles broadly. I'm actually delighted but can't possibly show it.

Alec recovers his composure and coughs for attention. "Sorry Freddie but HQ want you to cover the recce. They're bringing a replacement over now."

His smile disappears. "But they know I've got the afternoon off!"

All Alec can do is shrug his shoulders.

"Divvent worry love, we'll still be here when you get back. Alec will look after us an' we've still got two days together."

Freddie looks over to Alec who nods his agreement.

"Oh d........." His words are thankfully lost when an aircraft makes a landing and makes a noisy approach to the hut. He grimaces at me and mouths 'sorry'.

I take his hand as the noise dies down. "There'll be another time," and discretely whisper "and we still have tonight." I give him a peck on the cheek.

An hour later he leaves with two others to patrol the coastline. I'm left with Alec and the pilot who has just delivered the replacement. The pilot, Arthur, is much older than the others and sports a long moustache curled up at the ends. He is very talkative and I can tell, very traditional in his outlook. Our conversation is aviation of course but despite the heroics of the likes of Amelia Earhart and Harriet Quimby he vehemently disagrees with women flying. "Girls in the RAF, poor show, shouldn't be allowed, too interested in the latest fashions and hair styles." I have to bite my tongue - until it almost bleeds. I try and change the subject and eventually he starts chatting to Florence. I look at Alec who shakes his head, then smiles and gives me a supporting thumbs-up.

A sudden thought has obviously struck Arthur. "Who can take me back?"

Alec quickly replies. "There's no other pilot here but they'll be back in a couple of hours. Or of course, there's the truck."

Arthur's face reddens. "But I've got to get back, things to do, people to see and all that. I can't drive back in the truck, it'll take hours." He stumps off to check the hanger I assume to see for himself.

Chapter 26

Alec's story

One of our aeroplanes was written off today. Jimmy managed to land on top of a stray cow. The animal was concussed for a time then sprang up and strolled off as if nothing had happened. Jimmy was not so lucky and was rushed off for repairs.

The dreaded retired Squadron Leader Arthur Maynard DFC then paid us a visit, lucky us! He flew in with a replacement. Silly old fart going on about his first world war exploits. I wouldn't mind but I know most of it is made up. From what I've heard he never even met a German in combat. His only claim to fame seems to be when he managed to write off two of our own aeroplanes by landing one on top of another!

Poor Emily had to bear the brunt of his blustering. This is the girl imprisoned as a Suffragette and now has to listen while he ridicules women pilots. How she held her tongue I don't know. She's a perfectly able pilot having been taught by the best: her husband Freddie.

I had to smile when he realised there was no-one to fly him back to Ripon until the recce returns. He disappeared in a huff probably for a drink in the village pub.

I was left with Emily's children, Florence and Harry. Thankfully they had both been fed and were ready for some games. They are a real pleasure, Flo is cheeky always ready for some fun and Harry – well he's just a toddler, always trying to run then falling, picking himself up then crashing into something. They make a change from the everyday paperwork.

The three of us were on the floor reading one of Florence's books when I heard Old Gertie start up in the hangar. I groaned it could only be Arthur wanting to fly home. I knew this would create all sorts of problems. I also knew I couldn't stop him. The door opened and in walked the pilot.

I looked up and stared. He was wearing one of our spare suits complete with hat, gloves and goggles but no moustache!

"How dee ah look Alec."

"Emily?"

"Of course, who dee ye think it was?"

I couldn't speak. The suit disguised all her curves but not the smile. She lifted the goggles, I think, to make sure I recognised her. But I still couldn't speak.

"I'll take him te Ripon. Ah've been there a couple of times with Freddie so ah know the route. It's a clear day, just a breeze, yer problem solved."

I shook my head and my mouth must have dropped open. I found my voice and garbled. "But, but, I'll get the sack for letting you and you haven't got your flying license yet."

"Ah know that but as far as yer concerned ye thought Arthur had flown off himself without lettin' ye know. Our Squadron Leader will just think a pilot's just turned up te take him home and," she gave me one of her broadest smiles, "he'll never know ahm a woman."

"Until you speak."

She flashed another wicked smile. "I'll have to adapt me voice. I'll wait for him outside, fully kitted out fer when he comes back from the pub. He'll be delighted an' perhaps a little tipsy so that'll help the subterfuge."

She knelt down with children. "Sorry Flo I'll have te take that man back hyem. Will ye look after Harry an' be good with Alec."

"The one with the hairy face?"

"That's right pet."

"Ok Ma, Alec's readin' my book."

Emily turned to me. "There's more books in me bag like an' food includin' milk fer Harry if he needs it."

She left waving goodbye to us. I should have stopped her. It's all irregular, goes against all RAF's regulations and yet I so admire her for it. Of course, if it all goes to plan, he'll never know. Equality for women? Absolutely.

Soon after, she left soaring skywards, the Squadron Leader sitting oblivious at the front, Emily in the pilot's seat behind. I shook my head and actually laughed out loud. Who'd believe it? I suspect Freddie would.

"Now then kids, where was I?"

An hour later the recce patrol returned. The pilots were climbing out of their cockpits when Old Gertie followed them in. They gathered together to watch her land smoothly and taxi in. It was Freddie who walked over to speak to Emily. The other two thought it best to make themselves scarce. Very wise!

Chapter 27

I watch him stomp away, red in the face, clattering closed the flight office door behind him. His attitude towards women is desperate, unchanged over the centuries. He will never, ever understand. Liberation, equality will come but I wonder if I'll see it in my lifetime. Our conversation consisted of his life story, tales of heroism and bravery. No interest in what I may have done just an obvious lecherous study of my physical appearance.

Well I'm not having it. I know what I'm going to do. The RAF or the Squadron Leader are not going to stop me.

I can see the children are happy in Alec's care. "Ah won't be long, back in a minute."

He nods, I leave. Outside I can still see Arthur in the distance striding off towards the village. I follow him but only to the hangar and to the stores. The place is empty, the fitters must be with the aeroplane wreck. The flying outfits are hanging waiting and I wonder.

My plan is to fly him back to Ripon aerodrome, a larger base than here but it's nearby. I've been there a couple of times. I know the route and the landmarks. I've landed and taken off there. I'll be disguised in my full flying regalia. Gertie will need to be fully fuelled. It's possible, it can be done and it's illegal!

If I go for it it'll be my first solo or rather my first flight without Freddie. I'm nervous and excited. I've got this far and I know, if I turn away, the anti-climax will haunt me. I realise I'm going to go for it and I reach for the suit.

I check Gertie's controls from the ground, remove the chocks then climb aboard into the rear seat. Good girl, she's fully fuelled and ready to go. I go through the routine of starting, checking the instruments, cabin controls and warming her up. We taxi out of the empty hanger and make for the office. Alec must be wondering what's happening. I hope he's ok with a bit of child and baby-sitting.

I've confused the poor man. He didn't recognise me until I removed my goggles. Even my children looked surprised when they heard me speak. The be-whiskered pilot has no chance, he won't even give me a second look. All I have to do now is to wait his return so I sit tight and go through everything Freddie has taught me. I have to make sure Alec and everyone else is completely innocent of what I'm doing. It's all my decision and I'll take the blame, but I feel confident. The weather's clear, just a light breeze with a light cloud cover and no sudden thermal uplifts expected on the short journey.

Where is he? I have too much nervous energy. I need to walk, re-check the aircraft, inspect the runway, breathe deeply, anything to relax. My take-off will be watched by the fitters repairing the aeroplane and by Alec. The wreck has reduced the length of runway available but there's still plenty of space for me. I'm also hoping the recce patrol stays away until after I leave. If it returns before, that would be embarrassing. Freddie or one of the others would have to take over leaving me looking ridiculous.

At last I spot my passenger. As he gets closer, I can see he's been drinking, wavering off a straight line with the occasional trip. I reset my hood and goggles and give him a thumbs-up. I climb back into the cockpit and wait. He salutes theatrically as he passes and scrambles into the front seat. I don't wait any longer. I clear the brakes and we're off taxi-ing downwind, turning by the onlooking fitters and revving for the take-off. He's too busy fitting his own goggles to take any notice of me. He shouts *'I'm ready'* down the speaking tube and we're away. We clear the ground and climb steeply. There's no turning back.

We fly at 1500ft, well below cloud level. I need to see where I'm going but it's easy: find the Great North Road and follow it South. I relax and wonder if I can do some aerobatics but decide against it - perhaps a step too far! I see no other aeroplanes and after fifteen minutes Ripon comes into view just to the West of the road. I circle and see no activity. I check the windsock and safely land upwind. Yes, the best landing I've ever made. Then I taxi over to the group of huts'

"Perfect landing old boy, well done. Many thanks."

He lifts himself out the front seat and scrambles down to the grass. He gives me a big smile and a thumbs-up. I return the sign and give myself a big smile. If only I could strip off my hood and goggles and show him my long, curly mop. So tempting, if only, but I mustn't. I want to keep flying. This is so much fun. My flight back follows the same route, my smile glued on. Until…

There is a steady increase in noise. My smile disappears, is it the engine? I examine the dials, all looks normal. But the ever-increasing noise level is now frightening me. I look outside and my heart skips a beat. I see three aeroplanes; one each side the other directly above. My guilty conscious clicks in. I've been found out. They think I've stolen Old Gertie or maybe think I'm a raider armed with bombs. They're going to escort me somewhere for questioning. Oh God what have I done?

I study the pilot on the right-hand side and realise who it is and where they've been and where they're going. They're Catterick's flight just returning home and they've found me wondering around in the sky as if I'm on a holiday trip. At a signal they accelerate past me as if I was going backwards and I'm left watching their smoke trails. I know I have some explaining to do.

By the time I'm over the airfield I can see the three have already landed and have taxied over to the hanger. I skim the wreckage site and land close by. One of the pilots is walking determinedly straight towards me. I don't have to guess who it is even before he rips off his googles. He waits, arms folded, body taught. I want to stay in my seat but I have to face the music. I scramble down, stand in front of him and take the tirade of shouted questioning. There was no opportunity

140

to answer as he immediately turned and strode back to the hut, hands thrust deep into his pockets.

I lean back against the fuselage. I want to give him time to cool down. Is he upset because he didn't give his permission, because it puts the whole squadron in jeopardy or perhaps because I left the children?

"All of those but the main reason is that you're not ready to go solo." It's been fifteen minutes before he came out to see me still with Old Gertie. Fortunately, he has cooled down. "Lots of things could have gone wrong and you wouldn't know what to do or where to go." He lists the possible problems and I realise he, of course, is right. It was irresponsible of me. I drop my head in shame. I was stupid. I'm a Sister in a hospital piled high with responsibilities and I go and do something like that just because of the attitude of one man. I feel his hand searching out mine. He tips up my chin with the other and kisses my wet cheeks.

"It's mostly because I love you and I don't want to lose you."

I grab him into my arms. "Ahm so sorry."

"Come on, wipe your eyes. Let's go and have some tea." We start walking towards the hut. He pulls me over and whispers in my ear. "And that was a bloody good landing."

I can't resist a small smile. "Thank you. It was wasn't it?"

Chapter 28

"Come on, keep your kit on, I'll show you what to do when things go wrong."

We'd finished our tea and we had discussed the life of Squadron Leader Arthur Maynard DFC. The pilots and Alec were very dismissive of his World War activities. They had the idea that most of it was self-manufactured that he had done very little that deserved his self-acclaim. To me, it seems unfair. Setting aside his view of women as pilots, I cannot believe all the stories he related to me were all made up. In Flanders we treated many an airman with horrendous injuries. Terrible stories were told. It seemed to us that if you crashed you died or if you did manage to survive, the resulting disfigurement made you wish you had! No parachutes then or at least none that worked very well! Also, he's been honoured with a DFC. Surely that's not made up.

Discussing crashes, injuries and death isn't the best preparation for a flight where problems are set to arise. But I'm keen and rise to get going. I look at Alec to make sure he's happy with more child-minding. He smiles and nods.

"It's a pleasure Emily." He whispers to me quietly. "Anyone who can deceive old Maynard like that is my hero, or heroine." He gives me a cheeky grin.

I smile and reply. "Anyone who can please my two like you dee is mine." He colours up a little. Yes, he's a nice young man.

Half an hour of recovering from engine failures and operational malfunctions convinced me that I was foolish to think I could fly safely. Given there are no mechanical or weather problems, flying is easy but.......I was just lucky.

****

Two days later and we're on our way home. We so enjoyed our stay in Scarborough. It was so much fun we stayed for the whole weekend. Freddie's fear of the sea has reduced thank goodness. He smiled through repeated paddling, swimming amongst the waves and even a rowing boat escapade. The old castle and the gardens are magnificent. No wonder it was so busy, full of Yorkshire folk out to enjoy themselves. Well, there was a certain Geordie/German family who certainly did. We couldn't find any cheap lodging for the night so we stayed in the Grand Hotel.

Grand it certainly is. It's the largest hotel I've ever seen. It overlooks one of the beaches and is known as a Spa Hotel. Our room even has a tap for those who want sea water! Our room was plenty big enough for us including a cot-bed for Harry, a single for Florence and an amazing four-poster bed.

After the trauma and excitement of the first day and the squeeze into Freddie's apartment that night we certainly made good use of this wonderful bed. I love to recall sliding between the cool sheets and stretching luxuriously totally naked waiting for my lover. With the children fed and fast asleep I was looking forward to our night together by ourselves – the first for over two weeks. I well remember how he tip-toed out of the bathroom in his dressing gown and slowly pulled back the covers. I tried my best at a sexy wriggle. It was good enough to get him to strip off to start our night of pleasure, loving and smooching. Certainly, a night to remember and to recall over the next few weeks without him.

Florence was strangely quiet on our short journey home. We all had a lovely morning and caught an early afternoon train to get home at a reasonable time. She's normally full of beans, talking to other passengers, playing with Harry, but she obviously has something on her mind.

"Ye feelin' ok pet?"

She looks over to me wondering, I think, if she should ask a question. Eventually, she does and at the top of her voice for all to hear.

"Ma, what were ye an' Da doin' in bed last night?"

I whisper a quick reply hoping to divert her.

"Just sleepin' an' dreamin'. Shall ah read ye a story from yer new book we bought?"

She ignores my question and at her same volume. "But Da was squashin' ye an' ye were moaning. Were ye arguin' about me?"

I attempt another whisper. "Sshush, we were just cuddlin', that's all. Now, shall ah read for ye?"

"Ok Ma." Then, while I'm finding the page. "But it wes a very long cuddle."

"Now then, where were we?"

I just cannot look around me but I can hear some shuffling and polite coughing. Oh dear, who'd have children!

Arriving at Newcastle a woman from my compartment helps me onto the platform. I thank her and she smiles back. "Aren't children wonderful. You handle them beautifully."

I smile back and thank her again but I can't help colouring up. She walks away still smiling but to herself. I look down at my two totally oblivious of my consternation.

"Right ye two let's gan an' tell Auntie Millie what we've done on our holiday."

We walk carefully along the platform holding hands to catch the tram. I can't wait for her reaction when I relate our story.

Chapter 29

Monday morning and I'm back in my office. The same patients, same nurses and the same problems but I'm ready for them. Staff takes me round so I can check on progress. No surprises but she can't wait to let me know that Nurse Wright has been late 'every single day'. I ask her to send Wallace in.

I'm sorting my notes on the desk when I hear a quiet knock on the open door. I look up and there's an anxious nurse, eyes staring to the floor, hands clasped together in front of her.

"Come in Wallace an' take a seat."

She shuffles forward, sits down and continues to stare vacantly. Nothing's changed. Still hasn't brushed her hair, her new uniform stained, hat missing and I can smell she hasn't washed. I don't need to ask how's she doing.

"Wallace, there is a vacancy for a community nurse in the Hebburn an' Jarrow area. Ahm thinkin' of puttin' yer name forward. Ye have the right experience, canny with patients an' ye know the area. Ah think yer ideal for the job." I hand her the details. "Think about it overnight an' let me know tomorrow mornin'."

Her eyes light up as she quickly reads the vacancy schedule.

"Take it with ye. Now bettor get back te the ward. I'll see ye tomorrow."

She quickly rises, the schedule grasped tightly and heads towards the door. She turns before she leaves and smiles at me. "Thankye Sister."

I suddenly remember. "Hold on Wallace." I hold up another vacancy schedule. "Take this an' show it te yer Da. He may fancy a change."

I watch her during the morning and notice an improvement in her posture and in her general demeanour. If she does apply and fill the vacancy, she'll have the choice of living at home or staying where she is, in the nurses' quarters. Either way she has more flexibility – and a hospital bike! The opportunity of a porter's job in the hospital for her Da may allow her Ma to look after her children and further ease the pressure on Wallace. I suspect the wage on offer is less than in a shipyard and with unemployment rising daily, there'll be many applicants. Maybe a word in the right ear will help. I smile to myself, being a Sister has many an advantage. I realise I don't know him personally except that he stands up for his rights and that's not a bad thing, in my book.

Ideally for her family they'll grab both new challenges. If only one is successful then Wallace's life will improve, she'll regain her pride and she deserves it. A side effect will be to get Staff off my back, I hope.

****

The last two weeks have been taken up with working at the hospital without a break. I knew I had it coming, I love my work but I'm exhausted and really looking forward to a couple of days all to myself and my children. Near the end of my shift I can relax in my office but I'm thinking: I want to do so much but don't know how I can fit it all in. After my Flo and Harry, nursing is my top priority. Then, I so want to gain my pilot's license but that will take years. I'm frustrated that I can't take an active role in local demonstrations to fight for the rights of the workers and their families and in the back of my mind is the ambition to travel to America to see my family. I decide to talk it over with Millie. She's very settled. I think she's contented with her lot. Her long years in the Workhouse have blunted any further ambition. Being happily married with children and having no money worries has been her dream and that's what she's achieved. Lucky her.

"Yer still young Em. You've got time te dee everything but not at the same time. Be patient."

We're sitting in her back yard catching the last rays of sunshine with of course a steaming pot of tea and interesting looking biscuits baked today, children-assisted! She tells me to keep loving being a Sister, keep loving my family, keep flying and save up for a trip to America in one of the big ocean liners. But she says to let other people sort out the political issues, at least for now. She doesn't want me being locked up again and in need of fattening up like before.

"Ah know yer right Mills. Ye must think ahm off-me-head. Ah've got a wonderful job, an' ah have a lovin' family an' somethin' that keeps me feet on the ground, an amazin' friend."

"Who's that then." She looks serious and we stare at each other for at least two seconds before we smile, then laugh before we get up and give each other a hug.

"Was ah really that bad when ah got back from Holloway all those yeors ago?"

"Bad! ah hardly recognised ye. Ah didn't think you'd eaten anythin' in all those weeks away in London. Ah never told you this but when ah first went doon, the doctor took me aside an' confided that ye may not survive. Yes, ye were out of prison but the damage inflicted may be irreparable. Ah wes worried sick. Ah never told yer Stan either."

"Ah just felt so very tired all the time. Ah still remember ye singing te me in hospital. I'll never forget that. It brought me back into the real world. It might have been you that saved my life." Tears flooded my eyes. We cuddled again.

"So, ye were in dreamland an' my voice crashed ye back into reality, is that what ye were sayin'?"

I just smiled. "An' ye haven't stopped. Flo tells me yer always singin' along with some tune or other. She obviously loves te hear ye."

"Anyway, ye didn't need me singin' any more, you've fattened up nicely."

My eyes widened in mock horror. I drew in a breath and showed her my flat stomach. "Back to normal, what de ye think?"

"Ah wasn't lookin' at your tummy."

"Why aye, those will gan doon soon. Mind, Freddie prefers them this way but ah've certainly no chance in getting' into the latest tube dresses like ye can. I'll look like a barrel."

We continue to chat before I have to leave to get the children to bed. It's so nice to be able to confide in someone. I do feel so much better. I think I knew what I should do but I just needed re-assurance. I always know I can always rely on Millie.

Chapter 30

The day has dawned brightly, the sun is shining as if all the cares of the world have been blown away into another existence. The three of us are sitting at the breakfast table in our little kitchen. Flo eating her cereal, Harry feeding at my breast and me sipping at my tea with one hand.

Life is good. Full of hope and amazing opportunities.

There's a knock on the door. My eyes widen and I wonder who it could possibly be. I have to un-latch Harry and place him on a mat which immediately sets him off bawling. I adjust my dressing gown for decency and answer the door to reveal a messenger boy holding up a telegram. I take it, sign for it and close the door behind me while ripping it open. I focus on the writing:

'I regret to inform you that your husband, Frederick, has died in a freak air crash at the aerodrome. His body lies in Catterick hospital while funeral arrangements are made.

I can confirm Freddie served responsibly and diligently in his years in the RAF. He will be sorely missed by everyone at the aerodrome.

Air Commodore Brogan.'

I blink, then re-read the telegram. The message sinks in, I think I scream very loudly and continuously. I know my knees give way because the floor rises to meet my face. My brain is locked in a tunnel. I hear nothing, except a baby, crying in the background.

Chapter 31

I hear voices. They're shouting but I can't make out what they're trying to say. If I could just hear one voice but they're all talking at the same time. But I don't really want to hear what they're saying. It means I may have to do something. I don't want to do anything I just want to stay here in my tunnel, in my cave.

Now someone is pulling at my collar. She's insistent. She wants me to come out. She's calling me Ma. The other voices are now fading into the background. But I'm staying here. This is where I live and I don't want to leave. Everything is now quiet, no voices, no-one calling me. I want to stay here forever.

Now I hear the distant sound of the sea. Waves spreading up the beach then running back out again rolling the loose gravel with it. I can hear the gulls and the oyster catchers and the breeze bringing in the lovely smell of the sea filling and relaxing my whole body. I know all is well and above all this, there's singing. I remember the song. I've heard it before but a long time ago. I love it but it's getting louder and carrying me out of my place. I open my eyes I want to know who is singing.

"Hello Emily. We're all here for you: Your friend Millie and your children Florence and Harry."

I see them all looking at me, my best friend and my children. Then I feel a huge and growing wave of despair, my eyes fill with tears and my body heaves and starts convulsing releasing my tears to flood down my face. The memory of the telegram returns and my lungs produce a long howl 'No………

****

I'm sitting in the carriage as we return to Newcastle. The last few days have passed in a blur of emotion.

Millie came with us to the funeral, thank goodness, I so needed her support, we all did. We arrived at Catterick railway station and my favourite porter opened the door for us. I immediately could tell he knew what had happened. He saluted me, tears rolling down his wrinkled face. I could only hug him and say thank you. Alec was waiting at the gate with a car to take us to the hospital. He also gave me a hug. I knew this was going to be a very difficult time but Freddie will want me to be strong and not to break down.

For the first time I learned what happened. A reporter from the local paper was asked to write an article on the duties of the RAF in Catterick. It was suggested that he takes a flight to give him a feel of what flying is like. It was obvious he didn't want to but Freddie, ever convincing, persuaded him. That was the mistake. It seemed, soon after take-off, Old Gertie dived almost vertically into the ground. Examination of the wreckage showed that the passenger had grabbed the stick and pushed it forward. His hands were still curled around it in death.

That was the end of my Freddie, the reporter and Old Gertie.

My immediate reaction was: what a ridiculous way to die. You spend years fighting in the Flanders trenches avoiding shells and bullets and you die when some weak-minded writer panics. I know that's a ridiculous thought. It wasn't his fault. It's my Freddie who caused it. The most stupid, irresponsible, wonderful, loving, beautiful person I've ever met. How could you?

The four of us viewed the body in the mortuary. It was fully clothed in his RAF uniform, cap in his hand on his chest. There were wounds on the face I assume from burns. Millie looked after Flo and Harry and took them away leaving me alone with him. But it wasn't him. It was his body but my Freddie had left. I know I'll never ever meet someone so, so, I don't know. Yes I do, someone so perfect for me.

I stayed seated alongside the coffin. I was cursing him for being so stupid for ending his life so early. We should be enjoying our lives together, loving our children and each other and you go and do a ridiculous stunt like that. I was hurting, angry, upset, but gradually, these feelings started to fade. I could feel a presence. Something or someone telling me to live my life to the full. Don't forget my lover but be guided by his determination, compassion, his love of life. I smiled briefly and muttered: 'yes, I will.'

He was buried along with the war graves at Richmond cemetery. All the Catterick pilots were present along with the Air Commodore. Each praised his abilities not only as a pilot but as a man. Alec stayed with us throughout, helping with my two. I truly believe he will miss him more than most. He's a very different person to Freddie but I know they respected each other so much.

Before we left for the train, I went to thank him for all his help and support. All through he made sure we were looked after, in the right place at the right time but keeping his feelings buttoned up. I collected all of Freddie's possessions and saw he was leaning against the back of a chair looking out the window. I only realised his shoulders were shaking when I gently held them. He immediately stiffened and wiped his eyes on the back of his sleeve. I knew he had to get the grief out of his system. He's only a young man but he needed a cuddle. I turned him round and pulled him against my bosom, saying nothing. He in turn clasped his arms around me and cried. When his sobbing slowed, he released himself and looked embarrassed.

"Sorry Emily. He was my hero and so are you and I love your children. I always look forward to you coming to Catterick, we all do. You liven up the place. It won't be the same without you."

"Divvent ye worry Alec I'll be back te see ye. I'll never forget how well ye looked after my two, even little Harry. Ye allowed me te

fly. Ah knew they'd been in good hands. So, like or not I'll be back."
I gave him a kiss on the cheek making him colour-up some more.

"Thank-you Emily. Now, I'd better get you to the station. You
can't miss that train."

****

He dropped us off, waved and immediately drove away. His grief
wouldn't let him stay.

The train steamed in and we loaded up the extra cases with the
help of my porter. Before we left, he gave Florence a whistle and
Harry a green flag. I wasn't sure if they were a good idea. I also
wondered if the Railway Company would allow it. But of-course I
gave him a kiss on the cheek and made him colour up. I seem to have
this effect!

As we left, he saluted and we waved back. We chatted for a while
as we puffed our way back to Newcastle.

We're alone in our compartment. There's no conversation now, all
of us recalling the last few days. I sit back into the corner feeding
Harry while Millie holds Florence in her arms. I know my lover has
physically gone but I know he'll be with me in spirit keeping me
going. The next few days will be full of tears but I'll get on somehow
and make the most of my life.

Chapter 32

My life is the same each day:

I wake, my heart feels heavy, my brain is a void. I know what I have to do and I put on my smile and then widen it until it won't get any wider. I hum my song. It's a new one, a jolly one and is always on the wireless. At first just to myself, quietly: *'Yes we have no bananas.'* Then I increase the volume. *'We have no bananas today.'* I know all the words, back to front, inside out. Then I fill my bedroom with my voice: *'We have string beans and onions and cabbages and scallions.'* Before I wake Florence and Harry I get up still singing, put on my dressing gown and slip into the kitchen.

'And all kinds of fruit and say'. I light the gas and make my tea then hold my cup warming both my hands. *'We have an old-fashioned tomato.'* Between lines I take a sip and feel the hot liquid running through my body. *'A long island potato.'* I look out the window to the houses opposite and the brightening sky above, another day. Yes, that's good, it's going to be fun. *'But yes, we have no bananas.'* I hear a noise behind me.

"Can't you sing another song Ma. That one's boring."

"Morning pet. It's a happy song an' ah need te be happy. Come on, you as well, let's sing the last line."

I wave my hands like a conductor and she joins in half-heartedly. *'We have no bananas today.'* I hear a growing whimpering from our bedroom.

"See you've woken Harry now."

"Good. There's yer bowl. Get yer cereal an' I'll feed him."

This is how I get through each day. I have a schedule that must be kept from morning to night. This way I don't notice the heavy weight of my heart, the emptiness of my world. I must keep to my schedule. I've recovered from my deep depression. I'm out of it. Yes, I am and I'm never going to give it a chance to return.

We skip over to Millie's. Me pushing Harry in his pram, Florence trapped between my arms. My neighbours' wave as we pass. Some want to say something but I have to keep going. I can't be late. I walk straight in. She takes the bairns and gives me a hug. I give her a squeeze back. She can feel my tears. I wipe them away and blow them all kisses and leave. I know she's looking at me but I can't look back, I can't weaken.

At the hospital it's easier. It's business. Everyone has a job to do and everyone concentrates on getting it right. I take my ward round with Night Staff. I smile and talk to the patients, check the notes and make any treatment changes. There's a new patient in today, arrived overnight brought in by her daughter her Mum having fallen down the stairs. She's had concussion but she's certainly making a good recovery and with no other problems she'll be leaving tomorrow. Meanwhile she likes a conversation. I notice her broad Yorkshire accent and without any bidding from me she tells me she's from Scarborough and about her lifetime's work at the Grand Hotel.

I feel a jagged pain in my chest, my brain clouds over. I grit my teeth and try my very best to remain upright and smiling. I'm a Sister you have a job to do. Be professional, I mustn't let myself down. There's a voice in my head. It tells me to sit down and rest. She won't stop talking.

"Sorry Mrs Barraclough, ah need te get on but I'll come back."

I turn and head for my office. I feel light-headed and can't focus. I have to walk the full length of the ward. A nurse skips out of my way. I narrowly miss the central desk but skim some papers sending them fluttering to the floor. I can't hear anything, perhaps everyone has stopped what they're doing and are now watching me. I walk upright. I know where my office is but my face is wet, I must get there.

****

I love my cave, I love the sound of the sea, I.., but someone is with me, she's holding my hand.

"Emily, Emily, can you hear me?"

I open my eyes. I see Evelyn and wonder why she's in my cave. But it's not my cave it's my office in the hospital. Memories flood back, Scarborough, the Grand Hotel, my Freddie.

I grab her and pull her head down to me. I close my eyes; I don't want to believe what has happened.

"Come on Emily. I want you off the floor and into your chair. There's tea coming and we can have a chat."

I feel ridiculous. What am I doing on the floor? She helps me onto my feet and into my chair.

"Sorry Evelyn, ah must have fainted."

Two cups of tea have arrived. It's just what I need. I hold the cup with both hands. I can feel my face is wet. Embarrassed, I start to explain.

"I know, your Staff told me what happened. You know," she paused, "you haven't given yourself a chance to grieve properly. You're hiding it, it's locked away. You must let it out. It must be a terrible shock to lose your husband but think of all the good times you had and the love you shared. It'll be very sad but much better than trying to forget."

I stare at her then shake my head. "Ye know, after the funeral ah thought ah could just get on with me life. Then that depression hit me. Ah skulked around an' made everyone around me miserable. It wes down te me friends an' family, they dragged me out of it. But certain memories hit me like an express train."

"There's nothing wrong with memories Emily. Eventually you'll love recalling them. You'll smile and treasure them in your heart. They'll be yours and yours alone."

I smile to myself. "Do ye know the first time we made love wes in Flanders, in woods, very close te the front line. In fact, it wes a

156

German patrol that discovered us. Freddie managed te hide what we were doin'. Ah felt exhilarated an' petrified at the same time."

Evelyn laughed out loud. "That's typical of you. The first time we did it was at his parent's house during a party and it was before we were married. We actually used his parent's bed. We could hear the piano and the singing going on immediately below. We were both so nervous. It wasn't a complete success!"

I could only smile. "Evelyn, how could ye, an' before ye were wed. Ah guess it's got better?"

"Yes, it has. And at least we're married now." She blushed; I think embarrassed.

"Ahm pleased for ye both an' thanks fer yer advice an' the tea. Ah think ah needed both."

"By the way have Freddie's parents been able to come over?"

I shake my head. "No, not yet, but his Mother has promised. She wants te see us an' ah feel certain she wants te talk about her son. Poor Bridgette an' Wilhelm have now lost both their sons. Ah canna imagine how that feels."

"I'm pleased she's coming. It'll be good for both of you. Meanwhile young lady I've told your Day Staff that's she's in charge today and you're having the rest of the day off. No arguments and remember what I say. Let your memories free, talk to your friends about them and of course your Florence. You'll both feel better for it."

It's a lovely Summer's day and I walk and walk. Along the River and through the parks. I'm in my Sister's uniform carrying my cloak. It's as if I'm showing off but my thoughts are all in the past, with Freddie. As a grumpy patient in the CCS in Flanders, saving me from a German bullet, our rushed but romantic and tender love-making when he was on-leave. Then in peacetime, teaching me to fly, our bath together, his love for our children. So, so, so many beautiful memories I will never forget. He was never boring, always exciting, always caring and thoughtful. He was perfect, except he's not here with me. My face must be streaked with tears. I must look a sight but I don't care. I'm examining all my memories and then storing them away until next time. I feel very sad but strangely I feel uplifted for the very first time since his death. There's a spring in my step that's not forced. I look into the sunlit sky and thank Evelyn and then I thank Freddie for being such a wonderful person and giving me such a fulfilling life. I know I have to move on but I know I'll never ever forget him.

Chapter 33

We're well into Autumn now and I'm taking the longer but my very favourite route to work through the park. It's cool but quiet. Leaves are fluttering down in the breeze but I'm concentrating on a letter just received. It has a German stamp and postmark. I know who it's from. Last month, I decided to write, to encourage them to visit. I know it's a long journey and they have responsibilities but I know they'll both be hurting and I want to help, to talk. I'm sure I can take time-off work especially if they can set a date. It also depends on the political situation in Germany but the last I heard the economy was recovering, relieving the frightening tensions. I sit on a bench and, with some trepidation, I open the letter. The writing is beautifully crafted and in almost perfect English but what Brigitte says is both encouraging and concerning:

Dear Emily,

Thank you for your letter and I'm making arrangements. At first, I thought there was no time. I have so many responsibilities, duties, all filling my days but then I woke one fine morning and decided there and then. I'm getting older and need to break out of my routine. It will take me a while to arrange matters but I'm coming next Spring and by myself. Wilhelm is too busy at work and other things. Before I see you, I'm going to visit some old friends in Epsom then catch the train up to Newcastle and see my lovely daughter-in-law and my grand-children. I can stay in a hotel so you don't need to worry about me.

1923 has been such a wonderful but tragic year. Wonderful to see you all and then. Our poor Freddie.

Thank goodness Wilhelm had some time with him. It did make all the difference but what a waste of so many years.

Germany, I believe, is stabilising economically but the warring factions are still at each other's throats but I'm not going to go on about it. I hear enough, every evening, from Wilhelm.

Now I've decided I just can't wait to see you all again and your lovely country.

All my love,

Auf Wiedersehen,

Brigitte

I'm so pleased. I will reply tonight. I'm also relieved that she's going to stay in a hotel. I can't imagine her squeezed into my little flat with two bairns: me, Flo, Harry and the Countess queueing up for the bathroom – I don't think so!

This gives me a lift and I receive further good news when I get to my ward: Not only has Nurse Wallace Wright been accepted as the Hebburn and Jarrow Community Nurse but her father will shortly fill the Porter vacancy. She flew into my office before I could even sit at my desk. Her smile stretched from ear to ear, her cheeks pink with excitement. She was desperately trying to find a way to thank me without embarrassing herself so I just grabbed her, gave a squeeze and a kiss on the cheek.

"Ye deserve it an' ahm lookin' forward te meetin' yer Da. When dee ye start?"

I learn that she heard last night and they want her to start straight away. She needs training of course but to see her so excited was a real treat. Her smile and jaunty posture lasted all day giving the whole ward a lift, staff and patients alike. I even spot Staff Nurse McNamara giving her quick hug. Now all I have to do is find a replacement.

Chapter 34 - 1924

We're sitting by the ticket barrier at Newcastle station. Well I'm sitting, Flo is gazing at the comings and goings and Harry is, I hope, still fast asleep in his pram. I'm waiting to welcome Brigitte and help her across the road to the Royal Station Hotel. We've been here awhile, far too soon, but I thought, just in case the train arrives early. So, we're patiently await the Flying Scotsman and my thoughts have inevitably backstepped ten years to my one and only trip on this prestigious train. I was accompanied by four other Suffragettes full of excitement and anticipation. We had no idea of what we would have to do. If we knew then perhaps, we wouldn't have volunteered. But then perhaps not. It was all worth it despite everything that happened.

My dream ends abruptly when I lift completely clear of my seat as a huge locomotive suddenly shrieks then clanks noisily past blasting out a huge cloud of smoke and steam. As the fog gradually clears, I can make out a figure. It's a woman looking lost. Not any woman but a tall, slim, elegant lady, a Countess. There's no mistaking Brigitte, so different from the press of passengers leaving the train.

"Brigitte, welcome te Newcastle."

She turns, recognises us, smiles and holds her arms out. "Emily."

There's no formality, no shaking hands instead we give each other a warm embrace. We sit facing each other on the bench.

"Oh Emily, you look so lovely and Florence, how you've grown."

I notice the two-way affection between them both and listen to them chatting about what they've done and of course Flo's impending first day at school.

The four of us will have a full day together tomorrow but for now I want to take Brigitte to her hotel, let her settle in while I take my children to Millie's and then we can have the rest of the day together. I've been organised by my best friend: Cots, beds, food all arranged, all I have to do is to concentrate on entertaining Brigitte. Life is so much easier with a 'minder'.

The rest of the afternoon and early evening is relaxed. I can relate what I've been doing since we said goodbye in Munich over a year ago now. We talk of Freddie but, of course, under his christened name of Gunther. I refuse to hold back my thoughts and memories. I need to talk about him and gradually Brigitte unburdens herself. It's made life easier for me and I hope it can do the same for his Mother.

I can sense a change in the Countess. Before she was happy with her responsibilities at home and I suppose resigned to the needs of Wilhelm, but now!

She obviously has had an enjoyable few days with her friends in Surrey. "I've been painting the town red!" I had to laugh at her expression. She's obviously repeating something she's never heard of before but it does seem she's had a lively time.

"A whole group of us travelled into London and saw a show in Covent Garden called 'Primrose'. That was fun then," she paused and blushed slightly, "we went to a Music Hall at the London Pavilion. It was a bit naughty and....I think I had little too much to drink."

My eyes widen. "Really?"

"Yes." She went quiet obviously recalling the evening.

"And?"

"Oh, nothing happened, well, just a bit of innocent flirtation."

I can only smile. Here's the Countess of Feldafing admitting to enjoying male companionship. I know Wilhelm was her first and only boyfriend and I can never forget his own dablings with their maid. I think 'good for you Brigitte'. That's one in the eye for the Count. I shouldn't be surprised. She is a very elegant, sophisticated lady but who can produce a cheeky almost wicked smile.

"Does he have a name like?"

"James."

Probably I shouldn't but I want to know more. "Is he British?"

"Yes, he and his friends come from North London somewhere."

"What does he do?"

She smiles again. "He's a diplomat. That's how we got talking, with Wilhelm working at the German Embassy when we were in London. He works in Whitehall."

I don't want to ask any more questions. It seems too nosy but she continues.

"He's a nice man, very relaxed and has a lovely smile." She smiles remembering but then her mouth compresses. "But I don't suppose I'll see him again."

"He didn't give ye his details then?"

"You're terrible, but yes, he did."

"And ye gave him yours?"

She shook her head. "No, that would be a mistake."

I'm wanting to tell her she deserves a companion. Wilhelm enjoys himself why shouldn't she? But I bite my lip. It's not my business. She has to decide for herself.

I ask her about Wilhelm.

"After you left Germany, he was happier, more loving. But his mind is still full of politics. He's done a really stupid thing."

She sighs, I wait.

"He's joined the Nationalists. He doesn't believe their plans for the Jewish people. He says it's all a rouse to gain support."

"But ye divvent believe it?"

"No. Oh, I don't know. Maybe he's right."

I want to change the subject, get on to something lighter, happier. But she turns on one of her smiles and whispers.

"I've done what you recommended and I've been seeing a chirurg, mmm, a doctor, specialist you know. About my love-making problem. I've had a small operation and I'm now on medication and it's working." Her cheeks turn pink."

163

I grab her hand. "Good fer ye." I couldn't be happier perhaps the maid is not needed.

I let her know of our plans for the evening and hoping she'll agree. After hearing about her last few days, I think she will.

"We're goin' te paint this town red. It's not just London where ye can have fun." Her eyes light up. "Ah want te take ye to a jazz an' ragtime club. We can eat there, listen te the music an' dance if we want to. It's called the 'Speakeasy'. It's only just opened but ah've heard it's amazing. What dee ye think?"

Her expression gives her away before she answers.

"Oh yes please. I've heard the music, it's from America isn't it? I can't wait. You'll have to show me the steps."

I laugh. "Ye think ah know? We'll have te watch the others. I'll gan an' change out of these things an' come back fer ye. It's close by, we can walk there."

"Oh, will it be safe?"

I smile. "No angry Nationalists or Communists here Brigitte. Anyway, I'll look after ye."

We kiss each other on the cheek and agree to meet in an hour. On my walk back home I'm hoping I'm right. Newcastle is not without its drunks and troublemakers.

After a quick shower and a change into something more suitable I arrive back at the hotel. I wait in the foyer and casually people-watch. I rarely go out in the evenings and it's educational to see the different fashions passing me by. At this time of day evening wear combines with everyday clothing, tubular dresses with practical two-piece outfits. I note a group of men waiting by the desk doing the same as me then, as one, they look towards the staircase and stare. I follow their gaze and spot a tall, slim figure making her way carefully down. She's dressed in a sparkling, silken knee length dress below a cloak boasting a huge fur collar. I have to blink. It can't be.

She sees me and walks elegantly over. "Emily, what do you think?"

This beautiful, fashionable creature really is Brigitte. I can't speak. "I bought it in London."

I stand up and notice the group of men still staring. "Brigitte ye look amazin'. Ah divvent think Newcastle has seen such elegance before."

"Oh Emily, is it too much for an old girl like me?"

"Absolutely not. It really suits ye. Come on, we'll get over to the Speakeasy an' get the best table," I lower my voice to a whisper, "before those men's eyes pop oot."

She immediately starts to pull her cloak together looking embarrassed. I whisper "Divvent dee that. Show off yer canny dress an' yer figure." I gently take her arm and lead her out of the doors.

It's only a five-minute walk but I'm thinking I must look a frump alongside this slim creature. Shorter, twice the size and dressed in a style that went out-of-fashion years ago. Fortunately, by the time we arrive, I realise this is a stupid thought. Like it or not this is me and with my shoulders back and head held high we enter determined to have an enjoyable evening together.

I've heard it on my wireless set of course but the new music live is wonderful. My mind and body just tingle and I just have to get up to dance. I'm sure Brigitte is the same but I want to watch the experts first to pick up hints, but my hand is grabbed. A certain German lady can't wait. We take to the floor and I soon realise she's a natural. Jazz swing, Ragtime, Charleston, the band played it and we danced to it. I expected some surprised stares with two women dancing together but there's was none of that. Similar partnerships appeared and we just enjoyed ourselves without embarrassment. It's so uplifting, I feel free, unencumbered by tradition. We laugh, smile and make up our own routines only breaking off to recover and fill our glasses.

At our table we slump into our chairs, worn out, but Brigitte being Brigitte still looks elegant as always. How does she keep so composed, in control? I stir myself to look cool but fail in comparison.

I can't fail to notice groups of men looking at us. All are dressed casually in various colour shades so different from the stiff, formal apparel of just a few years ago. They talking amongst themselves. I anticipate dancing requests and sure enough, when the band sets off on a new jazz swing tune two of them come over. They're very polite and we both accept. My partner is smiley and light on his feet. Brigitte's is older, handsome and more serious, both are good dancers.

The rest of the night follows a similar pattern and gradually the joint effect of the music, the dancing and the gin cocktails are having an effect, on me at least. When a dance finishes my partners either tip their hats or give me a kiss on the cheek before walking away. Perhaps I'm not their type or maybe I'm holding myself back, too soon after Freddie. Brigitte's partners are different. Most kiss her hand romantically and ask for another dance which is usually turned down. However, I have noticed her first partner has returned several times and has been accepted with a smile. There's no doubt he's handsome in his mid-green casual suit and slicked black hair and there's no doubt they get on well. I have to admit they make a lovely pair together.

We're walking back to the hotel arm in arm. We've both really enjoyed ourselves. The music is still in my head and the cocktails are making me smile and stumble. Brigitte cannot remove her own smile or the pink colouring in her cheeks. I can tell she's making up for lost time. I can also understand she likes to recall a certain dancing partner.

"He's so light on his feet, and he's a singer in a band. He keeps fit and likes to play tennis."

166

I laugh. "Is there anythin' he canna dee?"

She smiles. "He's very nice. What do you think of him?"

"Well he never asked me te dance, so ah divvent know, but he's very handsome an' he certainly had an eye fer ye."

"No, he didn't."

I just gave her a look. "What's his name like?"

"Lawrence."

I made sure Brigitte was safely in her bedroom and happily relaxing drinking a bedtime brandy from the bar before I left the hotel to make my way home. She thanked me for a wonderful night and no matter how she tried she couldn't lose her smile.

Tomorrow's Saturday and I've arranged to meet her at 11 o'clock with Florence and Harry in the hotel foyer. Hopefully we'll both have recovered by then.

I step out of the hotel and cross the road to get a taxicab home. Looking out of the window I notice a car pull up outside the hotel and a handsome man with slicked black hair wearing a casual mid-green suit gets out.

Chapter 35

I'm sitting in my kitchen a pot of tea on the table. My mind is a whirl of worry. It doesn't help that I'm feeling the effects of last night's drinking and dancing. I have to get prepared for the day ahead then pick up the children before meeting Brigitte. The man I saw was most definitely Lawrence. I was in two minds: should I stop the taxi and warn Brigitte or consider it's none of my business and let them get on with it? In the end I stayed put and I'm now wondering what I'm going to find at the hotel.

If he is as nice as he appears then, good for you Brigitte, but if he's a chancer, only out for himself. Oh dear. I should be looking after her not putting her at risk. I mean what reasonable man would meet a woman at a dance then follow her to a hotel? He must be up to no good.

The more I think about what could have happened the more worried I am. I could find her murdered in her bed!

"Yer bein' too dramatic. Ah suspect they had an enjoyable night together." I've related what happened during and after our Speakeasy evening to Millie. "She seems to be Royalty. She's in her forties, certainly old enough te look after herself. She wouldn't have appreciated yer interference. She may have invited him anywa', after all she did tell him where she was stayin' like."

I'm not convinced. As we walk to the hotel my brain is going through what could have happened last night: rape, robbery, murder. I'm grumpy with Florence and Harry, which they don't deserve. I feel nervous. I'm not sure what I'll find when I get there.

Florence runs ahead and starts the revolving doors that shoot us out into the foyer. We're a few minutes late, my eyes dart around to find her. Thank goodness, she's there and she's still smiling. My tensions reduce, I wave and walk towards her. She looks happy, certainly very much alive.

I can't help squeezing her far too tightly. "Did ye have a canny night?"

"Yes, thank you Emily, it was just perfect in every way. And now I can spend the day with my lovely grand-children. Where are we going? You've been keeping it a secret."

My body relaxes completely. If there was a problem then she's certainly a good actress.

"Ah've booked a flight. Ahm goin' te take ye up into the sky."

Her reaction was of complete shock and horror. "Divvent ye worry. It's very safe an' you'll get first class treatment."

"But I've never been in an aeroplane."

"Ma's a pilot. She's very canny, everyone says so. She's promised te take me when ahm older."

"Well in that case Florence I'll let her take me." She turns to me. "It's something I've always wanted to do."

I explain that we're going to Catterick where Freddie was based. I don't mention it was where he died but I've planned a trip to his grave in Richmond. Alec has made the arrangements and will drive us there himself. It'll be a bit of a squeeze in their car but it's only a few miles.

We arrive at Catterick station where I introduce Brigitte to my favourite porter.

He gives a little bow. "It's always a pleasure to meet your daughter-in-law and her children." He pauses. I can tell what he's thinking. "And erm.. your son was one of the very best." His voice falters and brings a tear to my eye. However, Brigitte just smiles and takes his hand in hers.

"That's very kind of you. I appreciate that."

I can see Alec waiting by the car and we take our leave.

"What a nice man he is."

"Yes, he is."

"And he gave me an' Harry a green flag an' a whistle."

169

"Lucky you two."

Our flight is only really a few circuits around the aerodrome. No aerobatics just a few words through the speaking tube pointing out various landmarks then waving at the gathering outside the dispersal hut as we swooped overhead. Initially I have a few nerves tingling, after all, the life of Royalty was in my hands but we land perfectly and I can immediately see my passenger has enjoyed her flight.

"Oh Emily, that was so invigorating. You're magnificent."

"Ah wes taught by the best!"

She just smiles.

The next half an hour is spent chatting to the pilots and Alec. There's no embarrassment. Brigitte has a knack of making any conversation easy and relaxed. Part of being a Countess, I guess. She's certainly made aware how much Freddie was respected as a pilot and as a friend, by everyone. I take her aside.

"Would ye like te visit Gunther's grave. It's only a few miles away?"

"Yes please."

It's only a short journey which is as well, as six of us are squeezed together in a car made for four! We gather around his gravestone in the RAF section and we talk about his flying exploits and all the adventures we enjoyed together. Then five of us leave allowing Brigitte some time by herself, with her son.

We're soon on our train journey home. The day out has gone well but now, apart from my toddler, everyone is quiet, reminiscing.

Nearing Newcastle Brigitte takes my hand and smiles. "Thank you Emily I've really enjoyed today. I'm so proud of Gunther. I saw so little of him. I just hope he understood. I don't think I can ever forgive Wilhelm. What a waste."

"Thank goodness they built bridges last yeor. It made such a difference te him. The bitterness had gone."

I could see Brigitte is struggling against showing emotion. "Now then, have ye any plans for tonight? It's Saturday an' the Toon comes alive!"

Her expression changes she turns on her slightly embarrassed smile. "I haven't told you yet but I've been invited out to see a film. You see Lawrence came around last night to the hotel. You remember, the man with the green suit?"

My eyes narrow in mock suspicion. "Oh yes."

Colour flushes her cheeks "Oh no. He only came to invite me out tonight. We met in the foyer, then he went home."

I can only laugh. "Of course. Ah would never have imagined anything else. He seems nice. Ye have a canny time, ye deserve it, have fun."

To myself I thought how stupid I've been, thinking the worst. Not every man is a rogue. This Lawrence is obviously attracted to this sophisticated lady and wants to see her again. That's natural. His thoughts will change when he realises she's married and lives In Germany. Then it's up to them both. He's not taking advantage, they're both dipping their toes in the water.

****

It's Monday midday and I'm on the platform looking through the window watching Brigitte settle down in her first-class seat on the Southbound Flying Scotsman. She has a long three-day journey home stopping with her friends in Surrey and again in Paris but it's not a chore. She's calls it an adventure and she's right. I'm certain she'll meet and be entertained by many other travellers. She's a changed woman, still a Countess with responsibilities but determined to enjoy different experiences and not be beaten down by the expectations of men. I smile to myself thinking, we're very much alike.

171

Yesterday was a relaxing day for all four of us, no flying, no romantic assignations. Well not for me anyway. Just walks in the parks and alongside the Tyne, discussing everything from my work in the hospital to our hopes for the future. We called in to see Millie, Sam and Frank for an afternoon cuppa. Millie being Millie, is fascinated by European politics and poor Brigitte was bombarded with questions, probably something she wanted to avoid! But no-one would have guessed as she clearly described the situation in Germany.

Saturday night was clearly a huge success. Everything was 'wonderful' the film, the dinner and most of all, Lawrence.

"What a man. Punctual, kind and gentle but fascinating. Being a musician, he's been everywhere and has met so many famous people. He treated me like lady all night."

"But ye are a lady, a Countess."

"But he doesn't know that. I don't like to tell everyone. If I do, people change, they're embarrassed. Anyway, he brought me back to the hotel, we had a...now what did he call it, oh yes, a 'nightcap'. Then escorted me to my room and we said goodbye with a kiss and he left."

"Well that's nice."

That was Saturday night. What she didn't tell me until this morning was that they met again last night. She didn't volunteer any details except to say:

"Yes, he's very nice, very nice indeed."

No more details, just a very broad grin below pink cheeks and faraway eyes.

Chapter 36 - 1925

Two wonderful letters were delivered today, both from America:

To my Emily,

I'm writing this myself, with a lot of help from Davey. I hope you can understand what I'm saying.

Davey reads your letters to me and your sisters and they read their replies back to me. But he's now convinced me that I should learn to read and write myself. So that's what I'm doing!

When your first letter came, I couldn't believe it. You're still alive. I cried and smiled lots of times. I was so happy. And now you have three children yourself. You talk about Florence and Harry but never mention Mhairi. Don't keep it all inside. It'll be easier if you can talk about her. We're all heartbroken about your Freddie. He sounded so nice.

Well done on becoming a Sister in the hospital. I'm so proud of you. I bet you're knocking the nurses into shape and making the patients behave themselves.

And I can't believe you've been flying aeroplanes. You must be careful they always seem to be crashing.

We're doing well here in Scranton, Pennsylvania. Davey is now a Foreman at the coalmine and, by the way, he sends you his love as always.

Your sisters were thrilled to get your last letter. It arrived a few days before their birthday. Twenty-one, would you believe it. They dressed up really lovely for their party. Both of them taller than me and much slimmer. I've sending you a picture of them at the party. Don't they look so pretty? They send their love as well and they say they will write letters to you.

*This has taken me ages to write. Sorry about the crossings-
out. I hope you're proud of me.*

*I do miss you and your brothers, all of them. I hope and
pray that one day we can meet again.*

Goodbye my pet. xxx

Your loving Ma and Davey.

I cannot believe Ma is learning to read and write. I remember
trying to teach her but she gave up believing she didn't need it to look
after her bairns. We've been writing to each other ever since I learned
their address from Ettie. I study the photo. I can still recognise the
twins despite their change from young teenagers. I don't need Ma's
name-tags written below! They are very slim wearing their
shimmering knee length dresses and high heels and their curly blonde
locks set in a short modern style. Flo is smiling demurely while
Gertie is pouting suggestively. My heart aches to see them. I love
reading their letters over and over but I need to see them, to hug them
close. I want to be with them, my family.

I wonder about Mhairi. I keep her hidden from everyone. I don't
really know why. Perhaps I'm scared of releasing my heartache, my
shame. Will talking about her help me though, in the long term?
Freddie must know now. I wonder how he feels?

My other letter:

Hi Sis,

*Thank you so much for my birthday card. It came a week
early. The ship must have had a following wind.*

*We had a really exciting twenty-first. It was held in our
local Jazz club. Lots of our friends came and of course Ma and
Davey. I think we danced the Charleston all night. It's just
amazing, you must try it - but be careful of your poor old
bones! There were lots of good-looking men about. I haven't*

got a boyfriend at the moment so I'm on the look-out. Also, more exciting news, I've applied for a job with United States Lines. They have lots of Cruise Liners taking wealthy people to Europe including Britain. I'd be a waitress or maybe a maid or maybe something else. I don't really mind, it just sounds so different, sailing the seas, meeting lots of travellers. What do you think? It'll be a lot better than serving in a boring store in town. And, you never know, we might be able to meet in Liverpool or Southampton.

Ma and Davey are both well. By the way Davey is a great dancer. He made Ma go completely dizzy. It was all good fun though. I know Ma misses you and so do I and Gertie. She'll probably write but she's busy being an actress or trying to be. She goes to auditions but there's so much competition. I think she would be very good.

Love you Sis,

Flo xx

What a cheek. Old bones indeed. I put the letter down and go through my very own Charleston routine. Immediately I get a stitch and have to grip the back of a chair. I sit down on it thinking that I just need a bit of practice. Just because I'm thirty-two doesn't mean to say I'm past-it.

I read the letter through again. My wee sisters fully grown, looking at men. Then I realise I had a baby at eighteen. Maybe my twin sisters look after each other making sure no-one takes advantage of the other. I hope so.

I would dearly love to see her. Working on a Cruise Liner sounds exciting. So far away from the daily problems at the hospital and the deepening depression on Tyneside. But then I get realistic: working on a Liner is probably hard work. Me, I've got my two children and my work in the hospital is actually, really satisfying.

175

I've been a Sister now for over two years and I've got the ward how I like it. With the help of Evelyn, we've mixed up the patients so there's now no 'Poor' and 'Posh' separation. I've found more appropriate work for some of the nurses and even Staff Nurse Jean McNamara smiles on occasions. Yes, my daily routine is without too much hassle. Perhaps it's time to try something else. There, it's slipped out. I shake my head and wonder why I can't be content. Why do I need another challenge, a change of scene, another opportunity to make a difference? I don't know….but I do!

****

I'm walking back to the airfield office in Catterick after completing another thirty minutes of flying solo. Old Gertie's replacement trainer is being serviced so I've been up in one of the modern single seater fighters for 'testing purposes after repairs. Since my first flight with Freddie over two years ago I've had nearly forty hours flying time and that includes over ten hours solo. I've been taught the fundamentals of how an aeroplane flies and I've spent days in the hangar learning and helping the mechanics maintain the fleet. How I've still got away with it is down to everyone working here. But I do get the impression the RAF is changing. The Service is becoming more organised and, I suppose, a better managed business. Loopholes are being closed, more rules and regulations imposed, increasing need for inspections and reports. I feel at any time I will be discovered for what I am: a freeloader.

I love flying. To be alone high above everyone and everything else, in amongst the clouds sliced by sudden multi-coloured rays of sunshine beaming through is an experience few people have had, especially women. I read magazines telling stories of daring-doos of women in flying circuses in America and some setting world records flying over long distances. But generally, women pilots are very rare and, of those, most have the backing of a wealthy father.

I know I'm fortunate in many ways. I am lucky but I also know that you can make your own luck by being determined, having a go at something that looks impossible and not giving up easily. I will keep flying whatever it takes. Here at Catterick or in one of the flying clubs that are now springing up all over the country.

My thoughts bring a spring to my step as I pass over the hut's threshold to make sure Alec is coping with my three-year-old hooligan!

Chapter 37

I look up when I hear a knock on my open office door. Our regular porter is standing there looking nervous.

"Come in Mat. Anythin' wrong?"

He takes a few steps inside and finally after some prompting, he takes a seat.

"Is Wallace ok?"

He coughs and fidgets, he's obviously nervous about something. "Yes Sister, she's very well, thank ye. Umm.. Wallace only told me last night that it was yerself that gave me this job an' that it was ye that helped her get her home-visiting position. Ah wanted te thank ye."

I smile relaxing. "Ah only put a word in fer ye both. Ye did the rest yerselves. Wallace has always been an excellent nurse an' ah've seen how ye enjoy yer work heor. Yer canny with the patients. Ah've seen the way ye make them smile an' laugh. That's all part of their treatment."

"Thank ye, Sister." He's still looking nervous.

"There's somethin' else isn't there?"

"Er, well, aye, Wallace also told me about yer Suffragette work before the war an' how ye stand up fer what ye think is right. Ye see, ah still have a drink with the lads at Hawthorns an' there are still problems at the Yard but our Union rep is too shy, timid, ye know what ah mean, doesn't say what he should. The management just ignore him. Ah was just wonderin' if, maybe, ye could represent us?"

I'm completely taken aback. This group of men want me, a woman, to represent them to fight for their rights. My immediate reaction is to say No. But I can sense the lid I've locked down on my social justice demands, is releasing. Management have for years been subjugating their employees with all manner of unscrupulous changes: more work for less pay, holidays without pay, reduced safety checks. I have read about them, heard about them, then put them aside as something someone else can deal with. But now?

I can understand demands for ships, coal and iron have slumped but the changes they make are all one-way. The quality of life of the owners and management are unaffected. Not for them the inevitable reductions of food and clothing provision for working families or, in the worst case, dependency on local parish contributions. There has been no investment in new facilities in the busy pre and post war years. Now industry is suffering the consequences of foreign competition.

"Mat, let me think about it an' I'll get back to ye."

He gives me a broad smile. "Thank ye, Sister," he stands an' shuffles, "an' ah dee love me work heor."

"Good." I just smile then stare at his back as he leaves. I wonder.

****

Millie gives me a knowing look. "It's a wonder that you've taken so long."

I give her a questioning look.

"You've been dyin' te get back on te yer soap-box. Ye know ye have. I'd love te see their faces when ye walk in. But these are hard times. Reduced benefits are bettor than no benefits if the company closes doon."

"Ah know that. But there are alternatives, some give an' take. Also, some hit on their own incomes an' perks. It's all one way at the moment. Ah think it's important that each side understand each other's problems an' both have te make changes."

"Well good luck with that one. Ye de realise that if ye manage te change their attitude then all the other shipyard workers will want ye, te say nothin' of the miners!"

179

"If ah can dee anythin' then it might set a precedent an' the others will follow, lamb-like."

Millie gives me a worried look, takes my hand and speaks quietly. "Look Em, the Yard is not the hospital. Yer dealing with hard-nosed businessmen who take no notice of the Unions an' almost certainly will have no respect fer yer sex. Whatever the Suffragettes have achieved, men's attitude te women hasn't changed much. We're still just chattels who need a good slappin' te keep us in our place. My Sam is the exception of course an' so wes yer Freddie."

This is where I play my trump card. "Ah've met with a certain woman MP who'll support me. She's the MP for Middlesbrough but she used te represent Jarrow. She's a real go-getter."

"Ye divvent mean Ellen Wilkinson?"

"The very same."

"But she's a communist."

"No, she used to be in her student days but she's staunch Labour now. And, she has influence."

"And a reputation!"

"Good."

"Ahm meetin' some shop stewards, Mat an' the union rep in the Black Hammer next week te discuss our approach. Ah wes hopin' Millie, if ye could.."

"Why aye pet. Me days are a bit lonely now Florence an' Frank are at school with just blondie here. Te have all three fer a couple of hours in the evenin' is no problem an' ah've got my Sam te help."

"Thanks Millie. Ahm lookin' forward to it."

Millie shakes her head as if I'm totally mad but she doesn't have my desire to make changes. I may not succeed but I'm going to give it a try. I scoop up my two and we make our way home. I wonder what Freddie would have thought. He would warn me of the dangers but wouldn't stop me, even if he thinks he could! I know about the kidnapping and attacks on individuals in Germany but I don't understand why it should happen in Newcastle. There are no groups of intimidating Nationalist party members patrolling the streets. All I'm doing is helping two groups to compromise, to understand each other. Perhaps I'm being naïve.

I rarely go into pubs. The evening is warm, the sun is still shining but the brightness disappears as you enter 'The Black Hammer'. Inside it's dark, forbidding and stifling. The windows are stained a brownish-yellow and any light filtering through illuminates the great wafts of tobacco smoke. The whole place stinks of cigarettes and beer and, as far as I can see, I'm the only woman inside.

I manage to find the group of four and settle in to a corner with a glass of lemonade. It seems that Mat has told them what I've done in the past. The two shop stewards seem in awe of me, impressed and proud that I'm a Geordie like them. The Union rep is quiet, suspicious I suppose, understandably.

What surprises me is their lack of knowledge of the current order-book problems at the shipyards. I have to explain that during the years immediately after the War, the yards were fully employed replacing the British ships that were lost. But there was no investment and no export and, because of this, other European ship builders invested heavily in their own new yards and our export trade never re-appeared.

I outline some of my ideas: investment in new equipment, increase the range of work, different types of ships, diesel power replacing steam. Possibly working jointly with other yards to share facilities. From the point-of-view of the labour force: improved facilities, paid holidays, proper training. Basically, what I'm saying is a happy workforce works harder with fewer accidents and less mistakes meaning increased profits.

I want to get away from confrontation, accusations of failed contracts and shouting matches. Inevitably there will always be redundancies during hard times but a well-run business will always attract new work and good times will follow. I suspect it will take years to change the present static system. It may even take government intervention to break the old intransigent ideas and that's where Ellen will come in to her own.

I can't say the shop stewards agree with all my views, particularly the union rep who kept muttering under his breath. Either way it's clear their way has done nothing to solve the dilemma so basically, I can do no worse.

If all this has no effect then it's down to publicity to show the management is not open to new ideas and maybe this will force government to take action to protect the workforce and their families.

****

It's a week later and I'm sat at home, the children are in bed but I'm wondering what's hit me!

I had to take a day off work and arrived, with the two shop stewards, at Hawthorn's offices at 10.30. We left at midday. Anyone would think a meeting for nearly two hours was enough to have a sensible discussion but anyone wouldn't know we were kept waiting for most of that time. There was no welcome, no refreshments, no polite introductions.

Eventually three men appeared, two of them be-whiskered and the youngest clean shaven, all without any apology. They were the owner, his personnel manager and a much younger man who I was later informed was the owner's son. I introduced myself as the representative of the workforce. I briefly described what I thought was the current position with the trade and the disagreements between the two parties. Then suggested possible avenues to follow to achieve a compromise. I repeatedly requested some sort of response but only achieved shaking heads, guffaws and muttered insults.

"Have you finished young woman?"

I nodded. "Then I'll tell you what's going to happen." He nodded at his Personnel Manager who proceeded to detail the number of redundancies to be made, new longer working hours and cuts in pay that are going to be implemented.

"Dee ye not think my ideas will help rebuild confidence in yer business an' at the same time give reassurance to yer workforce an' their families?"

The Personnel Manager started to answer but stopped, his eyes flicking over to the Manager almost in fear. I could see why. His face had turned blotched scarlet and I could almost expect steam to blow out of his ears.

"Young woman, you know nothing about my business and the assurance of the workforce and their families has nothing to do with me. You would do better to stick to looking after your husband and making his dinner rather than sticking your nose where it's not wanted."

At that point the meeting became a slanging match. One of the Shop Stewards stood up, pointed and spat out words through clenched teeth. "Divvent ye dare insult this woman, she wes a Suffragette an' nearly died fer her trouble an' then saved lives as a nurse in Flanders while you sat on yer fat backside makin' yer fortune buildin' warships."

"So, she's a commie then, trying to stir up trouble."

At that point I got up, spread my arms and, determined to keep my voice calm. "Ah think it's best te re-convene when we've all calmed doon." I made my way to the door beckoning the others to follow.

Down the stairs the stewards apologised. They were obviously embarrassed for me. I thanked them for their support but that they shouldn't be embarrassed, I've had worse insults. Outside it was very warm and I had to loosen my jacket and blouse. Before we parted I told them that my next step will be to involve Ellen Wilkinson.

"Ye know her?"

"Yes, we've already spoken about this. She has a good deal of influence, much more so than any of us."

I could see they were impressed. I know the MP has huge support in this area. Before we parted company, I confirmed that I would let them know the results of my meeting. At the bus stop, a large car drew up alongside, the window wound down and I recognised the young man, the son of the owner.

He spoke in perfect English, no sign of a Geordie accent. "I have to apologise for my father. May I give you a lift?"

Immediately Millie's warnings raced across my brain. I shoed them away, he was the only one who had kept calm and he may have a different view from his father.

"Let me introduce myself. I'm Jake Morrison the owner's son. I think your ideas are interesting. I do believe we cannot go on without changes but my father is um..." he pauses looking for the right word, "stubborn, set in his ways. A bit of a dinosaur you might say. He wants me to take over when he retires but that could be some time, unless he has a heart attack first of course. You can see he's very excitable. Either way I will see if I can moderate his views a bit, drip-feed ideas."

We soon arrived at my flat.

"Any chance of a cup of tea and we can talk over some of your points?"

My uncertainty returned but again I submitted and we came inside. I slipped off my jacket and while he waited in the sitting room, I made the tea in the kitchen. He continued to talk about how the business could change, I relaxed, answered and prepared the tray for our refreshments. I returned still talking but he'd gone and before I could turn, I felt his breath on my neck and his hands slipped round my waist. My whole body stiffened.

"What are ye doin'?"

His hands slid up and grasped my breasts as he kissed my neck. "You know you like it."

I needed to keep calm and remove myself from his grip. "Well let me put the tray doon first." He pulled his hands away thinking he has a willing victim. I walked to the table, grabbed the cake knife, turned and held it to his face. "Ah think it's time ye left."

He was still smiling. "Come on, you live here by yourself, have some fun. Let me have that kn.."

"Cooee Emy, we're comin' in."

His eyes widened, his smile disappeared and immediately made his escape elbowing his way past my friend and three children.

I couldn't move or say anything. I just looked at Millie. I still had the cake knife firmly in my grasp. Millie took hold of my arm and carefully removed the knife before I slumped down on to the settee, head in my hands.

"Come on, drink this tea an' tell me all about it."

I related the whole sorry story to Millie.

She was not surprised at the Manager's attitude but was horrified of his son's actions. She kept repeating what I already knew but ignored. "Never let a man ye divvent know in te yer house. Ye could have been raped, again. He thought ye were an easy target an' would be pleased to accept his advances." I gave my excuses knowing they were pathetic. I was just stupid.

Millie laid down the law for rest of the day. "We'll play with the children, feed them an' put them te bed. Then I'll take my Frank hyem, leave him with Sam te deal with an' I'll come back. Ahm staying here the night. We'll have te see how ye are tomorrow mornin'. Ye may need another day off. Also, we have te decide what te dee about that little brat."

I'm now sitting quietly waiting for her return. I watch out the window at the street in the deepening dusk. I know he won't return but the door is locked and bolted. I know I was naïve and stupid. I also know I'll make him pay for what he's done and I know I'm going to make life uncomfortable for the management of Hawthorn.

Chapter 38

To relax me Millie is discussing world politics! Normally I would let the info in one ear and let it flow out the other but this was different. Soon after we left Germany over two years ago there was big trouble in Munich. The Nationalists made their move and tried to take over the city. It was their leader, Adolph Hitler, who had apparently tried to bribe other prominent leaders to join forces. Fortunately, they reneged on their promises and Hitler and his followers were beaten back but not before many had died and Hitler himself was arrested. It seems he was heading for a long prison sentence but it seems he has friends in influential places and he's been released already. Oh dear.

Brigitte has never mentioned this either during her visit last year or in subsequent letters. I can guess she wants to keep politics in the background. I don't blame her but I'm sure it casts a huge shadow over her life. Either way there's certainly nothing I can do about it lying here squeezed up with Mills in my bed. She turns to me, and inches from my face, she asks. "So, what's the plan now?"

"Ahm gannin te get the bastard somehow. Ah mean, who does he think he is? Ah must be ten years older; he should pick on someone his own age at least."

"Perhaps he likes matronly women."

I look at her but I can see she's smiling so I pinch her nose and poke her in her skinny ribs.

"Oy! Admit it you've plenty to grab hold of."

For the last two years I seem to be developing into Ma's shape all bosom and bum. Freddie would have loved me as I am so I've no incentive to diet. Maybe I should or wear something voluminous to hide my curves. But there's no way I'll do that.

"Ah canna change how ah am. Even if ah could ah wouldn't. People will have to accept me as ah am. It's my body an' ahm proud of it."

"Well divvent dee daft things."

"How dee ah catch a sex-fiend? Get a photographer an' lure him in? Now, where did ah get that idea from?"

We recall our master plan to catch Proctor the Workhouse Manager. It worked a treat apart from poor Millie who had to suffer his actions before he was caught red-handed so to speak.

"Retribution is beautiful an' then to cap it all ye got him killed-off by yer lovin' polis! Ah wonder if we can dee that again?"

"No, he's just a spoilt kid who thinks he can get away with anythin'." An idea suddenly blew into my brain. "If only ah could get him on my side, he'd be a useful ally."

"Yer not gannin te let him have his way, are ye?"

"No, of course not but maybe a bit of blackmail is possible or rather the threat of blackmail. His Da won't want the bad publicity of havin' a sex-fiend fer a son."

"He may not mind. Ah mean how dee ye think he got to be the boss? Through good works?"

"Mmm, maybe he'd be privately pleased but not if he becomes a laughing stock with his fellow ship builders."

"Perhaps we need the help of Charlotte an' her brotha. Does she still work at the Workhouse?"

"She got married in the War an' they were still there before ah had Harry but the last time we met they were plannin' te retire. We could try, they may not be able to help but it'll be canny te see them. They were so canny together.

Millie smiles. "Remember her moustache? And we used te call her 'Teddy' after the king. She terrified me all me life as a child. At least until ye arrived then she seemed te change."

I smile recalling my time in the Workhouse. "Divvent ye worry she terrified me at first an' me brotha Con. Of course, she saw how responsible ah was an' made me her assistant, then she changed fer the bettor. So, it wes all down te me! But ah guess the new manager helped. She suddenly dressed smartly, cut her hair stylishly an' shaved off her moustache. Ye see that's what a man can dee."

"All down te you indeed. But ah can see the similarity in shape!"

With that I roll her out of my bed. "Yer sleepin' on the floor fer that." She crawls back apologetically and we cuddle ourselves to sleep.

It's morning and I'm back at work leaving Millie with the children but my idea is still playing on my mind. I decide to re-visit the Workhouse this very evening.

****

"It's going to be extended to take more children from a Home that's closing down. Well, that's what they say anyway. Either way Jackie and me are planning on retiring but we'll see it through the expansion. I want to make sure it gets off properly. I will miss all the children. I know I will, but we have plans."

We are sitting in the very same room that she used when I was an inmate. It was always tidy but now it's been repainted with new curtains and floor rugs. In fact, the whole place has been refurbished with windows you can actually see out of and clocks that actually work! All so different. The child that opened the door looked cared for, wore shoes and had washed himself. What a revolution. Changes were being made when I came here with Millie and Frank before the War. We met to draw up plans to trap Proctor and show him to the world as the debauched sex-fiend he really was. Now I want to trap another similar person, much younger but still someone who needs a scare or more precisely be persuaded to help me.

"Oooh, what plans?

"Well, first of all we're going travelling. We want to see more of the world. Then come home here and have a family of our own."

My eyes shot up in surprise.

"No, not myself. That would be nice but I don't want to break the world record for the oldest woman to give birth. No, we're going to adopt two or three children, maybe from here and bring them up as our family. You can't say I'm not experienced. What do you think?"

"All I can say Charlotte is – lucky children." I feel overcome and get up and give her a kiss and a hug. "Ye gave me a start in life. Ye put in a good word at the hospital an' ah've never looked back."

"I knew you were something special. You stood up for yourself and the other children. I could see you really cared for them. I knew you would do well and now you're the youngest Sister in the hospital."

"Am ah?"

"Oh yes, I know the Matron very well. But besides that, if you hadn't made up that plan of yours, that demon Proctor would still be here and I would never have met Jackie."

"Well it certainly did ye a power of good. Ye changed so much. New clothes, new hairstyle."

"Yes, yes and I shaved!"

I blushed and just nodded.

"Now tell me about this Hawthorn boy and what you want me to do."

I related the full story of representing the workers, their rebuff and the unwanted attention of the Manager's son. Then shared my plan for getting the boy on my side.

"Well I don't know them myself but I do know someone who does. She spent most of her childhood here in the Home and I managed to get her employed there but she wants to leave. Guess why."

"No?"

"Yes. Continual harassment from many of the men including your boy. She has a shape like you but now she hides herself in baggy clothes as a disguise. This sort of thing happens all the time everywhere. To photograph her being molested by one of the staff may not have much effect. He'd probably get a pat on his back. But the Manager's son is different. Any such photograph in a newspaper or distributed to rival companies will cause embarrassment and his family won't like that. No, they won't like that at all and he'll know that. He's taking a risk now but a photograph? Yes, that may just make him do as you ask."

"But would she be willin' te be a victim an' maybe lose her job in the process?"

"It may even safeguard her job with the ever-present threat of exposure. She may even be promoted."

"Why not leave it with me. I'll speak to the girl and my brother of course. Do you have a telephone?"

"Yes."

"Ok, leave your number and I'll get back to you. If it works it will please me more than it pleases you."

We discussed possible actions before and during the reveal. She also agreed that I could involve Ellen Wilkinson but only as a last resort – if the threat doesn't work and we have to show everything in its full pictorial glory.

On my way home I picked up Florence and Harry at Millie's house and updated her of our plan.

"Ye scheming pair. Can ah dee somethin'?"

"Thanks, but no. Ye can be our 'problem-solver'.

"Ok then. De ye know this poor woman? She may not want te be the target of his lust again."

"No, ah only spotted a few women in the admin room before gannin into the Board Room. It could have been any of them, or perhaps all of them!" Hopefully he won't have a chance of full intercourse. Ah just want a photo of his trousers doon."

"Supposin' he makes a grab for the camera."

"With his trousers doon? No, ah suspect it'll be like at the workhouse: Discovered by the group, photograph taken an' camera rushed away fer developin'."

"It worked the first time, we were lucky. But again?"

"Any better ideas? Remember ah don't want to show the world what he's been doin'. Ah just want him on a lead. If he doesn't dee as ah say I'll give him a big tug at his neck. Remember before his lust took over, he was actually talkin' sense. Ahm hopin' this will act as an incentive te support me ideas like."

****

Soon after I met with Charlotte. There came an announcement from the Company. It confirmed what they said at our meeting:

Due to the lack of orders we have to make the following actions immediately: 10% redundancies to be made, remaining employees will have their pay rates reduced between 10 to 20% and the number of hours worked each day increased by one hour. In addition, there will be an obligatory increase in holidays to four specific weeks, all without pay.

There were no concessions at all. Our meeting in their offices had made no difference, surprise, surprise. Their lack of respect and no consideration of other possibilities made me angry and I felt determined our devious plan has to be followed.

Mat, our porter who asked me to help, is very apologetic. "Ah heard that ye tried yer best but they weren't listenin' but at least ye had a go. Ye can understand how the lads feel. They're just ignored."

"All is not lost Mat. Ah still have hopes."

He raises his eyebrows and shrugs. "An' pigs might fly."

****

My plan has to go ahead but I've decided I can't put some other woman in this situation. It's my idea and I'll have to be the temptress. I've met with Charlotte who I knew would try to dissuade me but I'm determined. I want to be in charge of the situation not some poor girl who's reliant on her job.

The plan is for me to make a meeting with Jake Morrison to discuss opportunities – for the workforce. Charlotte's brother Branwell will go in earlier in the pretext of taking publicity photographs and will hide in the company's Board Room. I remember well its layout. In the centre of the long wall is fixed a sign: *HAWTHORN SHIPBUILDING COMPANY* and below that is printed: *For all your Shipbuilding Desires.* To one side are a set of display boards for drawings. The former is to be the backdrop for the 'reveal'. The Boards are for Branwell and his camera to hide behind ready to leap out at the opportune moment.

The agreed date is in two days, at one o'clock i.e. lunch time, when most of the office workers are on their dinner break. It also coincides with my own. I have explained to Jake what I want to discuss. Initially he was uncertain but was persuaded that I've forgiven him for his approach last time and that the important business is to work out a deal that benefits both parties.

****

It's now the day and I'm cycling on a borrowed hospital bicycle to get there. I have discussed with Charlotte and Branwell all the possible problems and possible interruptions and agreed alternatives.

I'm dressed in my Sister's dress tightened with a belt to best show off my curves underneath. I also have my briefcase including all my notes of ideas to follow up. I'm also wearing my 'sexiest' perfume as described by Freddie. I do hope he's not looking down on me but I have to erase this thought from my mind.

At their offices I note Branwell's car is in the yard and he, by now, should be setting himself up behind the screens with his new camera. I wait while the receptionist advises Jake Morrison of my arrival. I look around into an office of empty desks I assumed vacated by admin workers and typists. There is just one woman present standing at the filing cabinet. She is slim and has to be over fifty years old, an unlikely target for the Manger's son.

The man himself appears at the door. He looks very smart in his tailored suit and trim haircut. He smiles and comes straight over to me smiling.

"Pleased to see you Emily, follow me to my office."

My first problem: it should be the Board Room. We go in, he closes the door behind him and gestures for me to sit at the table. His face is distinctly flushed, his mouth tightly clenched. Then with his head bowed he starts speaking.

"I want to apologise for my behaviour in your flat. It was never my intention I really did want to discuss possible changes at the Company. It's just that you…You're just too…" He shakes his head and looks up at me. "I'm just so sorry, so embarrassed."

I could almost believe him, but I don't.

"Thank ye fer that but can we discuss ideas now please."

"Yes, of course."

I take papers from my bag and start spreading them between us on his desk but he interrupts.

"Let's go in to the Board Room, there's much more space."

"Ok then." I smile to myself and follow him down the same corridor we walked before.

We sit down together below the large company sign. I remove my cloak and spread out my papers on the table. I purposely stand close to him occasionally pushing my chest into his arm also hoping he would smell my perfume. He takes no notice of me and concentrates on my papers. Indeed, he takes a step away so we lose contact.

I try another temptation and bend over the desk to reach for a distant paper but he doesn't give me a second look instead he reaches over and retrieves the paper for me.

He is behaving like a perfect gentleman unlike me acting like a whore. I give up and concentrate on my ideas. He is supportive and enthusiastic and finally promises to speak to his father. I thank him, take my leave and wait by Branwell's car ready to apologise. I feel such a fool.

He eventually appears after fifteen minutes and I explain my predicament. He looks surprised.

"What do you mean. I've got what we want. When you left, he went straight back in to his office followed by an office girl and straight into action. He didn't even properly close the door. All I had to do was wait my time and snap. Clear view of his face albeit with his eyes closed and the young woman completely topless and her skirt up round her waist thoroughly enjoying the moment."

My mouth gapes hardly believing what I've just heard. "But who wes it an' are ye sure she wasn't bein' forced?"

Well I don't know but, if she's the girl from the school, Charlotte will certainly recognise her. She wasn't hiding anything. As for being forced. I would say it was more the other way around. She didn't need any help getting her clothes off. They didn't even notice me with all the grunting going on! Come along tomorrow, I'll have the photographs ready by then."

I cycle back to the hospital trying to make sense of what has just happened. I even feel a little insulted not being able to tempt him myself and yet some other woman had no problem although, if it was the ex-Workhouse school girl, she would be a lot younger, or am I just clutching at straws.

That evening it was difficult to stop Millie injuring herself laughing.

"There's you actin' like a dancer in a revue bar while he tries te concentrate on yer papers an' then a floozie comes in an' gets her way in a second."

"Perhaps he doesn't like busty women at all. Maybe he prefers the skinny young girls."

"Oooh, de ye think so. Could ah try?"

"Young ah said."

There's nothing I could do but just laugh it off.

I trudge back to my flat with a bouncing Florence and an annoying Harry. I think my pride is hurt but, forgetting that, the reason why we started all this may still work. Before he played around with this young girl, he seemed intent on trying to influence his father. So, whatever was my plan we may still achieve the required result.

I'm now talking with Charlotte at the school. Not as bad as Millie but she couldn't help but smile, just a little.

"Oh Emily, just assume they had pre-arranged their meet and he didn't want to spoil it by molesting you just minutes before."

At that moment her brother enters waving two photographs.

"They're just about dry." He slaps them on the table in front of us.

I think both our eyes popped. There was no doubting the identity of the man but the woman I recognised immediately. She was not young, was of slim build and certainly not hiding anything.

"Branwell dear, you must have noticed how old she is, look she's wrinkled and saggy. I bet she's nearly my age."

"Oh, I don't think about that. All I wanted to do was take the photograph and get out."

"Ah saw her in the admin office. She wes the only one in there. Ah canna imagine why a smart young man would want te make love to a woman like that. Ah wonder if she's got some sort of hold on him."

"Maybe she's rich. But then so is he."

In the end we could only just laugh at ourselves and hope his desire to change the working conditions, bear fruit.

I will not describe Millie's reaction that night but I have to admit the whole episode is laughable. I now just have to wait for any reaction.

The following week I read with huge excitement another announcement from the company:

Due to altered circumstances, the proposed changes to the conditions have been amended: The proposed redundancies and the one hour increase in the working day remain. However, there will be no decrease in pay rates and the proposed unpaid holidays will not apply. In addition, the management team will investigate options to expand their expertise to other forms of steelwork fabrication to offset the reduced market for shipbuilding.

I cheered loudly when I read this. It can only have been Jake's doing. But there are so many questions: Why did he molest me? Then why did he not show any attraction to me in the Board Room? Is he really sorry? Then why did he have intercourse with a much older woman? For the moment I don't care. There is now some hope for the labour force and for the Company itself.

Chapter 39

A letter has arrived from America. I see the postmark and recognise the handwriting. I open it quickly hoping the news from my sister Flo is good. There's a big smiley face on the paper making me smile in return:

> Hi Emily,
> Guess what, I got the job with the United States Lines and my very first trip is from New York to Liverpool. I arrive in early June, the fifth I think it is and we'll be there for three days before we have to leave. I must see you. Can you get a couple of days off?
> Everyone else is doing well. They're all jealous of course, he he!
> Flo xx

My eyes widen when I read the short note. I kiss the paper. Will I see her indeed? Of course I will, even if I have to walk there. I'm so pleased. Going to see my sister for the first time in over eight years. She hasn't even said what job she's got. I bet she's a maid. I look at my calendar and realise the fifth is only two weeks away. I need to re-arrange my shifts and hope Millie will look after my Florence and Harry. If not, I'll take them. Whatever, I'm not missing this opportunity.

I have to change trains at Leeds but otherwise it's a straightforward journey all the way to Liverpool. The pace of the trip is slower than the London trains and I'm anxious to see Flo. She's going to meet me at Lime Street Station and I'm ridiculously nervous. We've already spoken on the telephone yesterday when she arrived. The timing has been agreed and she's already booked our room at a hotel but I'm still nervous.

The landscape along the way is of stone-built towns nestled into the natural rolling moorland hills. Tall smoking chimneys give evidence of busy fabricating processes within the huge mills alongside, also stone built. To anyone else it may appear to be a contented, happy combination of a working environment snuggled into the natural landscape. But I suspect not. The relationship between the Mill owners and their workers will be no different to those on Tyneside. I shake away these thoughts. This is no place for my biased opinions. I'm here for a treat, to meet my long absent sister. I'm going to enjoy myself and forget about everything else.

The land around Manchester is much flatter and covered in factories and houses criss-crossed by rivers and canals. The greying mist fed by the discharges of thousands of large and small chimneys remind me of home. Liverpool is similar but in the breaks between buildings I spot the wide River Mersey serviced by a flock of stork-like dock cranes feeding or unloading huge cargo vessels. It occurs to me that I might be able to spot Flo's cruise liner but no sooner did I have this thought when we dived into a cutting and almost immediately into the station itself.

My fellow passengers have been friendly and helpful. They seemed to love my Geordie accent and I think, asked me questions just to hear me speak. Of course, I smiled at their own accents so very different despite living in the same country. Once we stop one young man helps me down from the carriage, tips his cap and walks away with a "T'rah fe now, 'uv a sound as a pound dee." I can only smile, have a guess at what he said and walk down the platform to meet Flo.

I give the collector my ticket and I'm immediately targeted by an American accent. I turn and there stands a beautiful, tall and slender blonde-haired young lady with her arms outstretched. Of course, I recognise her instantly and we fly together in long-missed embrace.

I step back holding her arms and examine her up and down. "Well, if it's not me little sister Florence."

She laughs and does the same. "Well. If it's not my big, big sister Emy."

"Hey, just one 'big' will dee, thank-ye."

She can't say anything. I could see her eyes glisten and I know mine must be doing the same. We just embrace again and hold each other for a long time probably getting in everyone's way.

"Tell ye what let's gan fer a cuppa in a café. Ah've missed ye so much. Ah canna believe yer really heor."

"Me too, I am really here and you sound just like Mother."

We walk away across the concourse and into the first café we find. Fortunately, they serve coffee as well as tea and some cakes.

There is so much to discuss. So much has happened over the eight years we've been apart. It all comes out in bits here and bits there. We have written but letters can never give the full story. She particularly wants to know about Con, how he died and where he's buried. I want to know about America and what she wants to do.

"Scranton is all about coal mining and railways. Davey says it's doing well. It must be because there's loads of new folk moving in, some from Europe would you believe. It's a big town and has lots of dance and music halls. We've got a wireless so we can listen to music at home, it's amazing. Davey organised a telephone for us but Mother won't use it." She smiles and raises her eyebrows. "She thinks it's going to bite her. She jumps every time it rings and stares at it."

"But she's learnin' te read an' write isn't she?"

"She sure is. We're very proud of her really."

"That's canny but what have ye been doin' an' what's this job like?"

"Great. Since I left school, we've both been working in local stores and sometimes in factories in admin. They're all boring but this one's different. I thought I'd have to make beds and clean but they interviewed me and made me a waitress. They say I have the figure

200

for it." She flaunted herself, sitting upright and shaking her hair. "What do you think?"

"Mmm, ye divvent want te be just a pretty face an' ahm sure ye divvent need me te tell ye: men canna be trusted, well, most of them."

"Oh Emy, you sound like our Mother. Most of them are old and have their wives with them."

"Ah bet there are some younger men and, married or not, they may think yer fair-game."

She looked down at her cup and I could see she was fighting with her conscience.

"Flo? Come on, tell me what's happened."

She feigns surprise at my question. "Nothing, no nothing at all." Then sets her smile in place. I decide to leave it, for now.

I tell her my news most of which is a repeat of my letters I've sent. She picks up on my flying news.

"How do you keep flying with the RAF now that Freddie's gone?"

"Te quote an American expression: By the seat of my pants! Basically it's because of Freddie that ah can still borrow an aeroplane. The other pilots, mechanics an' Alec have known me fer three years an' they trust me an' let me continue. Ah suspect I'll be found oot an' I'll have te find somewhere else. But meanwhile!"

She smiles her eyes twinkling. "And who's Alec."

"He's me child-minder. He's a bonnie young man who looks after the admin at the aerodrome. He's great with Florence an' Harry, an' they love him. And no, there's nothin' more than that."

"Shame."

I off-load my case at the hotel then carry on discussing our separate lives while doing some sight-seeing around the city. We catch a bus to the docks to view the liner: *SS President Roosevelt.* She is enormous. She fills the dock with her huge red and black funnel soaring skywards.

"So, where dee ye sleep?"

"In the middle somewhere. I haven't got a porthole and I think it's below water level. But I only sleep there. Most of the time I'm running around serving people with drinks and snacks."

"Te their cabins?"

"Sometimes." She quickly moves on. "There's lots of entertainment on board: a band, singers and a comedian."

We walk back to the hotel arm-in-arm. She's slightly taller and very elegant making me feel a little frumpy, but I don't care. She's my sister and it's wonderful just being with her, making up for lost time. After dinner and a few glasses of wine we retire to our bedroom.

I think the wine has relaxed her as she reveals her worries. "Poor Gertie, she's a great actress but she can't get much work and has little money coming in. It seems you have to know the right people and there's so much competition, even in Pennsylvania. We're lucky to have Davey otherwise she'd have to get back to working in the store."

Inwardly I feel concerned about their welfare. Working in a store is not the best but at least it's steady and, most of all, they're not so open to marauding men. "What about boyfriends?"

"We've both had some, even shared one! Some are nice but nothing special, mostly boring really."

"Sometimes they're bettor that way."

"Really? Your Freddie didn't sound boring."

"He wes special. I'll never find another one like him."

"Oh Emy 'course you will."

I smile and say 'maybe' but I know I won't.

We cuddle each other in our bed.

"Emy you've got bigger boobs than Mother."

"What are boobs?"

"These." She grabs one of my breasts.

I laugh. "Having three children has something to do with that. Would you like to have children?"

202

She answered quickly, too quickly, "No."

"Any reason?"

"No."

"Flo, are ye gannin te tell me what happened on the liner comin' over?"

She thought about answering but decided against it.

"Ok Flo, ye divvent have te now. See ye in the mornin'. 'Night pet."

"Night sis."

I've recalled my day coming over and meeting my grown-up little sister and slowly drifting off to sleep when I feel her hand slip around my waist and her breath against my neck. "Emmy, are you awake?"

I turned to face her. "What's up."

"With the 'Prohibition' in America everyone on the boat takes advantage and drinks heavily. Anyway, I had to take a bottle of whiskey into a cabin for a couple. It was 1ˢᵗ class so they have to be rich. Well I went in and he was by himself. I could tell immediately he had already been drinking. I bent down to place the drinks on the table when I felt his hand on my buttocks. I shot up and backed away. But he rose from his seat and he had a 10$ bill in his hand. He said 'it's yours for a favour.' I looked at him, I mean I didn't know what to say. He undid his fly and asked me to touch his, you know, his thing. I just flew out the room."

I knew there was a problem. "Ye were right. Ye should have gone te yer boss an' told him straight away. Ah guess ye didn't?"

"I did. He said you should have done it and taken his money."

"Oh God Flo. Next time this happens just say 'no' an' leave. Because if ye didn't he'll ask ye te dee somethin' else, then somethin' more an' before long he'll be inside ye an' you'll be in trouble. No amount of money is worth it. On yer return refuse te deal with him, give the job te a man or anyone else. Ye must stay away, he probably asked fer ye personally. There's a lot of sick men about. Ah've learnt the hard way."

"Mhairi."

"Yes."

"Thanks Sis." Her eyes closed and I looked into her young innocent face. I thought 'you've got a lot to learn. We're making progress but men will always be men no matter what.' I made a mental note to warn her again tomorrow.

I waved her goodbye from the quayside as she mounted the access bridge. She's smiling, happy and hopefully a lot wiser. I also promised to visit America as soon as I can. If only. I have two children at home and they are my priorities. Either way how on earth can I afford the fare?

Eventually I get home having picked up my two. The phone is ringing.

"Hi Emily, Alec here. I thought you might be interested, there's a Flying Club opening up in your area – a place call Cramlington. I think it's just north of Newcastle. They've got two Cirrus Moths and are looking for some experienced pilots. It might be worth the trip. I can give you their telephone contact number."

"Ooh, thanks Alec, now yer talkin'."

Chapter 40

I'm looking at a new map of Northumberland and I've found Cramlington and unbelievably it has its own railway station. I've never heard of it and certainly have never been there but it's only about twelve miles away. I've got the telephone number scribbled down and I just sit down to ring when it rings before I can touch it.

I recognise the voice immediately. "Hi Emily, it's Jake Morrison from Hawthorns. I hope you don't mind me ringing you at night, but I've been speaking to my father and I've got a proposition for you." He quickly adds. "Sorry, no, that's the wrong word, mmm." The phone goes silent for a few seconds. "Basically, we would like to employ you to help promote the business and also to negotiate with the union shop stewards. What do you think?"

I'm amazed at the question. "Dee ye mean yer father actually suggested it?"

"Well no, it was only after a good deal of persuasion. But he's allowed me to employ you, but only if you're willing of course. It's probably better if I deal with him personally."

"Ye dee know ah have very little experience divvent ye? Ah've been a nurse fer most of me workin' life."

"I know what you've done and I know your views on relationships in industry. I've spoken to one of the shop stewards, who, by the way, is very supportive of this idea. Also, your nursing experience helps one of my own ideas to identify ways of reducing sick leave."

I'm so surprised. I have never thought about helping and representing employers. This would be a real challenge but then I still have this nagging doubt as to Jake's motives. I would have to handle it somehow but the whole idea appeals.

"Still there?"

"Sorry Jake ah wes just thinkin'. Can we meet, say tomorrow as before an' we can talk some more?"

"Of course, see you at 1 o'clock then."

The telephone goes dead but my mind is alive with possibilities. I would have to give up my Sister position at the hospital. But I know I'm ready to take on another challenge. I need to talk it through with Millie to make sure the child minding can be arranged but also, I think, to get her approval and encouragement.

****

My mind should have been on nursing but all morning I've been distracted by the offer from Hawthorns. Millie added to my enthusiasm last night encouraging me to demand a wage equal to my current income and perhaps a shorter working week to give me more flying time. Of course, like me, she has the same doubts of his motives, but we'll see.

I arrive and wait in the reception as before. As before the same woman is in the admin office. Everyone else, I assume, is away for their dinner. She looks over and gives me a look that could kill. I just smile and look away. I don't have time to wonder what's between the two of them.

After nearly an hour I leave, full of enthusiasm. He explained in full what my role would be and it sounds exciting. I would work with him to discuss options to expand the business and crucially to improve relations with the workforce. I can't wait to start but I know I have to give proper notice to the hospital or at least until they can find a proper replacement for me. Also, he seems very keen to be flexible with my hours. He's aware I have children and have other interests and the wage he offered is very generous. It all seems too good to be true. Crucially, like at our last meeting he behaved like a gentleman: no accidental touching, leering or inuendoes. Just two enthusiastic people trying to make a difference.

As I leave, I again notice the woman. She's now been joined by others but they don't stop her from giving me another of her 'looks'. That's her problem, not mine. She'll have to deal with it.

Back in the hospital I decide to speak to Evelyn. She's disappointed but not surprised.

"I'm going to miss our daily chats over dinner and you made such a difference to your ward, both our wards really. You'd better tell Matron but be warned: she doesn't like her staff leaving, well, the good ones anyway."

"Ah have really enjoyed workin' heor an' you've given me so much support since ah arrived as a student. Allowin' me to have all my bairns in here an' still employin' me afterwards. Anywhere else ah would have been kicked out."

"I remember discussing that with Matron. There was no disagreement we wanted to keep our best staff. It was unusual, I know, but you were worth it." She paused thinking. "How many years has it been?"

"Fifteen."

"Good heavens. I still remember when you and Millie Hardy arrived. So wide-eyed and innocent and so eager to please. I was worried at first, employing girls from the Workhouse. But you soon won me over and then, you went and joined the Suffragettes!" She shook her head. "And now you're going to sort out Hawthorns. Those men are going to have change their ways real quick otherwise they'll be in trouble."

She started pouring another cup of tea. "Emy, any news on Mhairi? You never mention her. I just wondered."

"No." I sip my tea and think of what Ma said in her letter. "But ah think of her, every day. She'll be a teenager now, fourteen. Ahm always wonderin' if she thinks of me at all. Ah divvent talk about her. Few of me friends know. Ah didn't even tell Freddie an' ah divvent really know why." I stop, I don't cry any more, I can't.

207

"You know Emily. She will think of you and wonder what happened. It may not happen until she's got out of her teenage years but she will. Everyone needs to know who their parents are."

I laugh out loud. "I'd like te know where her father is. I'd probably kill him!" I shake my head. "Perhaps not, but ah might kick him somewhere he wouldn't like!"

"I think most women have dreamed of that at some time."

We both laugh. It's good to talk and I feel better for it.

"You must keep in touch and by the way, anyone you recommend for your replacement?"

"Ah've thought about that. My Staff is retirin' soon an' anyway ah think she's too set in her ways. She's a canny nurse, but no." I suggested a couple of others on my ward. "But what about yer Staff?"

"Yes, she's good, I'd hoped she would take over when I retire but I'm sure she'd do well. I have an idea of a replacement for your Staff Nurse Jean McNamara – Nurse Wallace Wright."

I can only smile devilishly. "Oo wouldn't that be pure payback time?"

"It would, but I'm not joking. I've read her assessments. I think we both spotted her potential and the last two years have only reinforced my view. She's completely dedicated and she'll do well."

I feel strange, upset in a way, discussing my replacement. But I have decided to leave, I've burnt-my-boat and life here will go on without me.

Matron was upset but not cross. She stood up and held her hand out to shake mine but had a second thought and walked around the table and gave me a big hug.

"I always knew you wouldn't last the distance. Too interested in good causes. We were just lucky to have you here for a few years. But don't forget us and I don't have to say that you'd be welcome back anytime."

208

I feel overcome. For someone like Matron to say these things about me was heart-warming. I gave my thanks as I did with Evelyn and took my leave with a heavy heart. It's so nice to be appreciated.

I still have a few weeks while they find a replacement. I try to concentrate, be professional but my head is full of ideas for my new job. I'm often found diverted in my office staring out the window or writing notes on a pad. On one occasion Staff had come in un-noticed and had to cough loudly to get my attention and to ask 'if I'm going to do my round this morning at all?' Her arms were folded across her chest but fortunately she was smiling. We're both in a similar position: she's soon leaving to retire and I'm leaving for another adventure. I wonder if she's aware she's being replaced by Wallace Wright. I won't break the news myself but I'd like to be a fly-on-the-wall when she finds out! But maybe she's moderated – probably not.

I've managed to get away a few dinner times to meet Jake at his office to learn more about the business. He's shown me figures and graphs and certainly we do have a problem with orders and, noticeably, the amount of sick leave is high, certainly compared to the hospital. He did agree that I should formalise their haphazard system of treating and reporting accidents. I suspect the numbers are high and there seems to be little in the way of first-aid supplies and qualified staff.

I've met many of the women in the admin office including Ruth, the girl from the Workhouse Charlotte mentioned. She seems a lovely girl. Pretty with her long brown hair and startling blue eyes but quite shy. We compared our very different experiences while inside the orphanage. Also, Gladys the older woman who doesn't seem to like me at all. I'm acutely aware of her relationship with Jake and maybe she thinks I represent competition for his affection. On one occasion we passed in the corridor to his office. She couldn't hide her smug expression or her slightly unruly appearance. I could only smile as I dallied for a while before knocking just in case he needed to get himself re-organised!

The day has arrived. I'm walking to work and it feels very different. For the first time in years I'm not wearing a nurses' uniform. I may cycle in future but it's sunny and I just wanted to take my time and prepare myself.

My last day at the hospital was memorable. So many goodbyes, hugs, cakes and flowers, even from some of the patients. I even gave a little speech in a waiting room filled with all my friends from Matron down to the cleaners and porters. All a vital cog in the business of care for the needy. I promise to come back and of course I will. Friends are for life.

Now, I can take Florence to school, leave Harry with Millie and still have time to walk to work. Long shifts are a thing of the past.

When I arrive at Hawthorns the offices and the yards are full, busy and noisy and I'm eager to get going. Ruth gives me a wave and a shy smile as I go through reception and I find my very own office fully equipped with a desk, chairs, a padded table and a filing cabinet. Someone has tried to make it comfortable and it is but I want to make a few changes to suit me.

My first project is to clean it. Cobwebs, dust and rubbish have no place in a room that's going to be used for treating the injured. I want it as clean as my hospital room. I have an impressive view of the river but I wouldn't mind a few pictures on the wall and a place for my own photographs.

Jake comes in and formally greets me and shakes my hand.

"Give yourself time to settle in and let me or Alice, my secretary, know if you need anything. I've asked her to show you around the place." He turns to leave when he remembers something and turns back. "Oh yes. I know how you love your tea so I've got a special teapot, a good supply of leaves and milk to keep you going plus the odd packet of biscuits of course." He smiles and leaves.

I call out a thank-you and think how kind he is. So different from my first experience.

One of my habits and it's usually a pleasure is that at the end of each day and each week I think back and go through what has happened and try to learn from any mistakes. My first week started slowly but my days soon filled with activity. At my request, Peter, one of the foremen showed me around the yard. We have a 'small' freighter on the blocks. Small is not how I would have described it. The curved beams of the ship's hull reach high into the sky. Men working at every level on higgledy-piggledy scaffolding and high above everything, cranes swinging great plates into position, all is awe-inspiring. But over and above everything else is the noise, crashing of steel, riveting guns, shouts echoing around the growing structure. The workshop alongside is just as noisy. I think Hell must be like this and everyone inside Hell must be deaf!

I was certainly the only woman there and my uniqueness was noticed. Men stared, some smiled, others nudged each other communicating by sign language. The inevitability of accidents is obvious. I knew I'd be meeting some of them again in my treatment room.

Sure enough the day after my tour I had a stream of men complaining of headaches, sore bits and bruises. I soon cottoned onto that: I listened to their 'serious' problems, examined and treated their the 'injury' and gave them an earful before sending them on their way. I also had a word with Peter to pass on the message that I'm here to treat actual injuries not imagined. Of course, I know I'm a novelty and like anything new I'm open to their curiosity.

On the Thursday I was called out to a real injury. A man was caught by a swinging steel plate. He was apparently knocked out and was bleeding profusely. By the time I arrived he was conscious but bleeding heavily. Fortunately, work had stopped and I managed to make myself heard. The cut was small but deep needing stemming with a sterilised dressing and a neat bandage around his head. I was more concerned with possible internal damage. He was able to talk sensibly and wanted to get on with his work. But, to be on the safe side, I decided to bring him back to the office to have a drink and a rest so I could monitor his progress. He recovered well, just embarrassed with all the attention. Satisfied, I let him off an hour early with orders to rest, to keep the bandage on and to see me tomorrow to reset the dressing.

My mind raced back to the Clearing Station in Flanders in 1918. If a soldier was brought in with such a wound it would have had a quick clean, a bandage applied and he would be sent back to the frontline. No possibility of a Blighty ticket that's for sure. Times have certainly changed – and thank goodness.

Next week is going to be interesting. Apart from my medical duties and my weekly progress meeting with Jake I'm going to meet the Union rep and hopefully the shop stewards. I'll need my diplomacy cap on. It's a bit scary but I feel it's important that we have a much better relationship than previously. In addition, a certain MP has agreed to see me at home, in the evening. She seems to be keen to meet me. Certainly, it would be a privilege to meet her. I have followed her career closely, she's one of my heroes.

I now have the weekend to myself and my children. My plan is to take the train to Cramlington to see for myself what this new flying club is all about, 'The Newcastle Aeroclub'.

Chapter 41

We all arrive at the station at mid-day. All of us meaning me and my two with Millie and her young Frank. The porter points us hopefully in the right direction.

"Ye gannin te see them aeroplanes then?"

"Ah hope so."

"Yer very brave. Wouldn't catch me up there, safer on the ground." He taps the ground with his foot and laughs at himself. "Are ye gannin te watch them?"

"Hopefully ah can gan up in one of the aeroplanes."

As I expected his mouth drops. "Ye, with one of them pilots?"

Florence pipes up. "Me Ma is a pilot."

His eyes widen and then shakes his head as he walks away obviously wondering what the world was coming to.

On our way Millie asks a question. "Ah guess ye get that reaction a lot?"

"Ah rarely divvent bother te tell people. Ah get the same comments: 'What fer?', 'Ye should be lookin' after yer family.' 'It's not right,' an' so on. One day Millie, one day."

The aerodrome has a large collection of huts and hangers most seemingly abandoned. One hut is obviously much newer and in use so we make our way there. The two Moths are parked outside with cars lined up behind. A man in flying kit is studying one of the Moths. He's probably in his twenties and is unshaven.

"Hello, ah hope ye divvent mind us bein' heor but ahm lookin' to see if ah could join yer club."

He looks at our little group and looks bemused. "I'm afraid we don't offer trips at the moment but we might later, maybe next year."

"Ah was actually hopin' to join the club as a pilot. Ah have actually flown Cirrus Moths in Catterick."

He looks aghast. My heart sinks, I know I'd have to go through my usual explanation.

"Yes, ah've flown with the RAF."

"Solo?"

"Yes, fifteen hours now."

He looks dubious. He tests me. "I've got a problem with the aileron control cable."

I look at the cable, the problem is staring us in the face. "It's come off the pulley wheel, look. That could be dangerous in a turn."

"Blimey. You're right."

"The solution's easy. Just loosen the wheel fixing, refix the cable an' re-adjust the wheel back te where it should be. The cable may have expanded because it's new. Ye have te watch that."

He nods then looks at me in wonder. "You've not met a female pilot before have ye?"

He shakes his head. "No." Then realising he's staring. "Sorry Mrs..."

"Just call me Emily."

"Ok, Emily, come into the hut and I'll introduce you."

Five men altogether, different ages, size and shapes but all are aghast at a female pilot in their midst.

The eldest man sporting a typical twirling moustache introduces himself as Victor MacTavish in a broad Scottish accent. "I'll take ye up for a birl if ye like lassie. See howfur ye get on."

He escorts me to a separate changing room telling me of his time in the Royal Flying Corps. He reminds me of the Squadron Leader I flew home to Ripon years ago. He needlessly helps me into a flying suit and leads me out to the operational aeroplane its engine already throbbing.

I settle in to the front seat and as we make our way to the runway I wave to Millie and the children watching at the hut door. The men are gathered behind no doubt still wondering about my abilities. After a couple of circuits, he shows off some aerobatics, all in full view of the watching party below. I smile, he's showing off to the little lady!

He asks through the speaking tube if I would like to try a few 'circuits and bumps.'

I take over. I'm wanting to show them all what I can do. Probably irresponsibly I want to show-off. I take one small circuit to get the feel of the Cirrus Moth again then it's my turn for the aerobatics, all learnt from Freddie. Dives, vertical climbs, hard turns, spins and finishing with a complete loop and a low pass over the audience causing them to duck. I even fly over the railway station to wave at the porter but he's busy with a stopping train and may not have noticed.

My landing back on the concrete runway is perfect, I say it myself! And I taxi back to the hut.

I jump down and head for the hut to some applause from the viewers. I look back to see if Victor is ok but he's still in his seat. I run back and can see he's not moving. His head is slumped to the side, mouth open, eyes shut. I wave over the others and climb on to the lower wing. I can see he's unconscious but he's still breathing, thank goodness. Two of us pull him out and lay him on his side on the ground. He seems to have just fainted.

I learn that he has a 'dickie' heart and has had it for years. I feel mortified. He does recover but I could have killed him. Poor man, survived air battles in the war then I come along and nearly end his life showing off.

He recovered enough to join us for a cup of tea. We had to explain what happened and he saw that I was upset.

"Ah mind thinking ye had made it all up then when you started throwing the aeroplane around the sky ah got worried. Ah canna mind anything after we climbed vertically. I must hae just passed oot. It's not yer fault I should hae told ye about mah auld ticker."

215

I only learnt after that he only delivered aeroplanes and never fought any air battles. He was too old and even then, in 1916, his health wasn't good but they accepted anyone at that time. None-the-less I didn't need to show-of, it was a stupid thing to do. Poor Freddie must be ashamed of me.

Going home Millie has made unrepeatable jokes. The children don't understand why I'm upset, they think I'm just amazing. Even the porter, when he realised it was me waving at him from on-high, wanted to shake my hand. But I know myself I was just wanting to show women can fly aeroplanes as well as men, and that's just pride.

Thinking how irresponsible I'd been they were still keen for me to join the Club. Their aim is to teach and to entertain. That's commendable and I'm very keen to help. So, I will be back and help all I can.

Chapter 42

We soon get back to Millie's and we find her Sam with his feet up waiting for us, dinner ready. He is one of those rare breed of men that can actually help in the kitchen. He's a nice man devoted to his partner.

"Hi Sam, how's Armstrongs doin' these days?"

As usual he gives me a big smile and a hug but the smile soon disappears.

"Not good, oot on strike again. Well until Tuesday mornin'."

Millie moans and shakes her head. "What's happened now?"

He's laying the table and getting ready to plate-up the dinners. "It's only a local issue. Some men have been laid-off fer being late! It wouldn't have happened if there wes plenty of work. Least excuse an' they're oot." He turns to me. "Millie's told me that you've joined Hawthorns te work on new ideas an' at the same time workin' with the Unions."

"Aye, that's right. Me first week wes last week. I'll be workin' with the son, Jake Morrison."

His eyes raise but continues to prepare the table. "Aah aye, good fer ye Emily."

"And?"

He looks directly at me. "It's only, well…, it's just a rumour, but he has a certain reputation. But ahm sure it's exaggerated."

I look at Millie, who silently shakes her head. "That he's a womaniser. Yes, ah've heard about that as well. I'll just have te deal with it. But he's been a real gentleman so far."

"That's canny." He quickly changes the subject. "Ah think we need someone like ye at Armstrongs. It's all one-way. No negotiation. What they want goes an' that's it. Millie showed me Hawthorn's latest announcement. Still bad news but there is hope of a different approach."

I can only smile. Hopefully Millie hasn't explained the background in too much detail. I'm still embarrassed thinking about what I did.

****

My second week started with a meeting with Jake. This will be a regular update of what happened the previous week and plans and ideas to take forward in the new week.

I brought up an idea of mine that perhaps Hawthorns could join forces with another similar company in steelwork fabrication but making different products not just shipping. Perhaps in railways, bridges, buildings. Products that are currently in more demand. We have the workshops and the expertise and it would spread our trade over a wider market and avoiding the concentration on just shipping.

I feel a real outsider. I can't go into the detail of possibilities. I don't have the knowledge of other local companies and what's doing well and what isn't. But it's the principal of not putting all your-eggs-in-one-basket.

Either way it's set him thinking. Combining companies has always been considered but always in the same market – shipbuilding. It's seems to have tripped a switch in his brain. He's speaking as he's thinking, the possible options, the benefits, likely companies. His words are spilling out like a river in spate. I can only smile to myself. He certainly has enthusiasm and energy. I like that. It can spread so easily to others making life much more interesting.

"Yes, that's really got me thinking. I don't know why I hadn't thought of it before, it's obvious." In his excitement he grabs my hand. "Great idea." Then immediately lets it go. "Sorry."

The rest of our discussions are rushed through. His mind is elsewhere. I mentioned my meeting with the Union rep and with the MP but I'm not sure it sinks in.

218

"Thanks Emily, that's been very useful." He goes to leave but then turns back to me. "By the way, Alice told me how you sorted the men out last week with their feigned aches and pains and with the man with the concussion. Well done, you're going to be just great." With that he leaves the room like a whirlwind. I slump back onto my seat, pleased and surprised with his reaction.

I spend my dinner break talking to Ruth. She has a habit of staring in wonderment at me with her large blue eyes. I'm not sure if this is some sort of hero worship but she has a lovely smile and I can understand any man being interested.

"Do you have boyfriend?"

"No." She turns her eyes down. I feel she's thinking maybe of her experience with Jake. I wasn't going to mention it at all. I didn't have to.

"Mr Morrison Junior thought ah liked him. Once, in his office, he kissed me and um, other things."

"Oh dear". I was going to start my usual tirade of advice for telling men to stop, when she continued.

"We were caught at it by Gladys."

"Oh dear." My brain started to re-arrange previous thoughts into different places. "Dee ye like him?"

"Yes, but not that way."

"Has he tried it on since?"

"No. He actually said sorry afterwards."

"Good."

"But, ah divvent think Gladys likes me anymore."

She has a confidence issue. I try to put it into perspective. "Ah think Gladys has her own problems an' ah suspect Mr Morrison will be more respectful now."

She gives me one of her sweet smiles, "Thank ye Emily."

Now at Millie's with the children, I mention my earlier conversation with Ruth. We both realise the turn of events has been to

Gladys's benefit. She obviously likes Jake and she is using her 'embarrassing' discovery to her advantage – to get his attention. I recall the revealing photograph. She's bribing him. Thinking further: maybe this is the reasoning behind Jake's control of his natural, youthful womanising.

"Ye dee realise Emy that, as it turns oot, there was no need for Charlotte's an' yer great plan at all. Gladys did it fer ye."

"And ah was right: behind his wandering hands lies a desire to make changes to improve the company. Good old Gladys, ah should thank her!"

"Well, for yer sake ah hope she keeps at it. Unless of course ye get te like him!"

I shake my head. "He's nice but not like that. Either way, he's far too young."

"Mmmm."

I'm in bed after an interesting day. I cuddle my pillow, a habit since Freddie died. A silly thing but it gives me comfort. I think of Jake. I'm fond of him, clean shaven, good looking, respectful and kind to me, all the things I like in a man. Except he is much younger than me, at least ten years I would guess. I wonder what he would be like as a partner but I dismiss the thought. Probably not the best idea if I'm going to work with him every day. I start to drift off to sleep but I see a picture of a pair of soft blue eyes with a sweet smile below. This image is somehow comforting, relaxing. Goodnight Ruth.

Chapter 43

Ellen Wilkinson arrives at my doorstep just when I was reading a story to my two. I bring her in hoping she likes children. She does. I know she hasn't any but she's very easy with them and they're relaxed talking and playing with her. I can see immediately we're going to get along fine.

She comes in to the kitchen while I'm making the tea and we chat about the current political situation and the problems with trade generally. She has a soft Mancunian accent, rare in these parts, and speaks clearly and knowledgably. She's particularly interested in my new role in Hawthorns.

"Wow, I'm impressed. Looks positive to me. I read the two announcements from Hawthorns you sent me. The first was a typical forthright statement but the second showed that something had happened. A slight change in thinking. Was that your dealing?"

I relate our meeting in their Board Room and my later discussions with Jake. I avoid any mention of bribery planning!

"Well done you. Do you mind if I used the text of that second announcement to advertise the proper approach for a working relationship in a big company? I'll explain the background and of course I won't mention personalities. In fact, it will be an excellent advert for the company itself."

I agree instantly. It can only help my work although I suspect Mr Morrison Senior will still have reservations – but that's Jake's problem. I follow up with my ideas for the company and to improve the management/workers relationship.

She seems impressed and asks me to keep her informed of progress. It seems however that the situation generally is getting worse particularly in the mines. She cannot see an easy solution.

"We're suffering from lack of investment and cheap imports. But we must keep trying."

We retire to my small sitting room and I find she prefers a bottle of pale ale rather than a sherry. We swop stories of our Women's Suffrage days. She wasn't a Suffragette but certainly a keen supporter of the movement. I show her the newspaper article of me when I was released from hospital with Emmeline Pankhurst's comment.

"You're some woman. We need more like you. We've still got a long way to go."

I returned the pat-on-the-back. "An' yer the only female Labour MP, that's a real milestone."

She smiles. "And it's bloody hard work sometimes."

I offer her the only available bed for the night but she has to travel down to London tomorrow morning and needs to prepare before she leaves. But it was real pleasure and delight to meet her. I hope we can see each other again soon.

The following morning, I mention Ellen's visit to Jake. His eyes widen in horror.

"But she's a communist isn't she?"

I go through her life story again. "Not any more, she's staunch Labour an' what's more she supports what yer doin' here. She's gannin to use Hawthorns as an example to others. Looking at options an' all that."

"I don't think that'll go down well with my father. The other shipbuilders will want to kill him. Giving in to the labour force and all that."

"But Jake, we're not, ye wrote the second communication yourself an' that's all they'll see an' ah bet they've already seen it anywa'."

"It'll be like rubbing their noses in it. They won't like it one bit."

"Well that's just tough. We've got the labour force on our side an' if yer gannin te chase other companies te join us, they'll be more willing if they can see we're not riddled by strikes an' go-slows every other week. Either way, you've got te warn yer father an' tell him it's to our advantage."

"Oh God, this'll be fun. Better warn everyone there could be fireworks any minute."

"I'll come along with ye if it would help."

"Errr, no. I'll just say our second announcement is being recommended by the government as a way forward in industrial relations. I won't mention any names. I'll say it's out of our control, but on the good side it'll be good for business."

"Very diplomatic."

"Wish me luck."

"Board doon yer trousers?"

He just smiles, takes a deep breath and leaves. I do wish him luck but I think back to the times when I had to admit something to my Da. It usually meant a good hiding but that was it, no after-shock.

I can't just wait for his return, so I go to the admin office for some support or at least someone to take my mind off.

Ruth is there, as always, ready with one of her smiles. We chat generally but she can see I'm agitated.

"Tell ye what, dee ye fancy a drink in the town after work like."

I explain that it's not possible with my two in tow but it's a nice thought. She looks disappointed.

"Maybe another time then?"

"Yes ok."

Middle of the afternoon and Jake knocks, walks in uninvited and looking excited. "I don't believe it. He just said 'no problem'. He almost smiled then muttered something like 'it'll do 'em good! Wow that's real progress."

He shakes my hand. "What a partnership. Do you fancy a drink in town after work to celebrate?"

I say I'd love to but I can't with my two in tow!

"Maybe another time then?"

"Yes ok."

By the time I leave the office I have persuaded Millie to pick up Florence from school and keep all three for a few hours. We cycle in to town to a place almost hidden between two large shops. It was a 'bar' not a pub. A very different place, not dingy and full of men smoking cigarettes or pipes but a fresh smelling place with young people drinking wine or spirits.

"This looks canny. What would ye like te drink Ruth?"

Chapter 44

"Just ask fer me usual."

"Really, this is yer local?"

"Aye, ah only live a ten-minute walk away."

"And what is yer usual?"

"It's a Gin-Special, try it yerself. It's nice an' fruity with a kick."

My eyes lift. This girl is full of surprises.

I bring back two Gin-Specials but I'm not certain what went into it. Definitely gin but the 'fruity' bit looks like red wine to me.

Ruth is talking to another girl at the next table. She's probably about the same age. Suddenly I feel too old for this. I sip my drink and yes, it is fruity, but I can't taste 'the kick'.

She turns back to me and takes her drink. "Cheers Emily. That's me friend Sue. She works in a lady's shoe shop. Looks dead borin' te me but ah suppose she meets all sorts of customers."

"Cheers Ruth. This does taste fruity, it's canny."

She smiles. "Better be careful it packs quite a punch. Ahm used to it."

I wonder how she can afford it, but it's not my business. She's always looks bright and breezy in the mornings so it can't be that bad. We talk about work and the other women in the admin office and all the tittle-tattle. No surprises there. Then about where I was born and how I landed up in the Workhouse Orphanage. Her Da just 'buggered-off' abandoning all his family. Her Ma couldn't cope and she landed-up in the Home. But she enjoyed it. She said the food was better, the bed didn't have any bugs and Matron was nice. So, it worked out well for her.

After a couple of the Specials I'm feeling very relaxed and all thoughts about the age difference have gone. Sue joins us. I can't help but notice that both girls are similar. Not in looks, Sue is slim whereas Ruth is well rounded, but in their relaxed confidence and their easy laughter. They are good company and they make me feel ten years younger.

We stay about an hour and leave to find our ways home. The offer of a cup of tea is an easy persuasion to stop off at Ruth's flat. All three of us walk alongside the Tyne still enjoying our own company in the warm, late Summer evening. Sue lives closer and leaves but not before giving us both a hug and a kiss on the cheek. We cycle the remainder of our 'walk' and park them behind the block. It's quiet. On our way to her door Ruth takes my hand in hers then lifts it to her mouth to kiss it.

"I'm really pleased you've joined Hawthorns. You're a breath of fresh air."

I raise our joined hands and give hers a kiss. It seems so natural. Even when she stops and turns to face me, her kiss full on my lips feels right.

She takes me in and leads me up the stairs to her flat. It's small but brightly decorated. Instead of heading towards the kitchen she leads me to her bedroom and switches on a small bedside-lamp. I know what she's going to do but I can't stop her. I don't want to stop her. She removes my jacket, my blouse and underwear and takes my bare breasts in her hands. Then kneels down to caress and gently kiss them both. My eyes close enjoying the beautiful sensation throbbing through my body. I have so missed making love, gentle hands, damp kissing, the ecstasy of climaxing.

She releases me to pull back the bed covers and we help each other remove all our clothes and slide in. I'm in her hands. I've never made love to a woman so I'm going to learn and follow everything she does. As we kiss, her tongue searching my mouth, her hand slides down and her fingers slowly enter my body. I have to stop kissing to throw my head back and groan. She adds pressure, her fingers curl inside me and my climax takes over. I can do nothing except stretch

226

my hands behind my head and groan long and loud with long-missed pleasure.

"Wow, that wes just amazing. Now it's my turn on you."

"Not yet." She pushes back the covers to reveal my naked body. "Ye have a beautiful shape, large breasts, flat tummy an' a rounded bottom." She pushes my legs apart and inserts her tongue inside and slides it gently up and down. All I can see is the back of her head. I feel another climax coming. I pull her head closer adding to the pressure and my body starts throbbing again and I shriek loudly with even greater pleasure.

It's now my turn. I feel nervous as I try to arouse her. Her breasts feel firm, her slim waist curves out to sturdy buttocks and legs. I flood her body with small kisses but she pulls my head up.

"Take yer time Emily, there's no rush." We kiss mouth to mouth our tongues searching deep inside. I relax and try again this time my wet lips luxuriating on her smooth, soft skin. It must be working as I can hear the sound of her breathing. I enter her body and move my fingers as gently as I can. She slides one hand down and pushes against my hand moving my fingers further in and increasing pressure on her clitoris. It's working, her breathing gets heavier and I can feel her body throbbing against my hand. I'm ridiculously pleased for her and I repeat the process with my tongue as she did. It works again and embarrassingly I almost shout 'yes'.

All my nervousness gone we just cuddle and caress each other's bodies. I feel amazing, so relaxed and fulfilled. I've done something I never even dreamed of and it came quite naturally, with just a bit of help.

She's the first to move. "I'll make the tea now."

I watch her through the open door. She's still naked as if it's the most natural thing in the world. Which of course it is. I smile. "Good, that's the only reason ah came in!"

"Ye an' yer tea. Yer well known for it an' you've only been there a few weeks."

We sit at her table opposite each other drinking our tea still without a stitch on. It feels lovely, life's accepted rules abandoned. I can't help smiling. I look in to her clear blue eyes and wonder if she feels the same.

We have more fun dressing each other before I have to leave. Saying goodbye with a cuddle is not sad. We'll see each other tomorrow morning and every day after. Life is amazing, so full of surprises. I cycle back in the deepening dusk. I know I'm late but I feel like a schoolgirl. Totally ridiculous for someone over thirty but I do. I skid around corners, tear along the straights and then show-off by taking my hands off the handlebars and waving them in the air. People stare as if I'm mad. They don't know what I've just done. But they're right I am mad.

I apologise profusely to Millie and guiltily make up a story of frustrating delays. She seems relaxed about it and the children can't stop talking about the fun they've had. At the door we say our goodbyes but not before she whispers.

"Ye can tell me all about it tomorrow."

I can only smile and mouth 'ok' and blow her a kiss.

Chapter 45

With my children happily asleep it's my bath time. I lie back and re-enact my evening adventure. I wonder how I was so attracted to her. I've met and worked with lots of girls but never have I had this inner feeling right from our first glance. Maybe it's her smile or the way her eyes crinkle when she does. I realise she doesn't glance at all. Her smile holds you, follows you, she makes a connection that makes you do the same. I wonder as well if she has lots of girlfriends. She's obviously well known in her bar with her 'usual' Gin-Special. And the one aspect that stands out: she's very experienced in making love to women.

Pulling the evening apart like this is frustrating. Am I just one of many? Maybe she has another liaison tomorrow night and every night. I heave a great sigh. Either way, even if tonight is a one-off, I still really enjoyed the experience and will never forget it.

The morning after, however, is definitely one to forget. My head is thumping and my stomach is trying to decide if I should rush to the nettie or the sink. Florence and Harry choose this particular morning to upset each other. No matter what, I know this is all my fault and I tell myself to be patient and follow our normal procedure and get them to their destinations, well fed and dressed properly.

The morning is chilly and there are spots of rain but I am determined to walk to work. Hopefully the fresh air will at least clear my head. Apart from that I'm not confident of my cycling abilities in my present state.

I arrive and pass through reception. By this time, I'm convinced last night was just a one-off and I keep my eyes diverted away from the admin office. I enter my office and close the door behind me. I don't even make my chair when there's a knock. I think: Oh Jake, what do you want? I need a cup of tea.

"Come in."

A young lady comes in all smiles holding a cup in her hand and closes the door behind her.

"Ah thought ye might like this."

My heart leaps. "Oh Ruth, yer so lovely." I grab the cup, place it on my desk and take her in my arms.

She tells me that she couldn't sleep last night and it was such a special evening. My hangover has disappeared without trace and my worries have been blown away all in a second. We kiss and cuddle in between recalling our memories. Then agree to meet at dinner time for a walk, maybe in the rain, maybe in a summer snowstorm, I don't care.

She leaves and I drink my cool cup of tea. I'm rejuvenated and set forth with gusto to earn my living in this exciting place.

It's our dinner time walk and I learn what we can and cannot be seen to be doing. Same sex relationships are frowned upon especially by the churches. Ruth tells me that in some delightful countries it's punishable by death! We won't be going there then! Basically, we need to be discreet. No kissing, hugging or fondling in the street, office, shops or any public place. Interesting comparison with a man who can and does all of that to his girlfriend but a woman is limited to shaking her girlfriend's hand!

I certainly have a lot to learn.

I wanted to ask her around to my flat to meet my children but all this has made me unsure but I can't think why. Either way we have made a date. This brings up another possible problem: I will have to tell Millie and it has to be tonight. I know I just cannot keep any secrets from her. She's telepathic!

"Ok Emy, it's Jake isn't. He wants te marry ye. Yes?"

"No, yer so far away ye could be in Australia!"

"But there is someone isn't there."

"Yes."

230

"But that's great. It's been over two yeors. Ye canna be celibate all yer life. Now we're getting somewhere. Who is he an' what's his name? Ah know, it's that clerk chap from the aerodrome. Yes?"

"No. Alec is a nice man but, no."

I really don't know how to tell her. But I have to. I only hope she's not disgusted and abandons me.

"Millie, sit doon." Her smile disappears and her eyes widen as if waiting for some bad news. "Her name is Ruth; she works at Hawthorns an' she's lovely."

Her expression initially remains unchanged but slowly realization sets in and a smile grows until it stretches widely, ear to ear.

"She's a girl?"

"Of course."

"Oooh. How wonderful." She looks up to her ceiling in wonderment. "That's so typical of ye. Doin' somethin' different from everyone else. Pushin' back the boundaries an' all that. Ahm so pleased, ye must tell me all about her." She waits eagerly for my response.

"As ah said she's lovely an' ahm gannin te bring her here tomorrow afternoon if that's alright?"

"Alright? I insist."

****

Thank goodness. I sit back with Millie and we watch Ruth playing with Frank, Florence and Harry on the floor. She looks so much at home. I realise she must have lived with brothers or sisters before her Da left. I wonder if she misses them. I also realise I know so little about her.

I help Millie clear up in her kitchen. She whispers conspiratorially:

"She's wonderful. Such a happy person an' so relaxed with the bairns. Ah can also see she's very fond of ye, snatching at yer hand when she thinks no-ones lookin'."

I smile. "And ahm very fond of her. Ye know she was at our school, many years after us of course."

"No! You've got so much in common." She smiles, "the same shape as well. A couple of bookends."

I flick some soapy water at her. "Nothin' wrong with our shape. We canna all be slender lovelies like some."

The four of us walk back to my flat. Well, Harry's in his push-chair with Florence hanging on to the handle all controlled by Ruth. They're chatting together non-stop. It's as if they're all one family. To others I must look like their grannie. Perhaps I should dress younger, have a new hairstyle, go on a diet.

"Ye just dare. Yer bonny just as ye are." She smacks my rump for good measure. The children have at last settled down in bed and we're clearing the tea plates and cups.

"Ave never asked ye but where is yer family? You've never said anythin'."

"They moved away when ah was at the Orphanage."

"Where to?"

She looks uninterested. "Oh, some place called Croxteth. It's in Liverpool somewhere."

"De ye keep in contact?"

"Not much, the odd Christmas card." She changes the subject. "Emily, ah think ah need a shower, could ah use yours?"

I show her the controls and give her a towel. She's changed, she's become quiet, sullen, introspective. Mention of her family has struck a sensitive area. I've spoken about mine. Perhaps she's envious. Perhaps she needs to talk about them. I give her a few minutes to finish but the water's still running into the bath. I quietly open the bathroom door. Her back is towards me and she's holding her head in her hands. I throw off my dress and step into the bath still in my underwear. I slip my arms around her waist and hold her tight allowing the water to cascade over both of us. She turns, buries her head on my shoulder and releases all her emotion, her tears dilute, wash over our bodies and run away down the drain.

"What are ye like? Come in the shower with your undies on. Dear, dear, now get these off." She's obviously recovered and we wash each other all over.

"I've got more to wash than you."

"Oh really." I slap her backside. "What about this then?"

"Cheek!"

We dry each other and finish with a long sexy kiss exercising our tongues deliciously. We forget about our clothes and cavort around the flat completely naked. It feels so liberating. Inevitably we end up in my single bed squashed, relaxed and very happy. I'm determined to release her family demons but this is not the time.

Chapter 46 - 1926

By the end of 1925 shipbuilding reached a new low on Tyneside. Small companies have been lost, their yards now derelict, their staff out of work. Hawthorns have not escaped entirely but a deal with a local company from Wallsend has filled our workshop with locomotive fabrication. It's a growing market based on the growth of railways both with the railway companies and manufacturing industries. There have been the inevitable redundancies for some skills but growth in other areas. Jake's enthusiasm has reaped rewards and I believe he has even surprised his father.

For my own part there have been few problems with industrial relations. There are still mutterings but the shop stewards know as well as anyone the problems we face and the changes have been accepted. They have seen for themselves that management is doing its best to expand into other areas with investment in new machinery – a real change from the old, blind assumption that work will drop in from the sky. The working day has increased but the pay rates haven't dropped. A very different position compared to other companies. I don't need to be clever to know that the coal mining industry is heading for a big fall. Exports fallen through the floor, the coal owners demanding more work for a lot less pay. Small pits have already closed. There's talk of nationalization, which I believe could be a good thing, to get away from the grasping clutches of the greedy owners. But I have to keep my views private. I may be suspected of being a 'commie troublemaker'!

I guess being a nurse for many years I've concentrated on the health and well-being of the workforce and given advice on safety to try to reduce our poor injury and sickness record.

One of my successes I believe has been the works canteen. The better the food and drink, the healthier the workforce. I could see that our canteen was hardly used, most brought sandwiches for their

234

dinner commonly known as 'bait'. It was eaten in some corner of the workshop without any signs of hand-washing. No surprise then that stomach sickness was a common problem. Working with Agnes, the Canteen Supervisor, we now provide a healthier option at no cost. Commonly a stew with a chunk of bread and of course a mug of tea. Use of the canteen has multiplied. I mean, why not, free food and drink? It's been a great success but I'll have to show sickness has reduced which may prove difficult with the lack of past records. I also know this will have the side benefit of reducing the cost and time for the wives having to prepare their baits.

The toilets known as the 'netties' were disgusting. Dirty, no hot water and no soap. The office staffs' were little better. Men commonly didn't bother and used quiet corners of the yard or the Tyne itself! With Jake's approval, and he didn't really have any choice, the toilets were repaired and cleaned up, the ancient boiler replaced and, with the help of the cleaners a rota of cleaning and paper and soap replacement was agreed. This was done, almost magically, by re-organising existing resources and not costing very much more at all. It was all very obvious but no-one bothered before and standards just slipped over time.

My least successful change has been the introduction of ear defenders. I eagerly bought in a supply only to be told: they've never worn them and never will. Many of them are stone deaf anyway and have to communicate by sign language. They must be a great ball-of-fun at home! Either way I'll persevere. Try and get the foremen to wear them or at least the new recruits. Certainly, the women don them when they need to. It really confirms what I already know: men are a different breed altogether.

****

This Saturday morning we're off to Catterick hopefully for a flight. It's now March and if we're lucky the weather will be kind to us. Our two previous trips since Christmas, once to Cramlington and once to Catterick, have attracted only wet, misty weather totally unsuitable for flying. I still haven't proved to Ruth that I can actually pilot an aeroplane! I have shown her the details of my flights in my log book but I want to take her up and show her the delights of reaching for the skies.

On my last visit I introduced Ruth as my work colleague which, of course, she is, but no more than that. I could see the men there were interested. I had to smile watching them flaunt themselves. Something they've never done with me - I assume because of their respect for Freddie. Alec is different. I can see he loves the children and by his blushes I can see he likes me. I do like him, he's kind and considerate, good looking but he's far too young. I realise, of course, this is nonsense, he's older than Ruth.

On the train, while Flo and Harry read their books, I have a chance to talk about a recent letter from Ruth's mother. I took upon myself to make contact and her reply has caused upset.

I want to meet her and I want Ruth to come with me but she completely refuses. She threw a fit, shouting at me and trying to burn the letter. We've made up but she's adamant. The letter proved to me that her mother wants a reunion and has done for years. She has re-married and wants to explain why she had to leave her at the orphanage.

"Ah know the reason, she's an alcoholic, so wes me Da. Me an' me two brothas were starvin' all the time. We had te pinch stuff from market stalls an' shops. All their money went on booze an' nothing fer us. The only canny thing she did wes dumping me in the Orphanage. At least ah wasn't hungry all the time an' ah had some shoes."

She's speaking in a hushed tone but her deep hatred cannot be hidden from my children. They stare at her and I can see their normally lovely auntie has upset them. I change the subject. We can continue some other time.

Alec picks us up from the station. The Winter sun is shining but he seems diverted. His thoughts are elsewhere, my questions answered but without his usual smile. Oh dear, I want this to be a great day but it all seems to be going awry.

The other pilots and mechanics are pleased to see us, especially Ruth, and the Cirrus Moth is ready and waiting. Alec gets my flying suit whilst the others fuss around making sure my partner is kitted up suitably. The lucky pilot takes her outside for a tour around the aeroplane while I make sure the kids are happy and read the usual meteorological reports. I become aware that Alec wants to say something to me. He's on his knees with the children but keeps looking over. Eventually he gets up and walks over and clears his throat. Mine instantly ceases up. I think I know what he's going to ask.

"Emily, umm. I'm sorry to have to say this but I think this will have to be your last flight. You see the Wing Commander has had to draw-the-line. He knows you've been flying from here but because of new RAF regulations he can't hide it any more. It's all to do with new aircraft flight-time recording, pilot hours and so on."

I breath out relieved. I knew this was going to happen it was just a matter of when.

"Ah understand completely Alec, it's no surprise. Ave been so lucky for yeors, so many flights an' ye te look after me brood like."

I then realise this wasn't the only thing on his mind.

He re-clears his throat. "Emily, we've known each other a long time and I've realised how much I've loved seeing you and your children. The thought of not seeing you again is, umm…painful." He pauses but I know what he's going to say and I'm trying to think of an answer. "I was just wondering if we could um.. get married?" He looks at me and then immediately re-starts talking but much more quickly. "I'm nothing like Freddie. I only wish I was. But I could look after all of you and care for you, we could live in Newcastle if that's best. It's just that.. I think, no I know that I love you so much." He stops and looks at me waiting for an answer.

I can only tell him the truth. I can't give excuses. He doesn't deserve that. "Alec, ah think yer a wonderful person an' as ah've said before ah divvent know what ah would have done without ye but, ah have te tell ye' an' please keep this te yerself, Ruth is more than my work colleague. She is my partner, we live together, like a married couple."

"Oh um.., I see, sorry I didn't know. That's nice."

I stand up and give him a hug and whisper sorry. "But ah dee want te keep in touch. It's just that, as ah said, ahm more or less married already."

"I understand Emily and thanks for being so truthful. Lucky Ruth."

He's so nice and I feel so bad. But I know no man can match my Freddie now or forever. Either way, he's too nice. He needs a more homely person.

Fortunately, we're interrupted by Ruth fully kitted out followed by Regi, one of the pilots.

"How does she look, ready for the skies?"

"She looks perfect." I also thought: yes, perfect, in so many ways.

She's eager and impatient to get going. Florence stares at her in wonder while Harry's still concentrating on his picture book. Alec is pretending to look after them both but I can see his focus is elsewhere. I seem to be making two people I love unhappy but I know in my heart Alec can never have been the one for me and Ruth has to at least try and reconnect with her Ma.

Either way, I snap out of it. This is an adventure and I'm going to make sure Ruth enjoys herself.

I help her into the front cockpit, point out the speaking tube and how it operates, then explain the flying controls but warn her not to touch them, at least for this flight - a delicate issue considering how Freddie died.

We take off and I start a small circuit of the aerodrome. I look at the back of her head, her long hair flailing around below her leather helmet. I know she's my girl, my lover. I'm so lucky and want to give her a hug. Just a little difficult up here. Instead I send messages into the tube. She replies and waves both hands in the air. Yes, I'm so lucky, in many ways.

Not too many aerobatics. I think back to my first flight with Freddie. How nervous I was and how carefully he looked after me. Ruth seems calm outwardly. If she's anything like me her insides will be fluttering like giant moths. Yes, I'll look after her and hopefully forever.

Flight finished I help her out over the wing and down to the grass. She whips off her helmet and immediately flies at me with arms outstretched. I have to grab her in mid-air and the momentum swirls us around in a big embrace. I wonder at the thoughts of our watching audience but I don't really care. We need to enjoy the moment.

Her enjoyment is evident in the cascade of words and hugs for everyone. Thoughts of her Ma are forgotten, now stored away, temporarily, hopefully. It's now the turn of Jimmy, another of the pilots to take her away to help her out of her flying suit.

They're all aware it was my last flight and they all seem distraught, critical of the RAF bureaucracy and insistent that we should return as their guests. Over tea and specially provided cakes from the local village we chat about the RAF and its aircraft. It seems no matter who you talk to about their daily work there's always something not right with the management: pay, conditions, clothing, policy. Nothing is ever perfect. I believe the RAF is something the country should be proud of. They want to work for a Shipbuilder! There we are that's me following everyone else, slating their employers.

We say goodbye with lots of hugs all round. I wonder if this is really my last visit, I hope not. We start on our short trip to the railway station and I thank Alec for recommending Cramlington including my experience with Ex-RAF man Victor MacTavish.

"I think I know who you mean. He won't forget you in a hurry!"

While Ruth walks to the station with the children I hang back and hold Alec's hand.

"Sorry Alec. Ye are the last person ah want to hurt. But the best thing for us is to be friends. Ah won't forget ye an' we will see each other again." I kiss him on the cheek.

He nods and I walk away to join my party. I see him waiting by the automobile, then waving as the train arrives and takes us away. I wave back, oh dear.

"He does really like ye, doesn't he?"

I explain that he proposed and obviously I had to turn him down.

"Ah see ah've some competition with ye."

"Ye can talk. Look at those pilots fawning all over ye. Trying te help ye on with the flying suit."

"Yes." She paused and raised her eyes to the roof remembering. "They were quite handsome actually."

I give her an eagle-eyed look before her hand slowly slides over and holds mine tightly.

"Thanks for the day. It wes very special."

Chapter 47

Ruth stayed the night. It was easier for her and a great help with the children.

Who am I kidding? In truth we just wanted our favourite evening of reading bed-time stories with Flo and Harry, a cleansing, sensuous shower together and a super-sexy cuddle in bed. In my new bed in fact. It's larger so we don't have to sleep on top of each other!

I arrive at work feeling positive and raring to go. I smile and give Ruth a small wave as I pass her office, then notice Gladys. She normally ignores me completely or just sneers but this morning she has a smile for me. Not a pleasant good-morning smile, which few people have ever seen, but she wears a victorious, knowing expression. I ignore her. She's got her own problems. She's not going to spoil my day.

Into my office, my early cup of tea in my hand, I'm ready for the day. I spot a small hand-written letter in the middle of my desk.

> *Dear Mrs Mulligan,*
>
> *Just to let you know I've noticed you have an interesting relationship with one of the girls in my office. A relationship you may want to keep quiet. This may prove difficult without some compensation.*
>
> *I believe Mr Morrison will not be pleased to know his offices contain such un-godly goings-on.*
>
> *I thought perhaps £5 each week will ensure your revolting secret remains that way.*
>
> *G.*

My immediate reaction is to sort her out. I'm seething and have to hold myself down. How dare she. This is the woman who has a hold on Jake for regular intercourse for his moment of weakness with Ruth.

There must be a better way. A slanging match is not ideal in a working environment. I could meet her on our way home, out-of-hours. I could send her an answering note. I have to calm down before deciding.

I ring through to Jake. He's free all morning for a meeting.

"She's an evil woman." Jake colours up immediately as he reads the note. "You've no idea what she can do. She's completely poisonous." He's up on his feet, walking over to the window and back, then leans against his desk head in his hands.

"Jake, ah know she has a hold on ye an' ah know what ye have te dee te keep her quiet."

He looks up at me eyes wide with horror. "But, it's always at dinner time when the offices are empty."

"Jake, the girl she's talkin' about is Ruth. We're good friends. She's told me what happened with ye. Ah know what's gannin on."

"Oh god, what a mess. If my father hears about it. I daren't imagine. Now this."

"Ah think ye exaggerate the effects of your liaison with Ruth. Most men would certainly try the same, certainly they would dream about it. And, if ye divvent mind me sayin', yer father certainly has a wonderin' eye."

"Really? He would never have an affair. Mother would leave him."

"He may not go that far but it doesn't stop him lookin'. What ahm sayin' is that his reaction may not be as bad as ye think. After all, ye were both unattached. Mind, I divvent know how you managed it."

He smiles and shakes his head. "I closed my eyes and thought of someone else." His smile disappears and looks at me. He's obviously thinking about what I've said. Then slumps back down onto his chair. "What's best to do?"

242

"Ah divvent know her personal position but maybe it's about time te rationalise the admin office?"

"You mean get rid of her?"

"Yes. Is she married, children?"

"I don't know, she never speaks about a husband. Yes, she did mention a son, a young lad I think."

He smiles at last. "Perhaps I've over-reacted. It'll certainly be a relief for me. A huge weight off my mind." Then he looks at me. "What about you and Ruth?"

"We're just good friends, well, actually very good friends."

"Good for both of you. You deserve each other." He comes and gives me a shoulder hug. "I'll deal with it as soon as possible. If we're going to keep this company going, we don't need people like her."

****

By the end of the week her desk is cleared, her seat stands empty.

I'm not going to mention the affair to anyone. Job positions come and go all the time. It's not unusual. But I feel certain this isn't the last we'll hear from her. There is no doubt she's the vindictive sort. I foresee a note to Jake's father coming. It would be as well if Jake came clean with him before it arrives.

Despite what's she's done I still feel a sense of guilt and I hope she doesn't suffer from lack of income, at least not for too long.

Chapter 48

The newspapers are full of it. The BBC gives us information and opinion through our company wireless set and everyone on Tyneside is completely diverted by the news: The miners all over the country are on-strike. Not only that but other unions have promised to support them and are doing the same.

There are two distinct opinions:

Most of the newspapers and the BBC consider this act as disloyal to the country. They accuse the Unions of being led by revolutionary communists. Their aim is to bring down the Government.

Every other member of the general public I've met support the Unions. They've had enough. Unemployment is sky high and growing daily causing poverty not seen in my lifetime. Even those still in work have had their wages cut and their hours increased. There are groups of men standing at street corners with nothing to do, nowhere to go. Communities have to support each other sharing what little they have. There may be the odd communist but my work with the Shop Stewards proves to me that there is no desire to bring down the Government. All they want is a fair wage for a fair day's work.

It seems the Government have prepared for this action since last year. Coal stocks have been built up, the army and a huge squad of volunteers have been recruited to maintain crucial supplies and it appears newspapers and the BBC have now to print and broadcast only what the Government want. No alternative viewpoints are allowed. It is all one-sided. This way the general public outside of the heavy and transport industries are easily influenced. This is what is known as 'Martial Law' and it's disgusting.

Hawthorns have done better than most but the men's Union has been asked by the TUC to join the strike to show their support. I have to meet them and as far as I'm concerned, I'm on their side but I have to mediate. I can't just say ok go-ahead. I have to lay down the consequences. Principally no work, no pay. I can suggest showing their support by striking for one day per week and working maybe an extra hour each other day to maintain progress and to offset their loss of pay. There'll be no dire threats, like at some companies, that if you strike, you're sacked! I agree with the cause and I will support them as much as I'm able.

The meeting has been long and traumatic. Support for the miners is 100%, hatred for the coal owners and the Government is 100%. In typical Tynesiders' fashion they want to stick together and I don't blame them. A strike day has been agreed for early next week. Further strikes are dependent on what's happening elsewhere. The TUC are meeting the Prime Minister in London. Something may be resolved but with this Conservative Government, I have grave doubts.

It's past eight o'clock. I'm cycling home under the grey, gloomy sky matching the country's mood. I'm hoping Ruth has managed sorting the children. I know she doesn't mind. She seems very fond of them. She's still adamant she doesn't want any herself but that's more than fine with me. My mind suddenly diverts away from strikes and Martial Law onto Freddie, the father of my children. That wonderful man cruelly lost far too early. I see his face in my mind's eye but he looks worried, he's eyes are wide open, he's shouting. What's happening to me. There's a sudden movement from the side I look over a man is moving towards me he has a stick. He's going to hit me with it, but no, he thrusts it into my wheel and sends me flying high into the air. It feels I'm in slow motion as I somersault over the bicycle then speeds up as I crash into the ground, my head banging into a wall. I can't move, I must be dead, no, I can see the sky. Then a face looms blocking out everything.

It's a young man's face. He thinks I'm dead, he looks worried. He pats me on my cheek trying to wake me up but I've decided to play dead. I just stare vacantly in front. It's safer this way. He looks away and speaks to someone beside him out of my site.

"Ah think she's dead. Ah killed her. Oh God. You said she would just get some bruises, that's all. I'll hang fer this. What am ah gannin to dee?"

I hear a low growl. "It serves her right, the little bitch. Come on let's get gannin."

The face disappears and I hear faint running footsteps. I think I'm safe but I still can't move. Minutes later I hear more steps approaching. The same face appears. He's upset. I can see tears in his eyes.

"Ahm sorry. Ah didn't mean it. Please live, ah divvent want te be hanged." His head droops down and he starts sobbing. He must have heard a noise as his head shoots up, gets to his feet and runs away fast.

"Stop, come back."

Another man appears in my view. Much older and looking very worried. He reaches for my arm and feels for my pulse. He mumbles to himself. "Well at least you're alive although you're in a right old mess. We'll get you to a hospital."

A woman's face appears alongside, maybe his wife. "I'll get our automobile here. Is she alright to move?"

"I don't know but I don't think we have a choice. We'll pick her up in that carpet in the back."

I seem to be in safe hands but my sight is growing blurry and I slip away to another world faraway from here.

Chapter 49

Staff Nurse Wright's story

It was another late night. I should have gone a while ago but I still had reports to write. I didn't mind. I could have a lie-in the following morning. The ward was quiet, dinner had finished and the plates cleared away. Most of the patients were either reading or getting ready to sleep. It's always my favourite time, much quieter after the rush of the day. Sister had already gone for the night and all I had to do was complete some reports, recall the events of the day and consider if I could have done anything better. The hand-over had been done. The night sister was just making her tea before she started.

The telephone rang with a shrill which at that time of the night makes everyone jump. I'm told a patient is on her way up in our new lift and to give her the best treatment possible. This surprised me and I asked why.

"You'll see. She's a mass of bruises, cuts and sprains and she has concussion but as far as we can see no broken bones."

We have an empty bed. I went to check it before this woman appears. I thought it could be a result of domestic abuse or maybe an early drinking casualty, both getting more common. But why 'the best treatment'. Perhaps she knew her.

The lift door opened with a crash and the porter pushes her carefully into the ward.

"Sorry Staff, I'm still not used to this new lift."

I smiled at my father. "Alright Da. I'll help ye off with the patient."

He grabbed my hand. "You'd bettor look who it is."

247

I looked along to her face and gasped. "Oh my God, Emily, what happened?"

"She's been given a sedative Wallace, she's oot cold. The man who brought her in is a doctor. He said she wes attacked by a young man. He assumed he wes tryin' te rob her but she still had her bag around her shoulder. The robber must have been surprised an' scarpered before he could take anythin'."

I started to examine her. "I'd bettor leave ye to it. But look after her won't ye. She's a bit special."

I could only nod. She really saved our family. Both of us have her to thank for our jobs. There's no way she's not getting the very best treatment even if I have to stay all night.

But of course, all her injuries had already been treated so really there was nothing to do except wait for her to come around. I wondered who was looking after her two children. Whoever it was must be worried sick. I remembered her friend Staff Nurse Tanner but not where she lived. I had a brainwave: Sister Parker knows her. I ran down the stairs to her ward and with luck she was just about to leave for the night.

"Oh my goodness. Keep an eye on her and I'll call in and tell her child minder. But you say her injuries are superficial." I nodded. "Good. Then better get the details of the doctor who found her then ring the police."

I managed to get the doctor's details and rang the police. They're so busy with all this strike business but they did say they would try to visit in the morning. I climbed back up the stairs two at a time forgetting about the lift. The night sister was with Emily.

"She's stable but that head injury worries me. There could easily be internal damage. We'd better monitor her heart and blood pressure through the night. I've alerted the doctor-on-call. He'll come if there's any deterioration. You can get to bed now Wallace, get some rest."

248

"No, I'd like te stay. She means a lot te me."

"Wallace get back to your digs. We'll need you tomorrow, wide awake! She's in good hands. And that's an order."

I had to go. Maybe she's right.

"Goodnight Sister."

****

Nurse Wright relaxes as she makes her way back to the nurses' home. She passes an old woman done up in a thick coat and woolly hat, her hands thrust deep in the pockets. She wonders why she's wearing such clothing on such a warm Summer's night. But not for long. Her day is taking its toll and she needs to get some rest.

Ruth's story

She should have been back. I was expecting her by eight and was going to surprise her with dinner but now it was cold and congealed, her wine glass untouched. She told me the meeting with the shop stewards was going to be difficult and long but this was taking dedication too far. The children went to bed an age ago and all I really want now is to sleep myself.

There's was knock on the door. I thought, at last. I rushed down to let her in. She must have forgotten her key. I found a woman in a sister's uniform, slimmer and older than Emily.

"Sorry to trouble you but this is Emily Mulligan's flat isn't it?"

"Yes, it is. Ahm lookin' after her bairns while she's away."

"I'm Sister Parker from the hospital. I have to tell you that Emily has been attacked and injured on her way home. She's not badly hurt but she's in hospital. She's sedated and in good hands."

My hands shot to my mouth. "Ah must gan an' see her now. Which ward is she in?" I changed my shoes while I was talking. I muttered more to myself than to the Sister. My poor Emily and there's me moaning about her being late.

"She's in the Mary Seacole Ward but you don't have to...." I heard her speaking but I had to go, there and then. I think I shouted back, "the kids are asleep, there's dinner and wine on the table. Help yourself." I hope she's ok with that.

I ran most of the way and by the time I arrived I was hot and sweaty. I spotted the receptionist and asked her the way to the Ward and that I need to see Emily Mulligan. She pointed to the lift while muttering. "She's popular tonight, first her mother and now you."

The lift is slow but it gives me time to relax. Mother? Her mother's in America. Who on earth could it be?

The lift slowed and stopped. I slammed open the doors making the nurse at the desk jump.

"Mrs Mulligan?"

She pointed me in the right direction. "That's her mother there already."

I could see a woman in a thick coat looking at the patient closely one hand thrust deep in her pocket. "That's not her Ma." I started to walk over to see who it really was. In the dim light I saw her pull out something shiny, glinting then she screamed: "This is fer ye, ye revoltin', unholy queer."

"Stop." I started to run. I wasn't going to get there. The knife started its journey down to Emily's chest. I dived headlong, crashed into the woman and sent her flying over my now prone body and I heard the rattle of steel on concrete. I swivelled round and grabbed the knife.

"Give me that ye queer bitch." I turned towards her, the knife made contact and slid easily into her on-rushing body. I let go, she staggered then collapsed onto the floor her hands clutched around her weapon. Blood poured out of the wound in swelling waves. She

gurgled briefly then let go. Her hands dropped to her side. Her eyes stared at the ceiling, motionless.

Chapter 50

Freddie is speaking to me, in German. I haven't a clue what he's saying but he's laughing so I laugh with him. I study his handsome face standing there dressed in his flying suit. He turns away and looks at another woman and smiles. I recognise Brigitte, his Ma, looking elegant as always. She holds her hands wide welcoming both of us. We walk towards her but a flash of light stops me. I see a silhouette of an aeroplane within the flash. It's diving vertically. I shout, "pull her up, pull her up."

I hear a faint, distant voice in my ear. "Emily," then again, "Emily." My eyes open but I can't focus. I can't see what happened but I remember what happened and tears fill my eyes. I want to sleep. It'll be better when I wake up, all will be fine. Now I hear singing. A lovely soft voice relaxing me. I feel content. My eyes flick open and I see her, my lovely forever-friend Millie.

She kisses me gently on my cheek. I wince. She holds my hand, I wince again. Gradually I feel pains spreading all over my body. The worst is the back of my head. I go to feel it but there's something in the way.

"Millie, what's happened?"

"Ah divvent know where te start. What's the last thing ye remember?"

My brain is clearing quickly, the pains are sore and throbbing. I try to think back.

"Meetin' with the Union, ridin' me bike," I pause, "then, nothing. Why am ah in me bed?"

"Emy, yer in hospital. I'll get ye a cuppa an' I'll tell ye all about it or at least what ah know."

I look around and recognise my old ward but why am I here, in bed? I try to sit up but the many pains stop me. I gently examine my body. It's covered in bandages, there's a splint on my leg and another bandage wrapped around my head. I feel like I've been blasted by shrapnel in the trenches.

I hear footsteps and see a nurse approaching. I recognise her immediately.

"Wallace."

She gives the broadest of smiles. "Sister, ah mean Emily, ahm so pleased yer awake. Ye gave everyone a fright." She stops as Millie arrives with my tea.

"Come on then, tell me all about it. Ah wasn't drunk was ah?" They don't laugh at my effort for a joke. "Ah wes drunk?"

Millie sits down. "We'll tell ye all we know."

Wallace starts the story. "It seems someone attacked ye while ye were cyclin' home last night. A doctor an' his wife found ye an' brought ye heor. Ye had lots of injuries an' concussion. Ye were sedated an' you've been asleep until just now."

I takes me a while to take all this in but then I realise I haven't been home. "But does Ruth know an' how are my bairns?"

Millie continued. "Be patient Emy, Ruth an' the bairns are all safe. Wallace here got hold of Sister Parker te call in at yer house te let them know. It seems Ruth came rushin' over here leaving Sister te mind the bairns.

"Thank goodness. Dee ye know where she is now?" Millie and Wallace look serious, I feel worried about what they're going to say.

"Neither of us were heor when Ruth came in but from what we've been told," she paused looking at Wallace, "someone pretending te be yer Ma came in an' tried te kill ye, heor in yer bed."

"What, yer kiddin' me."

"Ruth followed her in an' realised it wasn't yer Ma. Then she noticed the knife an' stopped her."

Wallace continued. "In the fight this woman wes stabbed an' she died."

My eyes widen and I stare at them both. I have to be dreaming. All this can't be true, can it? "This canna be true, yer jokin', yes?" They shake their heads. I can't believe it. "Who wes this woman, does anyone know?"

Apparently, the police came, took statements from the night sister and some patients, removed the body and took Ruth away for questioning.

"Ah took over from the night sister an' she told me all this. She said the police will be here today te see ye."

I shake my head hardly believing such a story. "But ah canna remember anythin' except how me meetin' went, that's as clear as a bell. Also, ah remember cyclin' home. How's me bicycle?"

"Still there ah 'spect. Probably in bits like you."

Millie and Wallace have to get on with their day and left me to wait for the police. Word of my crime story spread quickly and I received a host of visitors all outside the proper times. I'll have to have a word with Matron – and thank her! Several used their dinner breaks, other nurses I know popped in and one unexpected visitor – a certain Mr Morrison Senior himself, someone I very rarely see. He didn't stop long but before he left, he said the nicest thing: "Mrs Mulligan I have to say you've made a difference to the Company, and my son Jake of course. Not just your ideas and dealings with the Union but the way the workforce respects you. We're doing a hell of a lot better than most companies around here and I want to thank you for your part in achieving that. By the way, Jake has come clean with his problem with one of the admin. I know how you've managed the problem together. He's learnt his lesson. See you soon I hope."

Between visits I concentrate trying to recall the attack but it's just a blank. I've learnt from Jake that Ruth has been given time off. He's not seen her but heard about the rumpus in the ward. She so deserves it. It seems she saved my life. I miss her and want to see her and shower and cuddle together. I close my eyes to visualise us together but all I see is a young man's face saying he's sorry.

That's it.

He's the man with the stick. My memory is clicking into place, thank goodness.

Two policemen came, both detectives. They seemed to be pleased to be in the ward. Maybe a change from dealing with walk-outs and strikes or maybe just the attraction of the nurses. I can now tell them my story from leaving the meeting, to the attack, the attacker and his accomplice to the doctor finding me.

They have already interviewed the doctor and my Ruth.

"But who was this woman an' why did she want te kill me?"

He reads from his notebook. "The woman is a Mrs Gladys O'Neill. She was recognised by Miss Ruth Adams. I believe all three of you work at Hawthorns. We believe she was recently made redundant. That seems to be the motive."

"The killing was in self-defence, there was a witness. Your attacker is most probably the deceased's son. We'll pick him up soon."

I hold my head and close my eyes. Gladys you stupid, stupid woman and you've left your son alone in this cruel world.

They go to leave but one of them adds, "Yer bicycle is at the station when ye need it, but ah think you'll need a new one."

As I had hoped after tea time Ruth came in with Florence and Harry. Poor Ruth looked pale and weary. The whole experience must have been so traumatic. Florence looked horrified by my bandages, Harry just stared and pointed.

"Ahm comin' home tomorrow hopefully an' ah want you two te tell me what you've been doin'." I whisper to Ruth before they leave. "We can talk more about all this then, but ah also need a shower an' a hug with me lover."   "Funny that, ah dee as well."

Chapter 51

"Dee ye remember the last time ye took me hyem from the hospital?"

We're walking home two days after my attack. Millie's got me with one hand and Harry with the other. I feel much improved although very stiff with just a couple of bandages. One over my knee protecting a stitched, deep cut making me limp but my head bump has reduced and the dressing removed thank goodness. Millie and Ruth have been 'holding-the-fort' in my absence but I'm ready to resume my life, well, nearly.

"No, when wes that."

"It was after yer Frank knocked me over in his cart an' ah sprained me ankle or somethin'. Ah remember because ah wes in a real grumpy mood about bein' pregnant with Mhairi an' ye got the brunt of it."

"Aye, ye old moaner, you've not changed a bit! That was a few yeors ago."

"Fifteen actually."

She looks at me knowingly. "Feel the same then?"

I nod. "One day."

"Ah guess Ruthie doesn't know about her."

"Ah didn't even tell Freddie," I laugh then look surprised, "an' who's Ruthie??"

Florence is at school so Harry has the both of us all to himself. Ruth is at Hawthorns today. "How's she been?"

"Ah tried te persuade her to stay off another day like but she's like ye, wants te get on with her life. Ah think it'll take time te get over her experience, we may see a reaction later."

At home we talk over our cuppas both watching Harry playing.

"Ye know he needs a haircut."

She's smiling she knows what I think. He's got lovely blonde locks curling over his ears. She thinks I always wanted another girl and she points to his hair and the odd pink clothes I've bought. But she's wrong, I love my little boy and why can't he have long hair and pink clothes.

"He'll be teased at school."

"But that's a yeor away. Ah might get it trimmed a bit."

"That's my Emy. Never thinks like anyone else."

"Me! An' who's livin' in sin then? Not married an' with a bairn."

She didn't have a chance to answer as the front door opens and in walks Ruth looking surprised.

"Ah called in at the hospital an' yer heor."

"Yes an' so are ye." I walk carefully over and grab her with both hands so pleased to see her.

"Well I'll be off then. Ah divvent want te spoil the reunion."

"Oh no ye don't." I take her hand. "This is what ah call a group hug." The three of us hold each other so tight, I squeal but enjoy the moment. Harry just looks confused.

Ruth can only stop for twenty minutes and the three of us talk through the drama of that night. Everyone in the admin office were completely shocked of course but not entirely surprised. She openly threatened revenge when she got her redundancy notice. My relationship with Ruth is now well known having been described in great detail apparently.

"Well ahm not gannin te deny it. We love each other an' they can accept it or leave."

Ruth takes my hand and looks me in the eye. "Ah completely agree an' ye know ah think they will accept it. They think the world of ye an' what you've done fer the company already."

We stand up and hug tightly. "Sorry Millie but we needed that."

"That's so nice. Hold on te that an' both of ye will be just fine. Ah must gan. See ye later this afternoon with yer Flo."

She lets herself out leaving us to fulfil our need for close contact. Just for her last few minutes.

Left alone with Harry during the week feels strange but this is my chance to give him all my attention. But of course, no chance, my mind drifts back to Gladys and her son. They were both there when her son attacked. No doubt ordered to do it by his mother. At first, she assumed I was dead but when her son told her I'd been taken away by the doctor, she decided to finish the job. I wonder how someone can get so eaten-up with hatred. Forgotten at first but now as clear as anything, I can never forget her boy's reaction. He was truly sorry. Probably thought it was a bit of a game. I might have got a scare and a few bruises but no more than that. No doubt he'll be locked up and by the time he gets freed he'll be tarred as a criminal and a life of crime to look forward to.

I decide that I must see him.

Chapter 52

I considered going back to work today. I felt much improved after a relaxing night with Ruth and almost sprang out of bed to sort the children. I walked them both to Flo's school and dropped off Harry with Millie, got home and promptly collapsed on my bed!! No, perhaps another day off is needed.

Mid-morning, I was woken by my telephone ringing. It was the police. They want me to identify the young man they've arrested as the attacker.

Good this is just what I wanted. I re-dressed and set off for the station. I know what I want to do. I hope they'll allow me to speak to the prisoner. I feel sure it will be Gladys's son.

Luck was with me. I arrived and Sergeant Stanley Symonds was on duty. I can surely persuade my ex-lover.

"Hello Emily." He smiled and we sat and talked.

"At first ah couldn't believe you'd got involved in another fight but then ah thought: she's an ex-Suffragette an' a Flanders heroine so ah suppose, yes, it's to be expected."

"All ah wes doin' wes cyclin' hyem." But I had to smile. I rather like this reputation I seem to have.

Inevitably we discuss the General Strike, the picket lines, the volunteer drivers and the army. He's aware that Hawthorns are striking tomorrow just for the day.

"Ye know Hawthorns have changed in the last few months. They used to be a real load of troublemakers." He narrowed his eyes. "Nothin' te dee with a certain Miss Mulligan ah suppose."

"Of course, one word from me an' they quake in their shipbuildin' boots! But ah have te say, personally ah agree with their decision te support the miners. Ye must have seen fer yerself the terrible poverty. If they dee nothin' it will get even worse."

"Officially ah couldn't agree but when ahm off duty that's another matter. I'd probably join them," he paused, "ermm.. that's between ye an' me. If the inspector got te heor ah would be oot on my ear an' no mistake."

I smiled seductively. "Stan."

He narrowed his eyes again. "Yes Emily."

"Well, ah feel certain ye have the right man in yer cells but would ye let me have a private word with him?"

He turns on his striking smile that always sent my inside tumbling. "Just for you. I'll give ye five minutes."

Oh dear, what a scheming little devil I am.

"By the way what's his name?"

"O'Neill, Patrick O'Neill."

He leads me down the stairs to the cells. Two of them house recuperating drunk troublemakers from last night's demonstrations. The third cell holds a young lad coiled up and wedged into the corner. He has his eyes closed but they flick open when he hears his door being unlocked. He gets to his feet; I think hoping he's going to be released.

"Someone te see ye." Stan turns to me. "Just five minutes now. I'll be just outside."

"Thank you."

He leaves and closes the outer cell door behind him.

"Hello Patrick, de ye know who ah am?"

He nods. I can see he recognises me and now keeps his eyes on the floor. I certainly recognise him.

"Can ye tell me why ye attacked me?"

Nothing.

"Why did ye want te hurt me?"

"Ye got Ma the sack."

"She told ye that did she?"

"Aye."

"Dee ye know yer Ma tried te kill me in the hospital?"

He nods.

"Dee ye know she wes stopped an' she died in the fight afterwards?

He nods.

"Ahm very sorry that happened. Me an' yer Ma didn't get on like but ah certainly didn't want it te end like this."

Nothing.

"How old are ye?"

"Seventeen."

"An' where did ye work."

"Armstrongs."

Our conversation continued in a similar disjointed way. It appears he's an apprentice boilermaker and like most apprentices they don't get paid. He has no close family. His father is away, left when he was born. No brothers or sisters. As far as I can make out, his only relative is a Grandma living in Jarrow.

As I go to leave, I tell him I will come and see him again. I could see he was wanting to ask something and I try to coax his thoughts out into the open.

"What will happen te me?"

"Ah divvent know yet. I'll talk to the policeman."

"Umm.. ahm sorry ah hurt ye. Ah thought ye were dead at first. Ma wanted ye dead. Ahm pleased yer not. Ma isn't, she wasn't very nice sometimes."

"Thanks fer telling me Patrick. Perhaps yer Ma had some bad, personal problems."

He just nods.

I leave feeling very sad for the lad. He doesn't deserve to be in this position.

"He has admitted te the offence but has the mitigating reason that his mother forced him. He could still be sentenced up to two years at a borstal school but ahm sure it will only be fer a few months. Ah also have his Grandma's details. She seems te be his nearest living relative. We need te contact her te arrange his accommodation at least until the court case. He canna stay heor."

I want to get back home to sort my own plans but Stan wants to talk about our time we spent together.

"I'll always remember that time we spent in yer family home on the coast. Ah suppose ah always thought we'd get married. Then ah went an' messed it up."

"Oh Stan, yer happily married now aren't ye. Ye mustn't have regrets."

"No, Sophie is kind, understandin' an' supportive an' she looks after me an' the three bairns. Ah canna ask fer more than that. All the same ah sometimes wish..." He runs out of words and just stares at the wall.

"I'd be too bossy fer ye. Ye know me, I'd be changin' my mind all the time, supportin' all sorts of good Causes. You'd get frustrated. Now ye have someone dependable an' loyal te go hyem to an' spend yer life with. You've done well, ye should be proud of yerself."

"Ah know an' of course ah do."

"Ah want te make a few calls an' I'll get back te ye as soon as ah can." I give his hand a squeeze and leave before he says anymore.

****

"Patrick O'Neil, aye he's one of our apprentices heor. Why dee ye ask?"

I'm speaking to a foreman at Armstrongs, checking up on the young lad. "Ahm afraid he's in a bit of trouble with the police an' ahm just checkin' his story."

"Ye dee mean the Patrick O'Neil who lives in Hebburn with his mother?

"Aye, he's the one."

261

"Well then ye surprise me. He's one of the best apprentices we've had. Punctual, polite an' hard workin'. Ah wish we had more like him."

"Really, well thanks fer yer help. I'll quote ye if ah may. It will help his defence."

"Ah wondered why he hasn't turned up for a few days. Will he be released?"

"Ah canna say at the moment but I'll get back te ye."

****

I've just got time to cycle to Jarrow to speak to his Grandma. Stan gave me her address but she hasn't a telephone so there's no alternative but to see her in person. I just hope she's in. I eventually find the street and house, a typical brick-built terrace with bay windows.

"Come in pet, ye look hot."

She has no idea what has happened so I have to explain everything. Fortunately, she makes the tea before hearing the news. She's now completely stunned.

I pour out two cups myself then wait for her to recover.

"Ahm sorry it's bad news, the police will make contact but that's how it is."

Gradually the story of the family unfolded:

"My daughter in law, Gladys, wes a very sad person. Paddy, that's my son, an' Gladys were completely smitten with each other. Gladys wes much older, maybe twelve years but they spent every day together an' of course the inevitable happened, she became pregnant with Patrick. They had te get married but the day after she had the baby, Paddy scarpered. He joined the Merchant Navy. It wasn't until five years later that he made contact with me. He wanted te gan back te her but she wouldn't have him. Ye see by this time she'd changed.

She had built up acquaintances! Lots of them, all young men. Ye know what ah mean. They used te pay her well fer her services an' she'd lost interest in my Paddy."

She stops to fetch a photograph from her bedroom.

"This is me son. He wes one of the first volunteers te join up in 1914. He didn't last the yeor." I looked at the snapshot of a soldier in his khaki holding a rifle, the like of which I've seen countless times before. Each one a treasured possession of their mother. Paddy looked to be in his mid-twenties and like in all other photographs, with the hope of adventure in his eyes.

She pours another cup for both of us.

"After the war finished, ah think she thought the young men lost interest. She got too old for the game although she kept trying! To bring regular money in she got a job at Hawthorns. Ah see her occasionally with Patrick. Ah suppose that's all finished now. Mind, she wes always a bit peculiar. Ah divvent think even Paddy knew what she got up te before they met."

"Ave seen Patrick. He seems a bright lad."

"Whey aye, he is. Not like most young men his age. He works at Armstrong's. He's what they call an apprentice. Doesn't get paid much though, if anythin'. He stands up fer his Ma, although he's probably a bit frightened of her. She's got, had, a horrible temper on her."

She's very willing to talk about her grandson and loves the idea of looking after him after his time in Borstal. Which pleased me no end, this was the main reason I came.

I had to leave so that I can pick up Flo, Frank and Harry. I want to float my idea with Millie and then with Ruth.

As it happens both were concerned that Patrick may want to take his revenge for his Ma's death. They also think he should pay for what he did. He's not a child. He should have known better. Anyone would understand that sort of act could end in a serious injury or death. Either way they both know I'll do whatever I decide no matter what other people think.

The advice has clarified my idea and I now look forward to my first day back at work.

This day has been continuous, exciting and successful but I am now completely shattered. My aching, sore and painful bits are telling me to slow down. I know what I need and I know who can provide it.

Ruth comes to my rescue. She strips me off and sits me on a chair in my shower and massages the complaining bits until the pains are history, especially my poor throbbing head. Other less painful bits are also given the treatment for good measure – well good for me anyway. I'm then carefully dried and special cream applied where needed and slid bodily between the bed sheets.

"Right Emy, you stay there while I have my shower."

I don't need to be told twice. It takes me seconds to drift into a deep, peaceful slumber, dreaming of some gorgeous, naked woman sliding in next to me and caressing my every inch sending me in to a world of extreme ecstasy. Another world completely.

Chapter 53

It's Strike Day.

I'll be joining the march from our yard and into Newcastle. Hawthorns premises have been locked and barred for the day. No-one is to be let in so the alternatives are to have a day off or join the demonstration.

The shop stewards have negotiated the timing and the route with the police and have liaised with other ship-building yards to meet on the Town Moor. It's a long march through Heworth, into Gateshead, over the Tyne Swing Bridge and to the Moor. Many of the Transport workers are already on strike but for this day they have agreed to run a limited service to help those who would find the distance a problem.

I can still feel many of my injuries but there's no way I'm going to miss the March. I'm going to be joined by Ruth of course but also Celia my ex-Suffragette friend from Sunderland, Rose, my ex nursing colleague and Millie which means of course Harry will be in his push-chair. More nurses will join us on the Moor although if we find each other it'll be a miracle.

We start at ten thirty outside the yard, collect some banners and hopefully meet my friends. So, with Ruth and the push chair loaded with Harry, sandwiches and the crucial tea flasks we set off for Hebburn. It's a bright day, no sign of rainclouds yet and I can feel the old, missed excitement of demonstrations coming back to me. The nearer we get to the start the more people are joining us, chattering and laughing. These events are good to release all the frustrations built up over the years. To make yourself seen and heard. To join in with others, so much more satisfying than just moaning with your neighbour.

There's a police presence but it's relaxed. There are no raised batons, no-one mounted on horseback. There are no soldiers, tanks or armoured vehicles. If you believed the newspapers you would expect heavy armed escorts at every march with violent clashes and hundreds of arrests. Unbelievably, it has been proven some of the photographs printed are actually reprints of those from the riots in Ireland or from the 1921 Black Friday troubles. Most readers will of course believe what they see in print. It's a completely disgusting ploy by the Government.

When we arrive, I head for my agreed meeting place and there I can see Rose and Celia already waiting. They don't know each other but I soon change that. They're excited like everyone else, dressed for a warm day and carrying haversacks on their backs packed with provisions. Celia has even brought her own rolled-up banner on the bus journey. She explains it's been used before during the miners' marches. It reads: *'Not a Penny Less not a Minute More'*.

They make a fuss of Harry of course commenting on his long blonde curls. They're just jealous!

Before we start a shop-steward addresses us through his hailer. People quieten down to listen. He reminds us that this is a peaceful demonstration. There must be no violence. This is to show solidarity with the miners and by doing this we hope to show the Government that we're all in it together and something needs to change. There's a loud cheer and with the placards raised we start our March in to the city.

I thought perhaps, as I work on the employer's side I should keep in the background. This idea lasted at least a minute. Seeing my friends holding their placards high right at the front was just too inviting. So, I join them and with Harry thrust before everyone in his push chair we start off on our journey to try to make a difference.

We feel like celebrities. As we walk through the towns, locals are already waiting for us either lining the route, standing in family groups by front doors or hanging out their windows. They wave and cheer, some follow on behind, some even come and shake our hands, pat us on our backs. There's so much so support.

There's so much need for change, there are no dissenting voices so different from my Suffragette days. Then, support was rare. Even women used to shake their heads and wonder what all the fuss was about. But we wanted change and eventually we achieved some of what we wanted and that fight still continues.

Into Gateshead and Millie joins us. She was worried she wouldn't find us in the crowd. Perhaps she should have known we would be at the front.

Traffic has been diverted while we pass through. Automobiles wait in the side roads, their drivers standing alongside waving. Squads of children race ahead, wave as we approach then go again until they need to return home.

Then it's on to the little swing bridge for our arrival into Newcastle. The bridge is dwarfed by the High-Level, road and rail structure to one side and the massive foundation works for the new Tyne Bridge on the other. When finished it'll be the largest of its kind in Britain. It's now being fabricated just to the South in Teesside providing valuable employment in Middlesbrough.

Crossing our river, our lifeblood, always keeps me from talking and it has the same effect now. There are no shouting chants, singing or cheers. Everyone seems mesmerised, taking in the structures, the views and our old River Tyne flowing serenely below us as we cross.

Our passage through Newcastle is joined by other groups heading to the Moor. Although busier the support is not so vocal. The pavements teem with shoppers and workers but they're going about their daily business not to watch us pass by. Still we wave our banners and sing and chant happily and proudly.

Arriving at the Town Moor we're guided to an area to hear the speakers. Most are miners' reps and some politicians. There is one particular politician I'm especially eager to hear.

I realise the walk has tired me and standing listening is not doing me any favours. Ruth, bless her, has found me a seat – on the steps around a statue, so I can still hear and see what's happening. It's a fascinating view of a sea of heads and banners being waved and groups of policemen dotted around. Groups are still joining us, even a double-decker omnibus arrives disgorging a large body of men. I watch them. They seem very keen, working their way through the crowd towards the stage.

The first speaker appears. He is one of the Miners Union reps. He has a strong Yorkshire accent but speaking confidently and clearly helped by the sound system in place. We cheer when he demands a fair hearing by the government and his promises to fight on until we get it. There are other shouts, inaudible at first but from this raised height I can spot where they originate. It's from the group of men from the omnibus. I concentrate and realise they're calling him a commie and telling him to get back to work. The noise level rises as other men nearby shout back. I can feel tension mounting. The police are reacting moving closer to the group. I see a photographer on the stage pointing his camera at the fracas. It suddenly occurs to me that all this has been set up to divert attention away from the main reason we're here. I stand up and locate our shop steward to tell him my concerns. I suggest he gathers others together and usher this group of men out of the Park. I grab Ruth, Millie, Celia and Rose together.

"This is a set-up, probably by the government. We must get at that photographer on the stage. If he gets away the photograph will be headline news in the papers."

With Millie left minding Harry the four of us are able to get around the side then around the back of the stage. By this time the speaker has stopped, waiting for the commotion to die down. We step up behind the photographer and surround him. He is certainly surprised to see himself cornered by four determined women, especially me, brandishing a small pointed stake I've found. He attempts an escape, but we grab his camera. I get close and whisper in his ear.

"Who are ye working fer?"

He's nervous. "No-one, ahm freelance."

I hold the stake very close to his genitals and stare in to his shifty eyes. "Really? An' who's gannin te pay ye an' that group of men tryin' te disrupt this meetin'? Now be careful what ye say."

He's now wide eyed, really frightened. He stutters. "Mr Price, Gallogate Securities."

"Really, surprise, surprise. Well I'll return the camera te him minus the exposed plates. An' ye can tell him he'll regret tryin' te undermine what we're doin' heor."

He steps down from the stage but before he moves away, he turns to us.

"He won't be happy, ye know."

"Look around ye. None of these will be happy with ye, Mr Price or that group of men getting' onto that omnibus. ah should watch yer backs very carefully."

He shakes his head and joins the troublemakers. The police have efficiently split the two groups avoiding any violent clashes. The omnibus passengers get on board and it drives away. We can get on with our demonstration but I feel exhausted, I'm shaking like a leaf. If he hadn't been so frightened, I don't know if I could have hit him where it hurts most. Ruth grabs me and flings her arms around me.

"Ahm so proud of ye. Ye even scared me. Ye looked as though ye were gannin te kill him."

"That was an act. Ah was twitchin' like a leaf inside. Ah think ah need to sit doon."

"Emily."

I looked up straight into the face of my heroine, Ellen Wilkinson.

"I saw everything you did. It's obvious to me they were making sure our demonstration was disrupted. Someone paid that group and the photographer and those pictures would have been in the papers tomorrow with the headline something like: *Strong opposition to the strikers* or *Strikers outnumbered.*"

I gave her the details of the funder. She grabbed my hand and shook it tightly. "I'm proud of you and I'm going to change my speech. I'll take the camera back. I know him and I'll make sure he knows who I am. See you after."

"Thanks Ellen an' good luck."

She walks to the centre of the Stage and takes the microphone in her hand and delivers her speech.

> *I've thrown my speech notes away. I want to concentrate on what just happened over there. I can tell you now, that group of men came specifically to undermine our demonstration. They brought a photographer to prove to the world that we're in the minority and that most people support the government in their move to stop this communist movement to take over the country.*
>
> *You didn't know that did you?*
>
> *I bet you thought you were here to support the miners in their bid to be paid a fair wage for a fair day's work. I wonder how many here want to take over the government? Perhaps you're all communists?*
>
> *Of course not, but that's what this government want the rest of the country to think and they have complete control of what is reported on the wireless and the newspapers. Well, they will have me to answer to in Westminster. We shall report in the remaining un-bias, fair-minded papers and make sure these get distributed widely.*
>
> *In addition, this proof of their action will be reported back to the TUC delegation currently talking to the government in Downing Street. And, thanks to the heroic*

270

action of this group of women, these photographs will substantiate our claim.

Please give them a round of applause.

I'm not going to say anymore except to thank you all for your wonderful 100% support for this Cause. There has to be a change and we're on the first step towards that goal.

I am going to add my thanks to the police for efficiently and calmly controlling any possible confrontation. I have no idea where these people are now, so be on your guard. If you are taunted, ignore them however much you want to argue our case. Just cross the road and go home.

Thankyou.

There follows a huge ovation for Ellen. I'm so proud with the four of us taking that very scary action. We climb down from the stage and start back towards our group from Hawthorns. Ellen meets us.

"I think you four are in for sainthoods."

She notices remnants of my bicycle incident still showing. "Have you been in the wars."

I certainly didn't want to go into any details and just said that I went over my handlebars and ended up battered and bruised.

She smiles as if she knows otherwise. "I bet the other person looks worse!"

I laugh enjoying the joke but I think yes, sadly she's a hell of a lot worse.

My adrenaline levels are still high as we listen to more speakers, eat our sandwiches and drink plenty of tea. Some of my nurse friends have found me, some even noticed my scene on stage. They were very impressed. They suggested I should be acting in a Shakespeare play in the theatre. I think not!

The final speech finished and with the last applause fading we make our way home. We're in good time to pick up our various school children then say goodbye to Millie, Celia and Rose leaving me, Ruth and the two kids to wend our way back to my flat.

"You'll be stayin' won't ye?"

"Oh, depends on what yer offerin'."

"The usual."

"Then ahm definitely stayin'!"

We laugh, walk arm in arm, pushing Harry who's actually fallen asleep and talk to Florence about her day at school.

With the children in bed we discuss the day's events.

"Dee ye think we've made a difference?"

"Ah hope so. Certainly made the photographer think a bit that's for sure. He didn't like the look of yer stick an' where it wes pointin'."

I laughed. "The 'family jewels' were certainly in danger."

Chapter 54

I wake early, Ruth is still fast asleep, her head on my shoulder, an arm across my bare chest and a leg over my bare legs. I think how lucky I am to have such a romance. My life has completely changed and my assumption, that I would never meet anyone I loved as much as I loved Freddie, has been proven wrong.

And my new love is a woman. It feels so natural and did even from the beginning. Who would have thought? We have to be aware that certain acts should be kept private. Pecks on cheeks, walking arm in arm are fine but no romantic, erotic mouth to mouth kissing even holding hands would cause surprised stares. But I don't care. When we're in-private we do what we like and enjoy ourselves.

I bend down, kiss her lips and place my arms around her. She stirs and our bodies intertwine and we share each other's warmth. It's a lovely feeling and I don't want it to end, ever.

****

It's my first day back at work. I am looking forward to it but I'm nervous about the reaction after yesterday's strike and I suppose following the tragic business with Gladys O'Neill.

I walk into the offices and immediately ahm surrounded by a swarm of happy women from admin. They know what happened yesterday and want to know more. I look behind them and spot Ruth at her desk smiling at me.

"Ok, let's gan back into the office an' I'll tell ye all ah know."

Ruth has obviously spoken to them before I came in but they want to know more. Some were actually on the march and experienced the excitement of the day.

"Did ye actually threaten the photographer with a stick like?"

"Well, ah really only wanted te encourage him te tell me who's payin' him. It wes just a co-incidence it wes pointin' at his nether-region."

They giggle like school girls, I smile over to Ruth.

"Ye actually know Ellen Wilkinson?"

"Whey aye, ah've met her before. She's actually one of me heroines."

"What's she like?"

"She's very canny. Hard workin', totally committed te the Labour Party an' fully behind this General Strike te get fair wages fer the miners like. Divvent believe the newspapers, she's not a communist any more. She doesn't want a revolution, overthrow the government or anythin' like that."

"Dee ye think the miners will get what they want?"

"Ah divvent really know enough about it. But ah do know the government is scare-mongerin'. They control all reports in the newspapers an' on the BBC. So, what ye read or heor is not real, it's made up. Keep believin' the only reason for this Strike is te support the miners fer a fair wage fer a fair day's work an' nothin' else."

"Ye feelin' alright now?"

"Much bettor thanks. But no matter ah wasn't Gladys's favourite, ah never wanted that te happen." I turn to leave and speak as I go. "Ah best get on, but many thanks for yer support. There may be another walk-out next week."

It's my dinner break and I'm on a mission. To save time I've taken a tram to the police station in Newcastle. I'm hoping Stan will be on duty but I find another sergeant behind the desk.

I give my details and what I want but he is confused.

"Ah divvent want ye te press charges against Patrick O'Neill that's all. Ah want him to be released without any criminal record. He's workin' as an apprentice at Armstrong's an' he can live with his Grandma in Jarrow. Ave met her, she's very willin'."

"But he nearly killed you. He's admitted to it and he's got to be punished otherwise he'll just do it again."

"He wes forced into it by his Ma. Everyone ah've spoken te who knows him says he's a canny lad. Ave spoken te him, he's very apologetic. Ah divvent want him treated as a villain in a borstal. He'll come out a lot worse than when he went in an' ah divvent want that."

"We've also got to think about the safety of others."

I feel exasperated but keep patient. "He's safer now than when he leaves after months or yeors with real criminals. Please release him. Ah can change me story te say: Ah wasn't concentratin', had te swerve te avoid him then hit a tree. If that's any easier for ye."

He rubs his chin with his hand. "This is all very irregular. I'll have to have a word with my superior. Have you got a telephone?"

I give him my number and suggest that he speaks to Sergeant Stanley Symonds. He can vouch for me. I ignore his eyebrow-raising reaction.

"I'll ring tonight te check you've done it. Thank you."

****

On my return to the Yard the receptionist tells me someone arrived to see me but didn't give his name. She said he spoke very posh, like the King.

I smiled. "That'll be him then. Knighthood fer me!"

"Lady Emily." That sounds nice.

I laugh and wonder who it could be. Charlotte's husband Jackie Charlton maybe or her brother Branwell. Oh well, no doubt I'll find out soon enough.

The rest of the day was spent catching up, not that much has changed: little movement on the shipbuilding work, plenty of work on the locomotive boilers. A couple of entries in the accident book. Minor incidents sorted by Ruth, my trained-up medical deputy!

"How are you Emily?"

Jake walked in looking relaxed. I repeated the same script as before. "How's everything here?"

"Good. Father knows about your actions on the strike-day. His 'fellow' ship-builders had great delight in telling him, no doubt gloating all over their faces."

"Oh, wes he upset then?"

"Not in the least. He was smiling as he told me. All he said was: That's some girl we've got. I think you've got him hooked and I agree with him of course."

That's nice, from both of ye. Ah wes terrified but ah wes right."

We went on to discuss our situation generally. It seems the company is doing well even so far as employing more labour to meet targets.

"Well we have a lot te choose from!"

He smiles but becomes serious. "I heard about you and Gladys O'Neill. I have to tell you that the day after your attack I heard from one of our staff that, before she left, she had threatened revenge for her dismissal. I could hardly believe what she did. What a vicious, vindictive woman she was."

"Ah think she had a long history of problems. She wes very bitter an' twisted."

"And her son's just like her."

"Now that's where yer wrong. It turns out that he wes forced te act by his Ma, but ah believe he's a good lad. He's an apprentice at Armstrong's an' the foreman there thinks he's great. Ave spoken to his Grandma who thinks the world of him. Ah just hope he doesn't get in with the wrong crowd."

Jake, like most, assumes Patrick is a bad lad. I'm going to make sure he gets a chance to show he's not.

Mid-way through the afternoon the phone rings, our receptionist tells me a certain police sergeant wants to see me. I smile to myself and ask her to show him in.

"'Afternoon Stan, welcome to Hawthorn's. Ye got me message then?"

"Ah did. Ye want me te release a young hooligan?"

"Yes, ah dee an' he's not a hooligan."

"Mmm how are yer injuries by the way?" He gives me a sly smile.

"Dee ye mean the bumps an' bruises his Ma told him te give me? Well they're doin' fine, nothin' an ex-Suffragette canna handle."

"Ah may have te see my superiors. Wastin' valuable police time. He may set up an enquiry, it may be a communist plot!"

Then I just knew he was joking. I give him my most charming smile. "Please."

He laughs and shakes his head. "He's already gone. Ah took him to his Grandma's myself an' he'll be back at work tomorrow."

I clap my hands, get up and give him a big hug and a kiss on his cheek. "Thank ye so much Stan. He really is a nice lad an' doesn't deserve a criminal record."

"Yer right as usual. Ah think he'll do well. It also reduces our workload with all this strike business. Now tell me truthfully Emily, how are ye? You've had a tough few days: fallin' headlong off yer bike, nearly stabbed in hospital an' threatenin' a photographer on stage. What are doin' fer fun tomorrow?"

"Ah needed a couple of days after Gladys's death but yesterday wes great fun and ahm rarin' te go."

He stares at me and slowly shakes his head. "Yer some lady. Try puttin' yer feet up tonight an' read a book or somethin'. No more adventures this week."

I can see he really does still care about me. I must put that rape scene to the back of my mind if not kick it out completely. I know it was a one-off and I have to forgive him.

Before he leaves, he continues. "By the way Sergeant Gately said someone wes looking for ye, somethin' about yer children, ah think. He says it might have been a teacher. Stupidly he told them where ye work so he may call on ye this afternoon."

"Ok, I'll ring the school from heor. And thanks again for releasing Patrick."

I don't waste any time. I ring the school and get through to the secretary. Florence is fine, no problem there. I ring Millie. I catch her just as she's about to leave for the school with Harry to collect her Frank. Again, no problem there either. I relax but I still wonder. I have to leave myself now to meet Millie so maybe I'll see this teacher there.

On the way out I wave at Ruth. I know she's meeting a friend and can't come around tonight. I also remind Wendy our receptionist: if the King wants to see me, then I'll be in tomorrow!

I gather my borrowed bicycle and ride away past a line of automobiles outside the office. Diverted by who this mystery caller is I have to swerve suddenly as one is driven off suddenly, as another adds to the queue. I head away back into Newcastle cursing my lack of concentration. I don't need any more bruises.

Chapter 55

Back in my flat with Flo and Harry I start making our tea: toast and jam with tea and fruit juice. Flo's job is to make the toast under the grill, not a big job but she loves getting the toasting just right, crispy but not burnt.

Earlier at her school I asked about my mystery man but they knew nothing at all about him. Something or nothing I suppose. Maybe he'll appear tomorrow.

After tea we head out for the park to enjoy ourselves on the swings and the roundabout. When I say enjoy ourselves, I really mean the children. To me it's a continual worry of one of them falling head first on to the concrete base. I well remember as a child doing all sorts of outrageous tricks, climbing trees, swinging on ropes and jumping off high walls. Ma and Da never seemed to worry they just bandaged me up when needed. But I'm all of a fuss. I think I have to relax. After all, I am a nurse so can patch them up easily enough.

A new adventure is the slide just installed. It's high, steep and there's a guaranteed bump onto the concrete at the end. Now I have to stand behind them making sure they don't fall climbing up the steps and then run around to catch them at the bottom. There's always a queue. This gives me a chance to chat to other mums while we wait our child's turn.

I've got to know many of them and the hardships they're suffering. I never mention my role at Hawthorn's. They know I work there but that's all. They wonder why I left my Sister's job in the hospital – a good steady job. It was a wonderful job but I don't regret leaving.

On the way back home, our road is busier with workers returning on their bicycles and automobiles. Children are still playing on the pavements but I prefer mine to be in the back yard, it's safer. Familiar vehicles now line the kerbs but I do see a different one parked opposite. The driver is inside smoking, reading a newspaper. He takes no notice of my little group walking up. He's obviously waiting for someone.

Now it's bath time. Then a story. These are my very favourite times. I always think back to when Freddie came home. How he used to play havoc with the water, soaking everything and everyone. Then, when they were both changed and ready for sleeping, how he used to read them stories putting on different accents and acting the parts to fit the tale. The children used to shriek with pleasure. I try to give them the same sense of adventure but I'm nowhere near as exciting.

I know they miss him, we all do. They still talk about him, about our holidays together and our visits to Catterick. Fortunately, my Ruth is great with them and, thank goodness, is here more often.

When I'm alone in the evenings I sit reading or listening to the wireless. I love the music programmes featuring the big bands and the new jazz. It's nearly always from America and I think of my family and how they're all doing. Another of my ambitions is to visit them but I really don't know how I could afford to. Turn to a life of crime maybe!

I'm half asleep dreaming while my other half listens to the music when there's a knock on the door. My eyes shoot open. Who could this be at this time of night? I look out the window the same vehicles are still all there, all seems quiet. I get up wondering, worrying, when there's another more insistent knock. Then I hear her.

"It's only me."

I'm so pleased and relieved. I run to the door to let her in. She almost falls at my feet but she's smiling, giggling even. All evidence of having had a good evening.

"Come an' sit doon. De ye want a cuppa like?"

She looks serious for a second. "No, ah want ye."

She makes her way unsteadily towards the settee and crumples down into the corner.

"Well ah want ye as well but ah think a cuppa first."

I bring in a tray of tea with some home-made cakes. I'm hoping this may sober her up a bit. But she's now fast asleep, feet up, head supported by cushions. She's looking a little dishevelled and there's a distinct smell of her gin specials. I can't waste the tea of course so I just pour a cup for myself, eat the cakes and look at her.

This friend of hers is probably in the same state. I wonder where she is or maybe it's not a she. The thought hits my heart like a hammer. She's a lovely looking girl, any man would fancy their chance. But she's here with me not with him. That has to be a good sign.

An hour later the tea's been drunk, by me, and the cakes been eaten, by me again and Ruth is still fast asleep. I know we have to go to bed.

I rouse her gently. Her eyes flick open and stare.

"Go away, get yer hands off me, go away. Yer not my type." She suddenly starts swinging her arms around clouting me in the head. I try to hold her, stop her from injuring herself and me. Eventually she calms down and drifts back into sleep.

I guess she must be reliving some difficult past experience – hopefully not with me. I have to get her into bed.

"Come on you, ahm yer Emily, get into the bed. Tell me all about it tomorrow." She opens her eyes, realises where she is and I help her undress. Naked, she slips in to my bed, then swings her legs out again.

"Ah have te gan te the nettie, sorry."

Must be at least ten minutes later she's out but looking ill. I remember Freddie saying that coffee helps in these situations. Luckily, I have some bought particularly for Ruth. Soon she's sipping at the hot drink. I'm just hoping it does the trick.

I steady her as she slips back into bed. She's now very apologetic.

"I'll just get myself ready an' join ye. Divvent worry, yer with me now." She gives me a wan smile.

A few minutes later I join her. She turns towards me. Her hands grab one of my breasts.

"Emily, ahm so sorry, ahm so sorry."

"Tell me all about it tomorrow. Try an' get some rest fer now." I kiss and cuddle her. She's still holding me as if she needs reassurance it's me. I can't sleep, too worried about what's happened. I never thought about asking who she was going to see. Obviously, he plied her with drinks and tried to take advantage. Eventually she releases her grip, thank goodness and drifts back to sleep. I place her head on my shoulder and hold her gently. We'll sort it in the morning.

For some reason I must have overslept. My bedroom is aglow, daylight pouring through the window. For some time, I'm confused, my curtains should be keeping me from such a rude awakening. I blink and with one eye half open I look out from the bedclothes. The sunrise is highlighting a human shape. I rub my eyes and try to focus. The shape is the back of Ruth, totally naked.

"Ah wouldn't stand there if ah were ye. You'll be the talk of the street."

She turns "No-one can see from doon there."

"Ah know but yer givin' every man a treat on the first floors opposite."

"Oh yes." She smiles. "Come an' join me. Give them somethin' te remember for the day."

I smile. "If they see me like this it'll put them off their cornflakes." I do get up and boringly put on my voluminous dressing gown but then, not so boringly, sidle up behind Ruth and wrap it around her so we're both inside. "That's betta – fer them an' fer me."

"Mmm fer me too!"

We cuddle for a while then. "You've made me forget what ah was gannin te say. Aye. Ah was watchin' the dark blue car opposite. It's just pulled up an' the man keeps lookin' over like. De ye see him? He's smokin' an' wearin' a hat."

I peer over her shoulder. I recognise the automobile as the one I noticed yesterday. "Ah saw him yesterday when ah came back from the Park with the bairns."

"That's a bit weird."

"Aye, it is. Now come away from the window. Ah need te get the bairns up." I carefully draw the curtains again for some privacy.

"We've got time fer a shower?"

"Might have te do with a quick wash over the sink."

She comes over, pushes off my dressing gown and fondles my voluptuousness. "Are ye sure?"

There's no way I can resist and we giggle and squeal as we hop in to the bath and wash each other under the warming shower water. Our faces are inches apart and we kiss. "Yer feelin' a lot betta ah see."

"Ah wasn't but ahm improvin' with every kiss an' cuddle."

"Ye gannin' te tell me about last night?"

The memory is obviously painful. She puts her head on my shoulder.

"Let's get dressed an' sit doon with a cuppa an' some toast. We've still got a few minutes."

"My friend is someone ah've known fer some time. He came with his wife, well ah thought she wes. We met in my bar an' we had a few drinks. She wes very well dressed, as thin as a rake an' had a very posh accent. She kept askin' me questions about where ah lived an' where ah worked an' all sorts, very nosy." She paused looking down at the table. "Then she asked me about ye."

My mouth dropped open. "What was her name."

"Roberta someone, ah forget. But she obviously knows ye or at least knows of ye. She wanted te know where ye lived, did ye have a family, what ye did at work, all sorts."

"What did ye tell her?"

"By this time, ah felt a bit tipsy like but ah divvent think ah gave any details. She wes certainly aware we were more than just friends."

"How."

"She groped me in the toilets. She said something like: Am ah as good as she is?"

"Then?"

"Ah must have blushed. She said an' ah remember this, she said: 'Just as ah thought. Thank you Ruth."

"Oh my God. What wes yor friend doin' all this time?"

"He looked sheepish when we got back, almost ashamed. Ah think they work in the same office somewhere."

As I'm trying to work out what on earth is happening when:

"Ma we're gannin te be late for school."

Chapter 56

My next day was an anti-climax, thank goodness. Ok, Florence was just a bit late for school, Millie had to wait around for me to deliver Harry and maybe I didn't quite meet my start time at Hawthorn's but from then on, my day was a standard day. Few problems at work, collected, fed and played with the children, listened to my music and bed.

Today has been the same until I get to work and there on my desk is the morning edition of the Chronicle. The front page emblazons in front of me:

Lesbians take-over Strike Demonstration

I could hardly believe what I was looking at. Below the headline was a picture of the speakers' stage showing a photographer being surrounded by four women, one of whom was threatening him with a pointed stick.

The text described how a small group of female sexual deviants tried to divert everyone's attention away from the miners' problems onto their own sad demands. Even going so far as threatening an innocent photographer with violence. A man whose sole intent was to truthfully report on the demonstration.

I couldn't believe my eyes, but it got worse. The story continued on an inside page. The text surrounding a picture of me with Florence and Harry. I recognised my street, very close to my flat.

I'm past being upset, cross, disillusioned. I just cannot believe someone would stoop this far down. I close my eyes, totally distraught.

I hear a lot of noise and movement outside my office. My eyes open and stare at the frontpage photograph. I examine the women and blink. It should show Ruth, Rose, Celia and myself and the photographer but none of the figures were true. I realise now it's a complete set-up. There are no other figures in the foreground, no police behind the stage and the stick was being held high in the air with a man cowering below. All very different from how it actually happened. There's a knock on my door. I'm so incensed I can't think about replying. Then another knock and without waiting for an answer in walks Jake. I see him and close my eyes perhaps waiting for some sort of criticism.

"Emily can you come into the boardroom please?"

"Now?"

"Yes please."

I get up from my seat and follow him. I think I'm going to be sacked.

He goes in first and I follow. I look, expecting a few of the Board members but the room is full to bursting. I'm shocked, they all turn and notice me and they start clapping and smiling and I don't know why. I look at them in a state of shock. I see the admin women, men from the yard and workshop, foremen and shop stewards. The noise dies down and Jake starts speaking.

"Emily we've all seen the newspaper headlines. We know it's a scurrilous attempt at blackening your name and Ruth's. Most of us were actually there and we know what and why you did what you did. We all wanted to show you that we don't believe a word of what's been printed and that we all support you. You and I will agree a response but this is to show that you two are not alone. All the company are behind you, we stick together."

The clapping re-starts. The people begin to leave and shake our hands as they go. I'm in tears, I see Ruth, her eyes reddened overcome with emotion. I say thank you so many times over and over. Slaps on the back, kisses on cheeks and words of encouragement. Like Ruth I'm totally overcome.

As the last person leaves. Jake suggests a cuppa all round. Speechless, all I can do is to give him a hug. Ruth does the same and we make our way back to his office to make plans.

"I mean what I said in there. I mean to expose those responsible for this set-up."

The three of us are now sitting comfortably around a table loaded with cups of tea and biscuits.

"Jake yer very kind te show how much support we have. Ah really did think I'd be sacked."

"Over my dead body. Someone's trying to undermine you, to get you disciplined to make a nonsense of what the demo was all about. You're an asset to this company, you both are. You deserve all the support you're going to get. Now then, have you any clues, anything out-of-the-ordinary that's happened since that day?"

"No, ah divvent think so, except, aye. The police told me that a man wes askin' fer me. He knew my name an' they told him where ah worked. He said it wes about me bairns. No-one actually came here that day. Ah checked with the school an' with me friend who looks after Harry, but no problems there. So, ah just forgot about it."

"An' another thing, we both noticed. A different car in the street parked opposite me house. There was a man inside smokin', ah thought waitin' fer someone. The first-time ah wes walking back home with Flo an' Harry." My eyes widen. "Ah bet he wes the one who took that photograph in the newspaper."

Ruth continued. "An' we saw the same car the followin' mornin' in the same place." She then paused, looking down. I knew what she was thinking.

"Ye can tell Jake about yer evenin' oot."

She took a deep breath and repeated her experience with her old friend and the thin woman. "She wanted te know all about me an' about Emily. Ahm afraid by that time I'd had a few drinks an' ah must have told her too much about us." She looked at me ashamed.

"Look, you've done nothing wrong. You haven't broken any laws. Do you remember her name? Your friend may know."

Her memory jolted into life. "Ave got it. It was Roberta someone, Prince, Price, yes Price, Roberta Price.

My eyes widened. "But that's man that photographer was working for on our Strike day. He worked for Gallowgate something or other."

Jake rocked back in to his seat, nodding, obviously pleased with himself. "Well, well the chickens have come home to roost!"

"Pardon?"

"Price is the lowest form of life. His main aim in life is to blacken anyone's or any company's name. Mention his name to my father and you'll see his face go scarlet in seconds." His smile gets wider, he laughs like a theatrical murderer. He shouts: Yes, yes. "Sorry ladies but this is great news for many people in Newcastle. Let me explain Price is employed by anyone who wants to discredit someone or some company's name. He'll do anything for money. He has no morals, no conscience."

We sit spellbound trying to understand Jake's implications. "So, he's workin' for someone who wants him te de their dirty work."

"Precisely."

"Then who?"

"It's quite often one of our competitors. But in this case, it's obviously the Chronicle. You'll know the government has put heavy pressure on all newspapers to write articles proving the support for the miners is falling and exaggerating the numbers of volunteers keeping transport and supply routes working. Those papers that don't comply find their supply of paper has been cut or stopped completely."

"In our situation, because of you two and Ellen Wilkinson they didn't get the coverage they wanted so they're trying to undermine you and taking the focus away from the demo."

"So, what can we do. The headlines are already out there?"

"Maybe a word with the police, our MP......"

I had to interrupt him. "Why aye, Ellen told me that she knows this Price man. Ah think ay should contact her, let her know the latest an' see what she can dee like."

"Even better." He paused. "Look, this is attracting a lot of attention on your friendship. I want you to know I believe there is nothing wrong, you're just two people who get on well together. It's different but Emily, in the short time I've known you, I realise you've been different all your life. You're a breath of fresh air. Let's show them we're not going lie down and take this rubbish."

We finish our tea (I'm not that different) and leave Jake's office to discuss what we can do.

"He gets really emotional, doesn't he?"

"He's so changed from the young man who tried te grope me when we first met."

"Really? Ye never told me that."

"Just the once, before ah joined the company. Ah threatened him with a vicious cake-slicer. But he grew up very quickly when Gladys threw a net over him. She demanded sex in return for keeping quiet about his constant philandering. He completely changed. The better for the company and for every female here."

"Well he's yer number one fan now an' no mistake. But how could he have intercourse with someone so much older?"

I smile. "He closes his eyes and pretends to be with someone else."

"Who?"

"Probably a young nubile young lady now standing in front of me. Well, I would. Anyway, this old girl in front of ye is gannin te talk with a few of me influential contacts."

Chapter 57

"Leave it with me. I'll get the paper and I'll see what our Mr Price has to say for himself. I'll also have a word with our worthy Police Commissioner." She paused. "Emily this Price man is vindictive. Please, you must take extra care of yourself and your children."

A shiver runs up my spine. Old heartaches wrack my body from toes to brain. "Thanks Ellen."

Work has taken second place today. Now I'm cycling to meet my friendly police sergeant at the Station.

"Ellen Wilkinson is right. Price is a horrible little man, capable of doin' anythin'. I'll talk te the inspector te see if we can de anythin' but take my advice: forget routines, gan te work at different times, divvent always stay at yer house, pick up yer bairns an' change how ye walk home, maybe take the bus, tram anythin' as long as it varies day te day. It sounds as though you've already spotted him. He drives a new Crossley. Keep an eye out fer it."

I cycle home bewildered. My children could be in danger. Florence could be snatched at school. Harry from Millie's house or yard. My action at the demo has put innocent people in danger. If this is the result of me being 'different' I just wish I was normal!

I get to the school early to speak to the teachers, to warn them. I'm putting a good deal of extra responsibility on them. Similarly, with Millie. I ask her to vary the route she walks to and from the school with Harry. She understands and threatens to kill him! She will let me know if she notices a motor car following her. I try and describe it but can only say it's dark blue with a soft top. He's a heavy smoker and wears a trilby. I'm sure she wouldn't recognise a Crossley if she ran into it, so, to know the unusual colour, should help.

On my way home, by a different, longer route, I stare into the motor cars as they pass by. I must appear very nosy but they'll have to put up with it. Poor children they don't understand why I've changed the route and why they can't play in the park. We have to make do with playing hopscotch in the backyard and kicking a football at a wall-chalked goal.

For the next two weeks I maintain my varied routine. Ruth stays with me most nights but on the odd occasion stays in her own flat after drinking a few of her bar-specials with friends. Neither of us have noticed the car again.

A small, easily missed note in the Chronicle showed that Ellen has made her mark. Jake had to point it out, it read:

> *It seems the women at the recent demonstration were expelling a group of anti-miner demonstrators who, it is said, were paid to be present. We apologise unreservedly for our incorrect assumption.*

It took a while for the newspaper to issue the apology, hidden away on an inside page as it was, but Jake made sure all Hawthorn's employees knew about it. That night Ruth and myself celebrate at home with a night of gin specials especially made up for us by the owners of her bar. We drink toasts to Jake, Ellen, the police, Hawthorns and anyone else. It is so wonderful to know that everyone has pulled together. A company in harmony. The strike has ended sadly with little gained for the miners. I just hope our harmony can spread to other industries.

The night ends of course with a giggling, warm, comforting shower and with long, naked and sensuous love making, on, besides and snuggled inside our cosy bed.

I must be getting used to the 'specials' as the following morning I feel fine and special myself. I try to climb over my still sleepy lover but she wakes and grabs me.

"Ye canna gan anywhere without these. You'll just have te massage mine."

"Oh well if ah have te." It's so nice to be so naughty. We end up kissing deeply and intertwining tightly. Life is so enriched. I know I couldn't live without her.

Surprisingly we do get to work on time. Ruth at eight thirty and me an hour later. We have our dinner break at a table just outside the office with some of the women from admin. We discuss the end of the strike of course. The newspapers are full of it with headlines broadcasting 'The Country has come to its Senses' and 'Communist plot Derailed'. The miners are still out but there's no support from the TUC. They've caved in. The Government have won. The families have lost. But it is a milestone. Lessons will be learnt. Like the Suffragette struggles we'll get there in the end. Nothing happens overnight but change will come.

Tonight, Ruth has some work to catch up with so I just have to make do with recalling last night's antics. I smile thinking of my personal good fortune.

I arrive at work the following morning bright and breezy. I look over to her chair but it sits empty. No bag, no coat, no cluttered desk and the most disappointing bit, no Ruth.

Chapter 58

Ruth's Story – Part 1

I so hate paperwork. I always put it off until tomorrow but tomorrow never comes. I've now got a pile high with bills, demands and letters to answer. I've drawn up a list of chores and my aim is to tick them off one by one but my brain wonders away to another flat not far away and I wonder how my Emily is feeling. I can't help myself thinking how lucky I am. She's so positive and determined. I want to be like her. My depressions are fading. No more drowning my sorrows in gin thinking what a mess my life is. Booze, rotten boyfriends, disloyal girlfriends, no family to help me. My Ma in Liverpool but it may as well be Australia. I picture Emily jumping onto the stage brandishing a stick at the photographer. I would never have done that, but now? Her lovely friend Millie has told me all about her past adventures in the Workhouse and in the Suffragettes and what she did in the War. And she's been a Sister in the hospital and even flies aeroplanes for goodness sake. She can do anything she puts her mind to. But then she manages to love me, a good for nothing, frivolous loser. But I'm not going to lose her. She's my life, guide and inspiration. She makes me feel that I do have a place in this world.

My mind drifts to the two of us making love. Her gorgeous voluptuousness as she calls her body. She's every man's dream but she's mine and no-one else's. I smile but I'm interrupted by a knock on the door. My eyes lift, this could be her. I run to open the door ready to jump into her arms, but it's not her. I recognise Roberta Price the thin woman from the bar who asked personal questions then groped me in the toilets. I just stare.

"What dee ye want?"

"Ruth, I'm here to apologise for my rudeness asking all those intrusive questions and then touching you. It was just too bad of me. I have to admit someone paid me. It wasn't your friend John. He had nothing to do with it. You see he works with me at the Chronicle. I used him to get to you. He was very embarrassed. I've also had to apologise to him."

"Who paid ye?"

"It was someone whom I owed a favour. If I hadn't done it, I would have been in a lot of bother. Look, I want to tell you all about it. It would help me clear my conscience and help you to understand why I did it. I've bought a bottle of your favourite drink and some chocolates."

"Come in then."

We sit facing each other over the table. She's drinking the gin, I have my cup of tea, I want to remain sober. The chocolates are between us. She starts her story. I've heard it all before: Unfaithful husband, she wanted to know who was his mistress, this man did the detective work. She keeps offering me a 'proper' drink, I refuse and just pick at the chocolates. She has a posh voice which drones on and on. I can't follow all of it. She uses words I don't understand. My mind wonders and her voice seems to fade in to the distance until I can hardly hear her at all.

I feel hands on my body. They're squeezing me then moving on, between my legs. I smile it must be Emily but she's being too rough. My eyes flick open, I see a man's face. He's looking at my chest.

"Nice tits on this one."

I want to push him away but I can't move my hands or legs. I want to shout but my mouth is choked with something. I can hardly breath. I keep still and listen. I hear the continuous rumbling of wheels on a road close to my ears. I must be on the floor of a car or a van, but why, how did this happen?"

294

"Keep your hands off her, you dirty bastard. She's not here for your perverted desires." I recognise her voice immediately.

"Alright, alright, keep your hair on missus."

"I'm not your missus. You're getting paid to do a job, nothing else."

It has to be nearly an hour. An hour of trying to understand where I'm being taken. The only sound now is the rumbling wheels, the man and the woman are quiet. Then for the first time the sound stops, the engine is switched off then a door opens. I hope someone's going to untie me. It's the woman who speaks.

"Give me that petrol tank."

The gurgling of fuel filling the car tank is loud in my ear. For the brief seconds between re-filling the car tank and re-starting the engine I can hear soft whooshing noises. The sea's talking to me, telling me where I am. But is it North or South of Newcastle?

"How much further to Alnmouth then."

There's a quick, hushed, menacing response. "Shut up you fool."

"Cor blimey, sorry for living, I'm sure."

Sometime later we slide to a halt on gravel, both doors open.

"Untie her legs and get her in there."

My legs have been stuck in one position for hours, I can hardly move but they have no choice. I stare at the thin woman. She stares back, a thin, evil smile splitting her face.

"You and your queer bitch lost me my job and my husband has buggered off. But I've got you." She taps her nose. "And I believe you're worth a little bit to certain people. If not, then I'll have the pleasure of seeing you rot and eaten by the rats." She looks over to the man. "Get this tart into the barn. I'll be back with some food and water and keep your filthy hands off her."

While she drives away the man grips my arms still tied behind me and pushes me hard towards the barn. I can see it's derelict, creepers covering the walls and hiding the slates on the roof. Inside the floor is *covered with old straw and patches of well-rotted dung. For the first time I realise I have to go to the toilet. I can't speak. I try to make him understand almost throwing myself to the floor.*

"You want to pee?"

I nod

"Come 'ere then." He unties my hands and removes my gag. "But I'll be watching your every move. So, don't try anything stupid." He points to the corner behind a brick pen wall.

I can't think of anything I can do to escape. I still feel very stiff and weak. He's stronger than me and, at the moment, quicker.

"What's yer name then."

"Why."

"Well if we're gannin te be heor for a while ah may as well know."

"Well you can call me Fred and that's all you're getting."

"An' what about Mrs Price then?"

"How d'ya know her name?"

I just shrug, but I think: Yes, I'm right.

But where does this get me. I've got no chance. This Fred is stronger and although he's not young he looks athletic so probably faster as well. At least I might be fed here. I sit down and lean back against the wall. I have to think.

Chapter 59

There's been no telephone call or any other message explaining why she hasn't arrived at work. That's very unusual for Ruth. I know she likes her work here and wouldn't just leave un-announced.

Dinnertime and I'm cycling along to her flat worried something unexpected has happened. Her door is closed but not locked, that has to mean she's inside. I bet she's had a heavy night and has slept in, unusual but possible. There's no answer to my knock so I let myself in silently and take in the scene laid out before me. Her table is cluttered with cups, glasses, teapot and a bottle of gin, none have been finished. On the floor alongside is a spilled box of chocolates and a chair turned over. Surely this has to mean a meeting disturbed. Her bedroom is empty but shows her usual unkempt look. I can't tell if she slept here last night or not. The bathroom still has her wash bag. There's nothing here that suggests she's gone away.

I pick up the chocolates and wonder who on earth could afford such a gift and why have they been spilled? I can't imagine Ruth leaving any. I'm sorely tempted and take one that looks especially delicious.

"Hello."

There's someone at the door. I quickly put the chocolate back into the box with the others and open the front door to see an elderly lady looking worried.

"Ahm sorry te bother ye but ah saw the door wes ajar an' wondered if Ruth wes ok. Ah live over the other side." She points to her door.

"Ahm actually lookin' for her. She should be at work at Hawthorns. Dee ye know where she is?"

"No, but there was a bit of a rumpus last night. She wes talkin' te a woman at the door fer some time then ah think they went inside an' it went quiet. But about half an hour later someone else came an' wes let in an' then there wes some crashin' an' bangin'. Ah could heor his voice much louder than the woman's but not Ruth's. Ah mean she's always been a quiet neighbour, a bonny girl, it wes so unusual ye see."

"Could ye hear what they were sayin'?"

"Just a few words," she looked embarrassed, "swear words."

"Wes it very late?"

"No, they didn't wake me up or anythin'. Ah suppose about 6 or 7 o'clock."

"Sorry ye were disturbed. Ahm her friend an' she didn't get te her work this mornin'. I'll call again tonight just te check."

"Oh dear, ah hope she's alright."

"Ahm sure she's fine but ah will ring her tonight te make sure." I leave feeling very unsure she'll be fine. This is so unlike her. Arriving back at the Yard, Wendy, our receptionist hands me a letter just handed in by a small, scruffy boy who immediately ran off.

Intrigued, I open it there and then. Inside the envelope was a letter on pink paper, the printing in fine writing.

Dear Emily.   **15th June 1926**

It was so nice of you to somehow persuade a local woman MP to demand my resignation from the Chronicle. I can't think how you managed that! However, as a reward I've managed to persuade a very close friend of yours to accompany me on a seaside holiday. Unfortunately, I cannot manage her safe return without money for her railway ticket. These are so expensive these days: £100. Soon a young man will deliver a package containing her clothing. Please give him a sealed envelope with the cash inside - as a reward.

**When I receive the 'fare' I'll be able to arrange
her homecoming. If not, then perhaps she'll be able to
swim home. Oops, I may forget to ask if she can
actually swim!**

**I will need the cash within three days to allow you
to make arrangements.**

**Yours lovingly,
A well-wisher xx**

**Ps: please don't think to ask the Chronicle for my
address. It's something I like to keep to myself.**

I have to read it several times before I carefully fold it and stare at
Ruth's empty desk through the glass.

"You ok Emily?"

Hearing her speak I look over trying to understand what she said.

"Emily?"

"Ruth's been kidnapped. This is a ransom note." I close my eyes.
I'm putting two and two together. This woman must have abducted
her, drugged or drunk or both and has her locked up somewhere - on
the coast, that could be anywhere. "I'm gannin to call the polis." I'm
hoping Stan's there.

"I'm afraid he's not on-duty today but if you're right this is a
detective matter anyway. Give me your address and I'll come round."
True to his word two of them are waiting outside Ruth's flat by the
time I cycle there. I let them in, show them the letter and they
examine the scene.

"Have you got a photograph of Ruth?"

"No, but I'll look around." I've been here so little I feel I'm being
nosy, intrusive but I realise they have to know who they're looking
for. I find an old family photograph. It shows the unmistakeable Ruth

as a youngster with two younger boys, her brothers at their parents' feet in their living room. It looks like a happy family gathering, probably a very rare occasion. It's no good for the police so I keep searching. I find an album. Photos are inside ready to be stuck to the pages. They show her much older, some with friends and one particular snap taken close-up with her head on another girl's shoulder It's very recent. I show it to the detectives. Their eyes light up immediately.

"Thank you we'll keep this for now."

I have to explain about the demonstration coverage and the newspaper set-up and who I believe are the culprits: Mr Price and the thin woman who questioned Ruth in great detail and who probably works for the Chronicle.

"We'll have a word with the neighbour, then, I think our first call be the newspaper offices. If you don't mind, we'll keep the letter and let us know if this parcel arrives." To my horror one of the policeman pops one of the chocolates in his mouth.

"No."

He looks at me in surprise and stops chewing.

"They may be drugged. Ruth wouldn't get drunk te a stupor by a little sip of gin."

He stands up immediately runs into the kitchen and leans over the sink retching.

"Take some water and rinse out your mouth."

The other man looks confused. "You know about this stuff then?"

"I was a nurse for many years, it's not unusual. I can't smell anything particularly but she obviously took something to knock her out."

****

I'm sitting at my desk worried sick. I can't think of anything else but my poor Ruth holed up somewhere probably tied up and scared to death. I jump when my telephone rings. It's the police or rather it's Stan. The detectives have told him about Ruth and he has made his own enquiries at the Chronicle. He has a contact there:

"Yer kidnapper is that Mrs Roberta Price and she is the wife of that Price man from Gallowgate Securities. Anyway, she wes sacked by the paper for that scandalous piece about ye an' yer friends at the demo. This was instigated by the MP Ellen Wilkinson. She wasn't happy! My contact says that her husband has left her an' with nothin'. Also, apparently, she owns a now, derelict farm near Alnmouth. My guess is that she's taken yer Ruth there."

"Ah must go now, de ye have the address?"

"Not so fast, this is a detective matter an' the kidnappers could be armed. Let them deal with it."

"Stan, it could be too late, ah canna wait until tomorrow. She could be injured, they could take advantage, anythin' could be happenin'."

The telephone went quiet.

"Stan?"

"Stay there I'll pick ye up at six o'clock, ok"

"Stan you're a dream."

"Mmmm, well ah hope it doesn't turn into a nightmare."

Chapter 60

Ruth's Story – Part 2

What would Emily do? She wouldn't just sit here doing nothing. I need to escape but how do I get out of Fred's clutches. He keeps looking at me, checking. I need to distract him somehow, but how.

I spot a stone block on a high window sill next to me. Perhaps I could hit him with it but he would have to be asleep and there's no chance of that. Maybe ...

"Fred."

He looks down at me.

"Why de ye like my tits?"

He looks surprised at the question and looks down at my chest.

"Cos they're big I suppose."

I stand up and hold my breasts up and stick them out as best I can. "Dee ye think so?"

He's now focused on them and looking nervous.

"Would ye like te hold them?"

"What are you gettin' at?"

I pull up my blouse and underwear revealing my breasts allowing them to swing down unencumbered.

His eyes light up locked on to my bare chest.

"Well ye can if ye want."

I can see he's nervous but he moves towards me and with one hand he holds one breast.

"That's nice. Hold them both if ye like."

He doesn't need any further invitation. He grabs them both, kneels down and starts slobbering over my nipples and starts mumbling. I look over to the block of stone. I'm trying to work out the best time to act when I feel one of his hands reaching down between my legs and stooping lower at the same time. That was the chance. I reach over and with both hands I manage to slide then grab the stone with my hands. He hears the noise and looks up as I smash the stone with all my strength into his startled face. This sends him to the floor but he's only stunned and howling in pain. Quickly I bend down, retrieve the stone and repeat the action to the side of his head with as much force as I can. I hear a sickening crack. There's no further movement or sound. I think I've killed him.

I don't want to check or touch him in any way. I re-dress myself and run out the yard to the road. All the while I've been here, I've not seen another car at all so I start running the way we came, alongside the sea coast. After ten minutes I slow to a walk. It's completely deserted, fields and woods to one side and steep cliffs on the seaward side towering above stony beaches. I say deserted but the air is full of seabirds swooping, soaring and calling all the while blending in with the crashing waves far below. The stiff breeze is filled with the smell of the salty sea. It's a beautiful place to enjoy an invigorating walk, but not today. I walk on listening, looking and hoping for someone, anyone who could take me home to safety, to my Emily.

Some while later I see in the distance a vehicle approaching from the South. They're obviously driving North but surely this is better than nothing. They could take me to the nearest town. I feel weary and sit on the grassy bank to wait. To my surprise I can suddenly hear a vehicle close behind me, its approach silenced by the wind. It slows down and stops, the driver appears and stands hands on her hips.

"Well, well if it's not the lovely Ruthie, a murderer of men."

My heart sinks as I realise who it is. I back away preparing to run, there's no chance of diverting her attention with the delights of my body.

"Don't even think about running. I was an athlete and can still run faster than most men." She draws out a knife from her belt and before I can react, she grabs my arm and holds me in a vice-like grip.

"Do you fancy a swim?" She nods down the cliff besides us keeping the point of her knife close to my throat.

I try to kick her but I feel pain to my cheek as she flicks her knife blade through my flesh. I scream and scream. I hear the vehicle approaching from the South arrive and the squeal of brakes. Price turns me round to face it, the knife at my throat. I see a policeman get out and from the other side, my Emily.

"I'm sorry but you're too late to save this one." She then notices Emily. *"Oh, it's your lover. She's come to see your dive to oblivion. How sweet."*

I see Emily looking around and into the car.

"There's only me, this little murdering bitch has killed my friend. That's two in as many weeks. I wouldn't trust her in bed with me if I were you."

She laughs manically but the policeman takes this chance to dive at her feet. She slashes at him hard. The knife cuts into his uniform, immediately blood oozes spreading quickly. But the action has put her off-balance and she steps back trying to steady herself. I take my chance and give her the hardest push I can muster. It's enough to send her cartwheeling over the clifftop, screaming. I watch her body smash in to the rocks far below then taken by the tide and repeatedly smashed into the rock face ensuring life has left her evil body forever.

"That makes three."

I turn back to the policeman who is being treated by Emily, tourniquets wrapped around his wound. I squat down beside them but gradually everything is fading and I'm engulfed inside a distant, peaceful place.

Chapter 61

We head off North and take the coast road. Stan's confident he knows where we're going. I've managed to contact Millie who readily agreed to look after Flo and Harry. Similarly, Stan has warned his wife of his late turn.

The road empties the further North we drive and we now seem to be alone in the world. Being Summer there's still plenty of daylight. I hope he knows where this derelict place is. I've travelled this way a few times going home but have no memories of any particular farms, used or not.

"We're gettin' nearer. Ah remember the steep cliffs te one side. Keep yer eyes te the left of us. Look, there's a car straight ahead. Ah think it's parked. If the driver's about we can ask him."

Approaching closer I can see two people talking. I try to focus. I can't believe what I'm seeing.

"That's Ruth. Ah think she's arguin' with that other person." They haven't seen us. Then there's a flash of reflected light from the two figures. "Stan, that other woman's got a knife in her hand." He accelerates the last hundred or so yards then slams on his brakes and we skid to a halt. I can now see clearly the woman is holding a knife at Ruth's throat. Blood is oozing from her cheek. Stan gets out and approaches them from the front, I get out and approach from the side. There's no-one else in the car or anywhere else. The woman notices me and starts talking but I can't hear what she's saying. Stan suddenly dives in and I see a flash of the knife and a scream from Ruth as she runs full pelt at the woman careering her off the cliff and onto the rocks far below. I can see Ruth is stunned and just stares down into the water but I have to see to Stan. Blood is seeping through the arm of his jacket. It has to be stemmed.

I carefully remove the jacket and do the best I can with strips of cloth from my petticoat. Stan has to hold the tourniquet with his hand reducing the flow to a trickle. Ruth seems to have recovered and kneels down with us but her eyes are staring, then start to close and finally she faints, collapsing headlong onto the ground.

I feel helpless. Stan can't possibly drive with his injured arm; my poor Ruth is out cold and I've never driven a car. All I can do is wait for some help and keep watch over my two patients. Eventually an elderly farmer arrives driving his horse pulling a trailer. I try to explain what has happened but he keeps looking at me and shaking his head.

"Ah need te get these two te somewhere warm an' with a telephone." I lie to save unnecessary questions. "There's been an accident an' ah need te report it te the authorities."

He looks at Stan and Ruth and then at the two unscathed cars. "Ok, ah live in a village along the way there's a telephone in the Fishers." We help Stan onto the seat besides the farmer and poor Ruth onto the back of the cart. I sit beside her supporting her head and stemming a small cut in her cheek. We head off slowly then accelerate to a canter. The farmer obviously senses the need for speed. Sometime later he shouts over his shoulder.

"Ye know ye look exactly like a girl who used te live in our village. A very pretty girl, now what was her name." He shakes his head trying to remember.

I look at him. There is something familiar about him. Then my brain clicks in at last. Of-course, the Fishers. The pub in my village. My eyes light up. "Jon Maxwell?"

"Emily Mulligan. Frank an' Ruby's daughter."

I cannot believe this. He used to be a fisherman. We have to shout our conversation over the noise of the horse and cart surging along. "Why have ye changed from fishin'?"

"Too old."

"How's Mrs Maxwell."

"Same as ever."

I have to smile. I should have recognised where I am. With new understanding the surroundings become more familiar and finally we descend down to my coal gathering beaches. I feel Ruth stir in my arms. I hold her tight and start talking about where we are and what I did when I was living here with my family. I know she's still only semi-conscious but I just want to talk. I feel Stan's good hand on my back.

He smiles at me. "Yer home Emily."